U0124392

濟慈名著 譯述

余光中

譯者序

1

浪漫主義在歐洲的發展，約在十八世紀末葉與十九世紀初期之間，大致上始於德國的狂飆運動，而終於法國的1840年代。英國的浪漫主義，若以華茲華斯與柯立基的《抒情歌謠》初版爲準，當始於1798年，若以法國大革命爲準，則始於1789年；而其結束則沒有異議，當在1832年，因爲那一年通過的改革法案，大幅調整了下議院的席位，廢除了萎縮選區的選舉權，並增加了新興市鎮的名次。

在英國文學史上，浪漫時期緊接新古典主義時期而來，三十多年後卻被維多利亞時期所取代。英國浪漫時期的文學，主要貢獻在詩，而其主要詩人之出現，可分兩代。第一代的先驅是華茲華斯和柯立基；遠在蘇格蘭的彭斯和近在倫敦市隱的布雷克，對當時的影響比較邊緣。第二代的後秀，依其出生爲拜倫（1788-1824）、雪萊（1792-1822）、濟慈（1795-1821），比起前一代平均要小二十多歲。巧合的是：這三人都夭亡，但晚生的卻早殁，正如濟慈自己弔柴德敦（Thomas Chatterton, 1752-1770）之句：「夜色忽至，緊追你的朝霞。」（Oh! how nigh Was nigh to thy fair morning.）

　　這三位詩人在文學史上往往相提並論，因為不但年齡相
近，而且都客死他鄉。但論身世，則前兩位都是貴族，濟慈
卻屬於平民，中產以下。論教育，拜倫出身劍橋，雪萊出身
牛津；濟慈未能入名校接受人文通才教育，所以讀古典名著
要靠英譯。論經濟，前兩位都世襲家產，無須工作，若竟欠
債，則要怪自己揮霍過度。論健康，拜倫雖有小兒麻痺症，
致呈微跛，卻以騎泳無礙來補救；雪萊敏感多病，溺海而
死，拜倫早夭，則是自己糟蹋的結果；濟慈卻是患了肺疾，
母親和弟弟均因肺疾先他而歿。論感情，則拜倫與妻不合而
豔遇過剩；雪萊再婚，法院因他不信國教而判他不得養育前
妻所出，其後他一直追求「理想女性」而一再幻滅；濟慈與
芬妮・布朗（Fanny Brawne）訂了婚，卻未能終成眷屬，深
感挫折。論親情，則拜倫與雪萊從不詠及父母，拜倫更與母
親不合，雪萊雖有姊妹，筆下也未提及；濟慈與兩位弟弟加
一位妹妹的手足之情卻可見於三首贈弟之詩，其中〈贈吾弟
喬治〉採用了雙行詩體，竟長達140行。論名氣，則拜倫名
滿天下，銷路空前，甚至深受歌德推崇，身後更與拿破崙相
提並論。雪萊生前和濟慈一樣默默無聞，死後卻享譽極隆，
但在二十世紀初年卻橫遭逆轉，毀多譽少；濟慈身後則先受
冷落，不久評價持續上升，迄今不衰。

　　三位青年詩人之中，拜倫與雪萊友情頗深，彼此評價亦
高。濟慈在英國病重，準備去意大利養病之際，雪萊曾邀濟
慈去比薩和他同住，但為濟慈婉拒。濟慈在羅馬夭亡後，雪

萊又寫了一首長近500行的輓詩（Adonais）來悼念。不到一年半，雪萊自己溺於地中海，屍體漂上沙灘，已經面目難認，僅憑袋中濟慈送他的詩集可以辨識，足證他對濟慈的看重。至於拜倫，應該沒見過濟慈，對他所知很淺。李衡在回憶錄中說他力勸拜倫一讀〈希臘古甕頌〉與〈夜鶯頌〉。拜倫卻表示不解何以有「聽不見的音樂」，而「滿杯溫潤的南方」又應作何解。濟慈倒是久仰拜倫的盛名，甚至在十九歲時用十四行體寫了一首〈致拜倫勳爵〉。

2

　　亞里斯多德論詩，是以敘事詩與戲劇為本的，尤其是史詩與悲劇，所以他在《詩學》中說：「是以詩之為物，比歷史更富哲理，更為高超：詩慣於表現常態，歷史則表現殊態。我所謂之常態，是指個性確定之人物按照或然率或者必然率，偶爾會有如何之言行……」因此西方的詩人總覺得在寫抒情詩之餘，一輩子不能不經營一部長篇巨著，來考驗自己的功力。影響濟慈很深的史賓塞、米爾頓、華茲華斯等前輩都各有傳世不朽的巨著，濟慈見賢思齊，發軔之初也雄心勃勃，先後嘗試了兩個長篇：《恩迪米安》與《亥貢亮》。兩詩都取材自希臘神話：《恩迪米安》長達4050行，《亥貢亮》也有877行；前者以月神Selene對美少年恩迪米安的迷戀為主題，濟慈自覺寫得太濫情，太雜亂；後者並未寫完，也因為作者自覺風格與句法太學米爾頓了，應該改弦更

張。後來濟慈仍寫出像《奧陀大帝》（486行）、《小丑的帽與鈴》（783行，未完）、《伊莎貝拉》（504行）一類的長篇，但始終不及《聖安妮節前夕》與《蕾米亞》評價之高，討論之盛。拜倫與濟慈都是英國浪漫主義的健將，可是拜倫的貢獻在長詩，《唐璜》與《天譴異夢記》之好評迄今不衰，但其短篇抒情詩並不出色，其中就算是佳作的寥寥幾首也遠比不上雪萊與濟慈；濟慈享年比拜倫少了十歲，但是在短詩與長詩兩方面都有不可磨滅的貢獻。

　　因此我在這本《濟慈名著譯述》之中，除納入了他的抒情短詩之外，也選譯了他的三個敘事長篇。他的短篇，以十四行詩與頌體爲主。於十四行詩他兼工意大利原體與英國變體，所以兩體我都選了，以示他的多才。於長篇，我所選的三篇分別以嚴謹的史賓塞詩體、明快的雙行體，與大開大闔的無韻體寫成，以示其諸體皆工，而且主題的背景也有希臘神話（例如《亥貢亮之敗亡》、《蕾米亞》）與中世紀傳說（例如《聖安妮節前夕》）之分。我這麼做，對身爲譯者的自己也存心有所激勵。

　　譯詩，是一件極不討好的工作。天生英文，不是爲給人中譯而設的，反之亦然。但是既要譯詩，就得像詩。首先，原文若是格律詩，譯文就必須盡量保持其格律，包括分段、分行、韻序。韻序往往不易，或根本不可能悉依原文，但至少應該有押韻，讀來有韻文之感。坊間許多譯詩都不理原文的格律，未免太草率了，太避難而意譯了。許多譯詩的分行，忽長忽短，非常隨便，一看便知是力不從心。現代詩人

如果學這樣的譯詩，恐無功效，反被誤導。在這本《濟慈名著譯述》裏，我盡量依照原文的韻序：例如在頌體中，前四行一定悉依原韻，但其後各行則有時為求自然，酌予放寬。在雙行體中，每兩行轉一次韻，就一定做到位，無可妥協。無韻體呢，解脫了韻腳的拘束，卻要防句法易趨散文化。翻譯有如政治與婚姻，也是一種妥協的藝術：無論是原文或譯文，為了成全大局，都不得不各讓一步。

我在本書的妥協，不外三類。第一，專有名詞如果太長，照樣音譯過來，不但失之冗贅，而且會使句長失控；這時我就酌予精簡，有時甚至意譯。例如〈致荷馬〉一詩，就有一系列的島群叫Cyclades，若加音譯，勢必動用七個字（席克拉底斯群島），句長便失控了。因為島勢排列如環，不但地圖上如此，詞典中也如此形容，我索性就把它簡化為「環形群島」。第二類是一行之中偶見某字只起襯托填空之用，並非原文必需，不譯並無大礙，譯之又恐句法太長，我就斷然捨去，以救句法，並保順暢。例如在〈夜鶯頌〉之中，第三段第五行Where palsy shakes a few, sad, last gray hairs, 我只譯成「麻痺得留不住慘白的髮莖」，至於a few和last三個字，就「四捨五入」，不一一照譯了。但是在同一段，其第三行What thou among the leaves hast never known，我若直譯成「你在密葉間所從未經歷的」，不免會失之空洞，而且難懂。所以為了上下文意，又正好有助押韻，我就譯成了「你在密葉間未經的世情」。第三，由於中文與英文先天思路不同因而句法有異，加以古典詩的句法頗

多倒裝，遂使譯者往往「臨句躊躇」，不知「順譯」與「逆譯」之間如何取捨。例如莎翁十四行詩第一一六號的名句：Let me not to the marriage of true minds / Admit impediments. 一般譯者大概會順勢直譯：

　　讓我不對真心的結合
　　承認被阻礙；

但這樣的譯法不但無力，而且不像中文。可能的譯法至少有半打；就我而言，最好的也許是下列的方式：

　　莫逼我，雖兩情已長相許，
　　卻認命甘休；

其中「逼」字也可作「令」或「害」；「情」不妨改「心」，「長」也可以不用。我的原則是：在保持中文自然的句法下，盡量按照英文的順勢（normal order）或倒裝（inversion）來譯，英詩如果是迴行（run-on line），我譯時也應之以迴行。非常歡迎認真的讀者，把我的譯文和原文對照並讀。

3

　　濟慈最早的知音與出版人，是李衡（Leigh Hunt,

1784-1859）。這位次要詩人在政治言論上頗爲激進，所以他推崇的拜倫和雪萊乃遭保守的刊物醜化，稱之爲「惡魔詩派」（Satanic School of Poetry）。　濟慈的意識形態並不激進，卻因李衡的賞識也被稱爲「倫敦腔調幫」（Cockney School），飽受《評論季刊》與《黑森林雜誌》的譏諷，勸他回去本行，做他的藥劑師傅。由於他體弱多病，加上早夭，所以相傳他是被罵死的（snuff'd by an article），雪萊甚至寫了長達495行的希臘式田園輓歌來悼他。其實濟慈不但意志堅定，而且頗有自知之明，早就不滿意自己的少作《恩迪米安》而屢圖改弦更張，所以亥賁亮主題的兩首長詩都未完成就擱了筆。

安諾德把雪萊形容成象牙塔裏一位無傷大雅的天使，許多評論家也把濟慈說成遁世自戀的唯美信徒，其實都把他們過分簡化。濟慈對法國大革命的反應雖不如拜倫、雪萊之強，但對工業社會現實生活之咄咄逼人，卻是耿耿於懷的，而且在他的名作裏不斷提起，與藝術之美形成難以兩全的對照。我們甚至可以把藝術、現實、死亡三者形成的不等邊三角形，用來探討他詩中縈心的主題。

詩人的自我，形而下則爲生活，形而上則爲生命。生活，幾乎就是現實的代名詞，同義字。現實之苦，到死亡就告終。所以死亡可以解脫現實，此即浪漫詩人「求死」（death wish）之念，亦即里爾克所慨歎的詩人生前如天鵝在岸上，死後才如天鵝在水上。所以死亡（mortality）能剋生活，而未必能一併剋死亡，但詩人的生命卻受制、受困於

生活，他的現實。

　　濟慈是詩人之中的美學家，他刻意要探討的，正是形與實（image vs. reality）、美與真（beauty vs. truth）、藝術與科學（art vs. science）、憂與喜（melancholy vs. joy）之間相剋相生的關係。他的五大頌甚至六大頌，不但語言高妙，聲韻圓融，美感飽滿，而且富於美學的卓見，真不愧是英詩的傳世瑰寶。〈賽姬頌〉的主題，是想像要憑藝術之功來為靈魂建一座神殿，以便靈魂接受崇拜，同時自告奮勇，要擔任賽姬的祭司，將晚來的賽姬拱上希臘文藝的仙籍神譜。〈希臘古甕頌〉要探討古代的一件藝術品所喚醒的世界，有多麼光彩同時又有何侷限，還要追究冷寂的田園藝術如何抵抗時光。〈夜鶯頌〉寫詩人神往與美合一，覺得鴉片與酒遠不及詩之想像，繼而又自覺趁夜鶯歌聲正酣就隨死神而去有多逍遙，終於懷疑詩之想像莫非是騙人的精靈，是耶非耶，夢乎醒乎，尾聲嫋嫋不絕。〈古甕〉與〈夜鶯〉二頌的第三段，都引入了生活的現實之苦，來對照能供他解脫的意園神樓，儘管只是片刻的安慰。如此一來，這兩首名作就多元而且立體了。

　　〈憂鬱頌〉在頌體之中雖然最短，卻最富創意，能耐久讀。此詩之哲理，在於七情六欲多為相剋、相生；其意似乎老生常譚，但到了濟慈神助的腕下（the magic hand of chance），卻噴發而成生動的意象，令人難忘。詩一開頭，紛至沓來的有毒藥草令人吃驚，足見他的藥劑學沒有白讀，實為雪萊所不及。第三段乃上升之高潮，擬人格的隱喻體系

不斷翻騰，到末行遽然收筆，煞個正著。

　　〈懶散頌〉詩中瀰漫的慵懶情緒，正如詩人在〈憂鬱頌〉首段所痛切指陳的：「陰影加陰影未免太昏瞶，／會吞沒靈魂清醒的痛苦。」此詩要到第三段才推出主題：濟慈窮於應付的三種煩惱：愛情、野心、詩魔。詩人表明，前二者他苦追而不得，後者卻是愛恨交加而欲罷不能。一直到全詩之末，他再度聲明不甘演自憐的鬧劇，並斥走虛幻的象相閒情。

　　〈懶散頌〉極少入選一般的詩選集，也非學者賞析的焦點。反之，〈秋之頌〉幾乎是一切英詩選集所必選，享譽之盛迄今不衰。全詩不過三十三行，分為三段，主題該是天道順時而變，不言自化，人在其中，樂之不疲。濟慈不做哲人，卻能將此意完全泯入意象與音調，用語言的節奏來呼應季節的節奏，依次把秋天的觸覺、視覺、聽覺演成生動的戲劇，詩藝之成熟恰似秋季之成熟。濟慈之六大頌加起來，也許還不及貝多芬或馬勒的九大交響曲那麼崇高渾厚，但在較小的規模上卻也自給自足，別有天地。何況濟慈當時不過二十四、五歲，並非大器晚成，乃是早熟的天才。

4

　　以上的論述，算是譯者對濟慈的總序。除此之外，我對所譯的各種詩體，從十四行詩、抒情詩、頌體到長詩，都各有分述，不再重複。濟慈在世，詩名未彰，知音寥寥，寸心

雖有自知，但自我的評價卻頗低調。在世之時，他曾自許，說死後將列位於英國詩家之間。臨終之前，他自撰的碑文只是：「墓中人的名字只合用水來書寫。」（Here lies one whose name was writ in water.）此語一般譯者都譯成：「墓中躺著的人，名字只寫在水上。」其實此語的in一字，應指寫作的方式，例如written in English，或者written in blood。

　　濟慈寫給弟弟的信，也像梵谷寫給弟弟的信一樣，常常述及自己的作品和創作觀，在文藝史和文藝評論上頗有價值。所以我在譯詩之餘，也選譯了他的六封信，以便讀者印證之用。附錄之中，有我1976年在倫敦國際筆會年會上宣讀的論文〈想像之眞〉，當時年會討論的主題正是濟慈致貝禮信中所言的the truth of imagination；本書所附，是我論文的中文翻譯。二十年後，我重遊英國，又攜妻女去倫敦西北郊外的漢普斯台荒地（Hampstead Heath）憑弔委屈的詩魂，事後寫了〈弔濟慈故居〉一詩。

　　〈如何誦讀英詩〉是爲有心細讀濟慈詩作的讀者而寫。這種比較專業的訓練，恐怕連在大學裏開課的某些教授也未必受過。我也沒有特別受過，只是教了多年英詩自然應該悟出其中的道理。詩而只解默讀，其靈魂不過只醒來一半，可惜了。

　　本書在譯文之後附錄相應的原文，有心的讀者不妨參照，當可受益更多。英詩的傳統常把相互押韻的詩句對齊排列，例如意大利體的十四行詩，在排列時按例總將第一、第四、第五、第八各行，齊頭對準，而含另一韻的第二、第

三、第六、第七各行縮入二格排齊。我的譯文在這方面並不照辦，以免視覺平添紛亂。這是就六大頌而言，至於《聖安妮節前夕》的史賓賽體，末行延長為抑揚六步格，則譯文悉依原詩格式，讀者請莫誤會是我自己失控。

本書之譯述，時作時輟，先後久達兩年，並分別發表在《聯合副刊》、《聯合文學》、《印刻文學生活誌》和上海文聯主辦的《東方翻譯》月刊，使用了各刊不少篇幅。在此容我向各位主編衷心致謝。

在十四行詩、抒情詩、頌體的分別「綜述」中，有時我將自己的譯文和卞之琳、穆旦的譯文對照評析。為免此書過厚，體系太難，卞、穆兩位前賢的譯文不能全引。讀者如有意進一步詳究，請參閱《聯合文學》月刊302期（2009年12月）或《東方翻譯》雙月刊總第3期及第4期（2010年1月至4月）。

余光中　2012年1月26日壬辰龍年正月初四於左岸

濟慈名著譯述　目錄

輯一

十四行詩

十四行詩綜述

1

　　十四行詩（sonnet，或譯商籟，古雅而且簡潔）大盛於歐洲文藝復興時期，源出於意大利，早在十四世紀的斐楚阿克，已將此體發展得相當完美。到了十六世紀又有名家洪沙繼起，對英國詩人也有重大影響。莎士比亞的前輩如魏艾特爵士與塞瑞伯爵，意譯斐楚阿克的十四行時，已經將之變體；到了莎翁筆下，變體成了常態，後人遂稱爲莎士比亞體（Shakespearean sonnet），又稱英國體（English sonnet）。後來的英美詩人寫十四行時，兩體都有人採用，一直到二十世紀，雖無文藝復興時期之盛，卻也未盡冷落，大師如葉慈、哈代、佛洛斯特、奧登於此體仍有名作，爲論者稱道。

　　僅論詩體，則意大利原體與英國變體均爲十四行；每行都是十個音節，等分爲五個音步，每音步二音節，前輕後重，這樣的一行在術語上稱爲iambic pentameter。兩體相異之處，在於意大利體全詩分成兩個部份，前半八行，稱爲octave，後半六行，稱爲sestet，簡直可比樂曲。相應地，octave有八行的空間來呈現詩的主題，sestet卻只有六行可以迴旋，其功用在於把前面的主題順勢發展，予以加深或

擴大，不然就是逆勢操作，加以變奏或修正，甚至反向翻案。這麼一正一反，往往演成「正、反、合」的發展，其中天地似小實大，而餘味無窮。所以華茲華斯稱此體「不可輕視」（Scorn not the Sonnet），因爲這小樂器能讓莎士比亞剖心，斐楚阿克療傷，又像一片桃金孃花瓣，讓但丁戴在額頭，光如螢火，卻能在暗徑爲史賓塞引路，而到了米爾頓手裏又變成一支號角，其調能振奮人心。

　　但是英國體的十四行，在架構上卻大不相同：不再承襲意大利體的一主一客，相輔相成，而是「大放而急收」，前面的十二行分成三個「四行段」（quatrain），最末的兩行簡直像急煞車，爲前面的十二行下一個定論（conclusion）。例如濟慈的〈當我擔憂〉，在文法上全詩只是一個完整句：前面的十二行半全由三個副詞子句（adverbial clause）構成，每一子句佔四行，都由副詞when引進，正好符合三個「四行段」的要求。一直要到詩末的第十三行與第十四行，眞正的主句（main clause）才出現：主詞是I，動詞是stand和think；其實末行Till...do sink又自成一個附屬子句。最末這二行半當然不是結論，但是仍有總結前面三個附屬子句懸而未決的情境之功。

　　最後說到十四行詩的韻序（rhyming scheme）。意大利體的韻序一共動用五個韻：前八行爲abba / abba，後六行比較自由，可以是cdcdcd，也可以是cdecde或其他安排。英國體則相應其本身的結構，押成abab / cdcd / efef / gg的七韻序列。這樣的韻序比起中國七言律詩一韻到底來，要複雜得

多，對譯者的要求也更苛嚴，可說選第一行的韻腳時，就不得不考慮全詩的韻序，簡直是「牽一韻而動全詩」。

2

　　濟慈一共寫了六十一首十四行詩，相當多產。這產量比起英國浪漫主義的宗師華茲華斯來，當然只算小巫，但是華翁的八十歲三倍於濟慈的二十五歲還不止，而且他中年以後的十四行比之前之作都較遜色。量與質，未必能成正比。美國現代詩人莫美若（Merrill Moore）寫的十四行超過一千首，又如何呢，他仍不算是大詩人。反之，米爾頓一生只寫了二十四首十四行，因爲他氣盛才高，格局恢弘，用力以史詩巨著爲主，所以他的十四行多以特殊場合爲主題，正是歌德所謂的occasional poem，大半因事而發，乃能言之有物。也因此米爾頓的十四行氣盛而溢，每每會像無韻體一樣多見迴行，而且跨越前八行與後六行的「楚河漢界」。〈失明述志〉（On His Blindness）一詩是一佳例：十四行中竟有八行是迴行，第八行更一鼓作氣，從octave跨進了sestet。濟慈受米爾頓影響頗深，例如他的十四行〈如果英語〉，在第八行末本應收句至少稍頓，卻變成迴行，無論文意或文法都要等下一行才有交代。〈艾爾金大理石雕觀後〉的第四行也以迴行告終，要伸入第五行才能斷句。

　　濟慈寫十四行，頗得力於前輩史賓塞、莎士比亞、米爾頓、華茲華斯的啓發，六十一首作品之中，三分之二以上是

意大利體，不足三分之一是英國體。難得的是：兩體他都留
下了佳作，甚至傑作。例如〈初窺柴譯荷馬〉、〈久困在都
市的人〉、〈蚱蜢與蟋蟀〉、〈當我擔憂〉、〈亮星啊，
願我能〉等篇，都是一般英詩選集必選之作。其中〈初〉、
〈久〉、〈蚱〉是意大利體，後二首則是英國體。濟慈這麼
年輕，竟然兼擅兩體，真是難得。我所譯的二十首之中，自
己最喜歡的卻是〈艾爾金大理石雕觀後〉。此詩十四行中竟
有一半是迴行，尤其是第四行末，看來似乎是煞尾句（end
－stopped），後面一行卻接踵而來，氣勢流暢，呼應明快，
簡直像一對偶句（couplet）了。凡此種種，皆有米爾頓之餘
風。此詩前八行儘管自稱week而又gentle，骨子裏卻不甘屈
服，自有一股不可磨滅的豪氣。果然到了後六行，氣勢越來
越盛，聲調漸次升高，有如樂曲中的crescendo，終達末行
的高潮。我每次朗誦，都自覺會意氣風發。可惜此詩在一般
選集中，入選率不高。

　　我翻譯濟慈的二十首十四行詩，對他的詩體盡量緊貼；
但有時為了避免湊韻而失之勉強，我也會略加變通，在意式
與英式之間，權宜取捨，不以律害意。其實濟慈自己有時也
未能緊守格律，例如〈重讀莎翁《李爾王》〉這一首，末二
行是：

But, when I am consumèd in the fire,
Give me new Phoenix wings to fly at my desire.

前一行只有九個音節，其中the其實在快讀時算不上一個音節。經濟慈將consumèd加上被動式符號後，才勉強湊成十個音節，以符「抑揚五步格」之要求。至於後一行則長達十二音節，已變成「抑揚六步格」（iambic hexameter）了。原作既不合規定（例如Addressed to Haydon之二，其第十三行只有五個音節），譯文又何必拘泥呢？因此在我的譯文裏，每行字數一律在九字到十一字之間伸縮調整，才能配合原作的眞正語境。

〈致柴德敦〉寫於1815年，是濟慈極早的少作。柴德敦（Thomas Chatterton, 1752-1770）是上得了英國文學史的最短壽詩人，不滿十八歲就因見棄於文壇而自盡。他死於華茲華斯出生之年，華翁在〈果決與自立〉一詩中慨歎詩人在世，每始於喜悅而終於絕望，特別提到柴德敦與彭斯。濟慈寫此詩時才十九歲，未必想到自己也會夭亡，只是惺惺相惜而已；可是「夜色忽至，緊追你的朝霞」豈不是也應在他自己身上？幸運的是，他畢竟比柴德敦多活了八年，才能趕寫出更多傑作，在文壇的貢獻更大。這首詩是正規的意大利體，我的譯文也完全跟上原韻。倒是濟慈自己受害於英文本身的限制，能選的韻腳有限，不得不把misery和eye勉強相押。

〈久困在都市的人〉（To one who has been long in city pent）一詩，起句就套用米爾頓《失樂園》之句（As one who long in populous city pent），也有點像柯立基〈付夜鶯〉的一行（How many bards in city garret pent）。這是

首意大利體十四行，寫城裏人下鄉一日之遊，雖爲直敍，卻娓娓動聽。前八行（octave）寫晝遊，後六行寫暮歸，一開一闔，遣詞典雅，節奏流利，段落分明，多音節的長字（firmament, languishment）尤其暢快。但是後六行（sestet）就慢了下來，用兩個迴行（–an ear, –an eye）來煞車。小小的濟慈在結構上最會安排：整首詩只用了三整句，前四行一句，中間四行一句，末六行一句，井然有序。中間四行文法不可回頭，一回便尾大不掉。When引入的漫長子句不堪照單全收，放進中文裏來。常見一般只會「照搬」的譯者遇到諸如where men...的句法，不知所措，只知譯成「在那兒，人們……」，此關若參不透，譯筆永遠難成正果。又如gentle tale of love and languishment，若只知直譯，勢必冗長如「描寫愛情與爲愛憔悴的溫柔故事」，十四字之多，也是尾大不掉。我只用四字就解決了六個音節，不讓句長失控。本詩最美的兩句該是with an ear / Catching the notes of Philomel – an eye / Watching the sailing cloudlet's bright career，尤以第二句更美。晴朗的晚空，一片流雲旋生旋滅，其生命不過轉瞬之間，故云bright career。一片微雲，流逝天際，cloudlet極言其小，sailing則極言其漂游之輕逸，更含白帆趁風的意象，所以我用「一帆流雲」來概括。

　　穆旦是一位很不錯的譯家，可惜中文還不夠好，可以應變的籌碼不足。例如六、七兩行的Fatigued he sinks into some pleasant lair / Of wavy grass...，首先fatigued無論如何

不應譯成「滿意」，然後sinks into若譯為「深深躺在」，當較「懶懶」為佳，因為sink正與後文的lair互相呼應。Lair乃獸穴或窩巢，原是名詞；pleasant lair乃形容詞加名詞，我用動詞加副詞化開了，但此意在穆旦的譯文裏卻不見了。同時wavy grass穆旦譯成「青草的波浪」，未免太坐實，太重了。Catching, watching穆譯只是「聽、觀」，沒有錯，但不到位。我稍稍加工，譯成「追聽、望斷」，當較像詩，也更合濟慈的豐富感性。流雲那一句，濟慈原意應該不止「飄過」，而是雲生雲沒只在指顧之間，並非再看已經在空中掠過，而是再看竟已不在了。如此解釋，才能配合後文的mourns和passage。

　　至於此詩韻腳，前八行是abba, abba，只用兩個韻。穆譯勉強譯成abba, cddc，未免打了個對折。後六行是cdcdcd，穆譯充分對應，我卻把末二行互押，倒成了英國體了，不算到位。

　　〈初窺柴譯荷馬〉（On First Looking into Chapman's Homer）是濟慈最有名的十四行詩，幾乎見於一切英詩通選。濟慈二十三歲那年，十月某夜在亦師亦友的柯拉克（Cowden Clarke）家中，共讀柴普曼（George Chapman, 1559-1634）所譯荷馬史詩，十分驚喜，通宵不眠。次晨濟慈徒步回家，草就此詩，上午十時柯拉克即收到他快郵傳來這首傑作。此詩結構非常嚴謹：前四行說作者曾讀遍古典名著，後四行說只恨尚未得窺荷馬之天地；末六行用兩個比喻來形容得賞荷馬英譯本之驚喜。

　　欲譯英詩，必須熟悉英文文法，深諳中、英語法之差異究竟何在，否則譯文不像是詩，不是失之生硬，便是流於油滑。例如英文（或一切西方語文）常用代名詞或其所有格，並不妨礙詩意；反之，中文詩就絕少用這些。李白絕對不會說「抽刀斷水它更流，舉杯消愁它更愁」。王維也不會說「我獨在異鄉爲異客，我每逢佳節倍思我的親人」。

　　濟慈這首詩用了十二個代名詞及所有格（I, he, his, its, which），我的譯文只用了兩個。穆旦的譯文用了八個。穆旦譯了許多西方詩，習於西方文法而不自覺，所以他自己寫的詩也頗西化，其一現象便是不知省用代名詞。其實鄭敏、馮至也有此病。我的譯文少用這些代名詞，所以每行字數較省：可以自限不逾十一個字，而短行也不會少於九字。穆旦的譯文因爲費詞，所以每行常達十二字。此地我所譯濟慈八首詩，都自設每行上限爲十一字。吾友施穎洲譯文每行以十字爲上限，未免束縛過甚，語氣太促。其實莎翁十四行詩，也常見一行含十一音節。即使濟慈此詩，其十二行He stared at the Pacific–and all his men也含十一音節，只是Pacific讀快了勉強可以二音節計而已。

　　此詩仍是意大利體，但是穆譯仍將前八行押成不規則的abba, cddc，想必是無奈而非故意。其實「國、者」也不成韻。

　　第四行的which是指western islands，穆譯作「它們」，最敗詩意。第七行的breathe its pure serene，其serene一字源出拉丁，意爲「清淨的天空」。穆譯把生動可感的breathe意譯爲抽象的「領略」，可惜。原文前八行在意大利體本應自

給自足，以句號點斷，穆譯句長失控，竟向末六行的sestet去借用半行，仍應歸咎於功力不夠老練。這樣的功力在自己創作時也就會捉襟見肘。第十行的swims形容星光在望遠鏡中飄忽不定，最爲傳神；可惜穆旦又淪具體爲抽象，反譯爲平凡的「發現」。也就難怪我們讀他自己的詩，也常有「理勝於感」之憾。第十二行his men穆譯作「他的同夥」，也不準確。

〈寒風陣陣〉與〈致柴德敦〉完全一樣，是傳統的意大利體。寫於1816年11月，作者與好友克拉克夜訪李衡於漢普斯台地（Hampstead），要徒步五英里以上才能回到倫敦的寓所。顯然，濟慈在李衡家裏讀到米爾頓爲弔劍橋同學金愛華（Edward King）溺於愛爾蘭海而寫的悼詩Lycidas，又看了斐楚阿克獻給情人洛娜的十四行集。

〈蚱蜢與蟋蟀〉寫於1816年底，也是正規的意大利體。當時他和李衡比賽，看誰能在十五分鐘內完成以蚱蜢與蟋蟀爲主題的十四行詩。結果兩人都如期成詩，但濟慈先交了卷。濟慈之作用前八行描寫夏天籬邊草間的蚱蜢，再用後六行轉敘冬晚火爐畔的蟋蟀，一起一接，完全符合意大利體的結構。其實寫蟋蟀只用了四行，剩下的兩行卻用來描寫爐邊人在暖氣中聽來，竟幻覺蟋蟀之鳴像在夏天的草坡上聽蚱蜢之歌。這正、反、合的一波三折，贏得寫濟慈傳記的美國女詩人艾米・羅威爾的讚美，說結句之美不但在詩藝，也在詩思。

〈快哉英倫〉是意大利體，結構非常均衡。前八行octave之中，前四行坦言自己愛國，住在英國已很滿意，後

四行語氣一轉，說南歐的高爽晴朗也令我神往。到了本詩後六行sestet，則其前三行先說明英國柔順白皙的少女固然可愛，但是南國拉丁女郎的激情與健美，加上睇人的眼神，似乎更迷人。前八行說南國的地理與氣候，後六行說南國的佳人，都用本國情況來對照，真是高妙。

〈艾爾金大理石雕觀後〉（On Seeing the Elgin Marbles）的主題，是英國駐君士坦丁堡大使艾爾金勳爵，擔心土耳其與希臘衝突會損及希臘文物，乃取得土耳其當局許可，將雅典神殿的雕飾運去英國，1816年由英國政府買下，供大英博物館展覽。濟慈在博物館瞻仰由這些石雕傳承的古希臘壯觀，不勝神往，乃賦此詩。

前八行寫詩人面對古文化的真蹟，震撼於其神奇壯麗，對比之下，更自覺此身之病弱渺小，正如一隻病鷹仰羨滿天風雲，卻無力飛騰。不過他並不久耽於自憐，遂告訴自己不應溺於自憐之縱情。病鷹望天之歎也不全然是比喻。這些石雕、柱飾的真蹟原是採自巍峨的神殿，而神殿更矗立於雅典山頂的衛城。詩人可以設想，此身若在現場瞻仰，不知有多磅礡。末六行把場景由近推遠，轉實為虛，把想像的光輝帶回空羨的惆悵。為什麼會有眩暈之苦，是因為濟慈既不懂希臘文，又無緣親訪希臘，只能徒羨神殿之高，衛城之峻，而無力高攀。學者認為此詩是對無限與永恆之讚歎，當然也說得通。不過濟慈之詩藝出眾，往往在於他能以近喻遠，以實證虛，而不淪於抽象空論。其實末三行就地取材，可以理解為是回到現場，先寫古蹟歷盡兩千多年的滄桑，再寫衛城、

神殿俯臨大海，在「西風殘照」之下，廊柱簷角投下了曳長的古建築陰影。

　　此詩仍是意大利體，穆譯仍然未能對應前八行大開大闔的abba, abba，失職了。原文前四行勢如破竹，推進到第五行末文句才煞住，顯然有米爾頓之風，穆譯倒是跟上了。只是mortality譯成「無常」，不夠準確。三、四行的 each imagined pinnacle and steep / Of godlike hardship，穆譯是「每件神工底玄想的極峰」，不但失之過簡，而且語意不清。Pinnacle和steep兩個名詞，非「極峰」所能概括。Godlike hardship也不能僅僅以「神工」二字來支應。倒是原文只占半行的tells me I must die，穆譯卻變成整行，詳略之間分配失當。

　　後六行穆譯失誤不少，簡直不及格。第九、第十兩行brain和heart的對比，在穆譯中完全看不出來。Dim怎麼可譯「極盡」？The heart的意思也不能逕以「我」來抵充。更嚴重的是末四行，關鍵在於濟慈省略了（在英文文法上可以用do代替的）一個動詞：bring。因為前文已用過bring，所以到後一行就只說do了。末四行的文法脈絡應該是：So do these wonders bring a most dizzy pain that mingles Grecian grandeur with (1) rude wasting of Time, (2) billowy main, (3) sun, (4) shadow of magnitude.穆旦沒有看出這一層關鍵，遂令焦點模糊。「我看見的是灰色的波浪」，整句譯得唐突難解。原文在with之後，勢如破竹，是一連串密集而來的受詞，穆譯竟用一個修正的「卻」字阻在其間。Billowy怎麼

能譯「灰色」，也很奇怪。

〈詠滄海〉又是一首工整的意大利體。主題上，前八行寫海洋本身，後六行則勸世人，在疲於市井的繁瑣與喧囂之餘，不妨去海邊靜坐冥思。前八行的音調頗能營造驚濤拍岸繼而風定浪靜的聽覺。八行之中，四個韻腳（swell, spell, shell, fell）加上till，will一共六個曳長的 l 尾音，頗能暗示風潮起伏之感。另一方面，破空而來的重音逆移（desolate, gluts twice ten thousand caverns, Hecate）更加強了驚濤駭浪壓捲層疊之勢。尤其是Hecate頭重腳輕一連三聲急驟直下，聽覺的感性特別到位：換了是同樣月神之名的Cynthia，Diana或Phoebe，就不會有這種效果。

〈重讀莎翁《李爾王》〉是意大利體的變奏：前八行韻序abba，abba遵守傳統，後六行卻變成cdcdee，是英國體了。我的譯文完全到位。此詩以莎翁悲劇傑作為主題，更加上濟慈重讀悲劇的感受，古今相彰，人我交感，十分成功，處處都有伏筆。詩末的「鳳翼」呼應詩首的「華羽」。濟慈重讀《李爾王》，深感慘烈焚心，故云「蹈火而過」，終於「在烈焰中耗亡」，但願能從劫灰中重生。烈焰的意象不但來自悲劇，更扣住了濟慈自己的肺病。Consumed意為「耗盡、燒光」，其名詞consumption有「肺病」一解。就算此詩寫於1818年初，作者肺病情況才初現，但母親早已死於肺病，弟弟湯姆當時也將死於此疾，他自己是醫科學生，當然知道難以倖免。就算他不知道，也可稱為「一語成讖」吧。第八行The bitter-sweet of this Shakespearian fruit，如果

直譯成「這個莎士比亞的又苦又甜的果子」，不但太累贅拖沓，而且不像詩句，更押不上韻。把bitter-sweet移到句末，就可解決了。可見譯詩，有時還得重組原文句法才行。

〈當我擔憂〉（When I have fears that I may cease to be）是一首英國體十四行，也是濟慈極有名的短篇傑作，論流暢圓融，絕不遜於莎翁。結構嚴整，段落分明，一氣呵成：全詩在文法上只是一完整長句，前面的三個四行體（quatrain）各為一副詞子句，以when引入，主詞要等到第十三行才從容出現，卻由主動詞think引進第四個副詞子句Till love and fame to nothingness do sink。前呼後擁，陣勢好不井然。這種嚴謹，這種功力，這麼年輕，是當代詩人能企及的麼？

英國體的十四行，在結構上是三個四行段，加上結論式的雙行，韻序則為abab, cdcd, efef, gg。穆譯大致遵行，但末段的「你、的」和「思、裏」卻押得勉強。

有趣的是：穆旦的譯文比我的淺白直露。淺易如能做到「清水出芙蓉，天然去雕飾」，反而更高明。不過新詩的主流曾是白話詩，譯詩一向也以白話為主。問題在於白話比文言「費詞」，在翻譯時往往冗長、直硬，以至句長失控，反而不如文言那麼精簡而有彈性。所以文言修養不足的詩人譯起詩來，每每捉襟見肘，周轉不靈。穆旦的弱點正是如此。何況濟慈去今已近二百年，他的英文也自有些文雅，誰規定譯二百年前英文，必須用今日的白話呢？濟慈生年與龔自珍相當，定庵當時寫的是七言律詩，典雅可與十四行詩相提並

論。我當然無意用律詩來譯十四行，但是認為譯詩的時候，若能文白相濟，就多一張王牌，方便得多了。

我們不妨做一個實驗，看看穆旦的「全白」跟我的「白以為常，文以應變」相比，其間有何得失？這首When I have fears that I may cease to be，我的譯文〈當我擔憂〉用了141字，穆旦的譯文〈每當我害怕〉用了165字，比我多出二十四個字；平均他每行比我多用一點七個字。他每行多則十二字，少則十一字，我多則十一字，少則九字。此外，原文的代名詞有九個，包括七個 I，兩個 it。穆譯則有八個「我」，兩個「它」；我的中譯只有六個「我」，一個「其」。穆譯有十二個「的」，外加一個「底」；我譯只有六個「的」，外加一個「之」。可見我所省去的字不是形容詞尾的「的」，就是代名詞。詩貴精簡，其道端在刪去冗字贅詞。反諷的是：我用字較少，詩行較短，反而較有彈性，也更好懂。

原文gleaned my teeming brain，令我們聯想到米勒的名畫「拾穗者」，因此teeming brain自然隱喻豐盛的秋收。穆譯仍然反其道而行，淪具象為抽象，何況「思潮」之為物也很難「蒐集」。更何況後面的「穀倉」原承豐收而來，如何能接「思潮」。可惜一子落錯，全局受損。至於charactery，乃冷僻字，意為「按字序」，尤其是alphabetical order；穆譯「在文字裏」，令人不解。Starr'd face用動詞轉化形容詞，比starry face生動，但中文難以表現。穆譯「繁星的夜幕」，淪臉為幕，又把抽象代具象，誠

如王國維所病，「隔」矣。我譯爲「星相」，取其有面相
之聯想，當較近原文。「傳奇故事的巨大的雲霧徵象」一
句，連用二「的」，失之冗長，「雲霧徵象」也生硬難解。
「以偶然底神筆描出它的幻象」也不足以捕捉magic hand of
chance的妙處。我想，這種種不足穆且也許並非沒有自覺，
但是他可能更苦於安排韻腳，爲了湊韻，只好扭曲句法，更
難照顧詩意了。

　　濟慈此詩寫於1818年1月底，此後他寫十四行詩便傾
向英國體，少寫意大利體了。又詩中所稱fair creature of an
hour，一般以爲是他的戀人芬妮（Fanny Brawne），其實
是一位無名的絕色佳人，四年前的夏天他曾在馥素館花園
（Vauxhall Gardens）驚豔一瞥。除本詩外，濟慈還爲了這
千載一遇的女子另寫了兩首詩。

　　〈有贈〉也是一首莎翁體，譯文亦步亦趨。但在句法
上，前四行組成的第一段（quatrain），其一、二兩行Time's
sea...the sand乃主句，三、四兩行Since I was...of thy hand乃
附屬子句：這四行如果一路順譯下來，會不像中文，所以我
倒過來，把附屬子句置於主句之前。全詩末二行，依莎翁體
的規矩，應當互相押韻並且獨成一句，爲全詩做一結論。但
在這首詩末，這一句話卻從第十二行就已開始，所以我的譯
文也依樣處理。濟慈自註：〈有贈〉的對象爲一淑女，他
在泰晤士河南岸的馥素館花園（Vauxhall Gardens）驚鴻一
瞥。學者認爲：濟慈十四行詩〈當我擔憂〉（When I have
fears）中的fair creature of an hour就是她。〈有贈〉寫於

1818年2月4日，五年前是1813年；濟慈認識芬妮卻在1818
年10月底，所以fair creature of an hour不可能指芬妮。

〈致尼羅河〉寫於1818年2月4日，是濟慈和雪萊、李衡
三人比賽的結果。時限是十五分鐘，濟慈和雪萊及時交卷，
李衡則過了時限，卻不失爲佳作。我的譯文頭兩行是倒過
來意譯，若是直譯，簡直就會不知所云。我把swart nations
譯爲「黎民、群黧」，正合了中文的原意，成了雙關。第
十行 'Tis ignorance that makes a barren waste / Of all beyond
itself：此地的itself是指抽象名詞ignorance，穆旦譯成「只
有愚昧才意度自己以外／都是荒涼」讀者一定看不懂，倒
不如挑明了說是「異邦」。本詩是依意大利體，不過b韻以
beguile與toil相押，並未對準，倒不如我的譯文。濟慈和雪
萊都未到過埃及，卻都題詠了此一古邦，此亦浪漫主義神馳
遠古與異域之特色。雪萊的Ozymandias我也譯過。

〈致J.R.〉的對象是賴斯（James Rice），濟慈的好
友，濟慈說他是「我認識的人中最有見識甚至最有智慧的一
位」。詩人自恨人生苦短，何況他註定會更短於他人，所以
但願時光可以常駐，賞心樂事可以長享，而平淡的現實也可
藉浪漫的東方來美化。此詩韻腳並不穩健：space和haze未
能押準，Ind和bind也押得勉強。

〈致荷馬〉用的是英國體（亦即莎士比亞體）十四行，
我也完全追隨其韻序與段式，並以末二行雙押。「連環群
島」的原文是the Cyclades，如僅譯其音，恐得動用五個漢
字，甚至七個（席克拉底斯群島），倒不如迻譯其希臘文原

義。這一群島嶼在希臘東岸外海組成一圈，據說荷馬出生
於其中一島。濟慈的主題是強調天才目盲而心開闊，所以
天神宙父（Jove）為之掀天幕，海神（Neptune）為之撐波
蓬，而牧神Pan為之闢森林。三界都任其自由出入，豈不等
於Diana，既是月神，又是獵人之保護神，又是左右潮汐的
Hecate了。末二行把前文十二行做一總結，十分莊嚴。

　　〈詠艾爾沙危岩〉乃蘇格蘭南部的蕞爾離島，因火山爆
發而升上水面，所以濟慈說它前身在海底，後身在空中，
前身只識水族，後身可棲鷹隼，詩思熔地質學與想像於一
爐。此詩穆旦也譯過，可惜他竟未細看題目，把Ailsa誤為
Alisa，譯成〈詠阿麗沙巉岩〉了。

　　〈寫于彭斯降世茅舍〉寫於1818年11月11日，第一行濟
慈就自稱This mortal body of a thousand days，怎麼能確定
自己的陽壽只剩下一千天了呢？一千天只有三年欠三個月，
後來他死於羅馬，是在1821年2月23日，距離此詩寫作之
日，才兩年又三個半月，果然壽命不足千日：未必是一語成
讖，因為他自己是醫科出身。在此詩寫作前四個多月，濟慈
已寫過一首詩，叫做〈弔于彭斯墓前〉。他對苦命又夭亡的
詩人，例如柴德敦與彭斯，都倍加惋惜，誠如雪萊在悼濟慈
的長詩Adonais所云：「為他人的苦命流自傷之淚。」（in
another's fate now wept his own.）

　　〈致睡眠〉的主題，既是歌頌睡眠也是懇求睡眠。詩
人、藝術家等多思敏感，容易失眠可想而知。濟慈多病，當
然亟須安眠，肺病患者呼吸不順，尤然。德國諺語便說：

「病人睡得好，病體已半療。」難怪濟慈請求睡眠恩賜他「黑甜之鄉」，並說：「啊，溺愛的睡眠！肯否相助，／趁你頌歌未完就讓我欣然／合眼，莫等到阿門才將罌粟／催眠的慈悲撒遍我床畔。」第十一行的conscience我故意譯成「俗念」，所以curious conscience譯成「多事的俗念」。俗念在此地是指：人在醒時，萬念起伏，多半是世俗名利得失的雜念。《漢姆萊特》中丹麥王子始於To be, or not to be的那一長段獨白，便有Thus conscience does make cowards of us all之句：conscience如作「良心」解，則「良心令人怯懦」便說不通。濟慈狀物敘事，務求感性飽滿，所以常用動詞的過去分詞來做形容詞：這首十四行中，例如passèd，oilèd，hushèd等字，都不可唸成單音節。另一方面，第三行的embower'd其實應該唸成三音節，可是濟慈竟把第二個e省去，這麼一來，這一行只有九音節了，不應該。

〈如果英語〉既非正規的意大利體，也非英國的變體，更難稱兩者的調和、變通。韻腳次序極亂，排成abca, beca, bceded。我的譯文稍加收拾，排成abba, acca, dede, ff，前八行近於意大利體，後六行卻是不折不扣的英國體。濟慈此詩之主題，是勸英國詩人要把十四行體（商籟）寫好，就不可草率敷衍，而要改弦更張，全神以赴，務必使片詞隻字都發揮效果，切戒妄用枯枝敗葉來織桂冠。如此，繆思的桂冠至少由她自己作主來採織，遠勝過由庸才來劫持操縱。

〈名氣〉是一首中規中矩的英國體十四行，我大致亦步亦趨，包括韻序。年輕的濟慈病體和愛情皆無保障，經濟不

穩，詩名未彰，對於成名當然是十分渴望的，所以寫過兩首以〈名氣〉爲題的十四行。此詩乃詩人自勉自慰之詞，大意是說名氣無理可喻，越求成名，越與名氣無緣，不如順其自然，不卑不亢，反而能贏得她的青睞。濟慈追求的盛名未能及身而遂，這一點，他在〈當我擔憂〉一詩中也似有預感，在〈懶散頌〉的第三段也有涉及，稱之爲「野心」（Ambition）。

〈亮星啊，願我能〉（Bright star! would I were steadfast as thou art）也是英國體，學者一向認爲是濟慈最後的作品，在航向意大利的船上，由他親筆謄於畫家塞文所讀的莎翁劇本，亦即〈情人訴苦〉（A Lover's Complaint）對面的空頁上。晚近的考證卻認爲成詩日期應提前到1819年底，置於同一主題同一詩體致芬妮的情急之作〈苦求你給我慈悲、憐憫、愛情〉（I cry your mercy, pity, love – ay, love!）的後面。

穆譯每行長度，在十三字與十字之間，我譯在十一字與九字之間；他共用了164字，我只用了141字，差別與When I have fears一詩相同。這也許要歸因於穆且未能節省，例如首句的bright star，譯「亮星、明星」即可，何必非用四字，把詩行拉長到十三字？七、八兩行的new soft – fallen mask of snow，原文只有七個音節，穆譯「飄飛的白雪，像面幕，燦爛，輕盈」，卻用了十二個字，何況「燦爛」也未能對應new，更無端重複了首句的用詞。此外，moors譯成「漥地」，也錯了：漥地水濕，能積雪成面具嗎？

第十行pillow'd upon譯「枕在……之上」即可，何必費詞說「以頭枕在……之上」。Ripening譯「酥軟」未免稍俗，且有「酥胸」的浮濫，倒不如直譯「成熟」。下一行its soft swell and fall，其中its是指胸脯，譯成「它」沒錯，但不合中文想法，也不美。倒不如歸於「它」的主人，直接挑明「她」好。我逕譯「她」，應該更好懂吧。第十二行in a sweet unrest未必僅指詩人「心中」，更可能是指或是兼指詩人枕著這麼一個活枕頭，起伏不安，而又樂在其中吧。末行live ever譯成「活著」，是不夠的；awake for ever也不能只譯成「醒來」。

濟慈專家海若德（H. W. Harrod）在1989年牛津大學版的《濟慈詩集》評註中，指出此詩前八行的bright star，是說北極星，這孤高不移的氣象來自莎翁的一一六號十四行詩，還加上《凱撒大帝》第三幕第一景六十至六十二行。其實濟慈一樣崇拜米爾頓，以北極星開端時也應難避免華滋華斯以北極星喻先賢的意大利體十四行〈米爾頓，此刻你應在人間！〉（Milton, thou shouldst be living at this hour!）。海若德認為此詩以標榜北極星的孤高自遠開始，卻以戀情的入世狎近結束，失之勉強。我也覺得詩人又以星象高曠遠矚、堅貞自許的氣派為志，又以愛欲沉醉寧死溫柔之鄉為歸，又要求永恆，又不捨當下，由octave逆轉而入sestet，矛盾未能統一，意境難稱圓滿。

致柴德敦

柴德敦啊！你的命多悲慘！
憂傷之寵兒——苦難之子！
眼神過早被翳於夭逝，
天才與雄辯竟不得大燦。
喉音莊嚴而自得，也竟然
過早消失於殘韻！夜色忽至，
緊追你的朝霞。如此去世，
像蓓蕾半開被寒風摧殘。
都過去了：你已經就位
在至高的星穹，向眾星運轉
唱得多酣暢；聖樂誰能損毀，
渾忘世道無情，人間不安。
你的美名下界有善人相維，
不容輕菲，更流淚以澆灌。

久困在都市的人

久困在都市的人應感到
最稱心是凝望那晴豔
而開朗的天顏——喃喃祈願
向著笑容廣闊的青霄。
誰比他快樂呢,他多逍遙,
倦了,便躺在起伏的草間,
窩得好樂,而且讀一篇
優雅的故事,講為情苦惱。
傍晚的歸途,一面追聽
夜鶯的歌聲,一面望斷
一帆流雲燦爛的生命,
可惜匆匆溜失的一天:
竟似天使的淚珠,全程
寂寂垂落透徹的太清。

初窺柴譯荷馬

曾經我暢遊金色的領域，
名邦與古國也見識了不少；
而去過的許多西方列島
古詩人曾向日神獻祭。
有一片廣土常聽人提起，
說深思的荷馬曾經領導；
卻無緣吞吐其中的靈妙，
要等到柴普曼的洪音壯語：
於是我有如夜觀星象，
忽見有新星游入眼底；
又像壯哉戈達士鷹目奮張，
俯瞰著太平洋——而眾兵丁
都面面相覷，充滿了驚疑，
肅然，立在達利安的峰頂。

寒風陣陣

寒風一陣陣，遍地在低吟，
四周的枯樹一半已落葉；
滿天的星斗看來很冷冽，
我還有好幾里路要步行。
但我一點不在乎多淒清，
或風吹枯葉颯颯而不絕，
或銀燈點點高照而不滅，
或溫馨的家還隔著遠程：
只因滿心洋溢著友愛，
剛才得覽於小茅屋裏；
說金髮的米爾頓盡吐悲辛，
悼他的愛友李西德溺海；
說動人的洛娜倩披青衣，
而專情的裴楚客燦戴金頂。

蚱蜢與蟋蟀

大地的歌詠從不沉寂：
當百鳥被烈日曬得頭昏，
都躲進樹陰，有一種歌聲，
一籬接一籬，沿新割的草地，
那是蚱蜢——他領先發起
夏天的盛會——他的歡騰
永遠不告終；就算已玩睏，
也可安憩在清涼的草底。
大地的歌詠從不中斷：
落寞的冬晚，當寒霜把萬籟
都噤絕，爐邊就唧唧清揚
蟋蟀之歌，因室溫而高囀，
在半醒半寐的人聽來，
就像蚱蜢在草山吟唱。

快哉英倫

快哉英倫，我本已心滿意足，
不想出國觀賞異國的青翠，
也不望異國的清風來吹
祖國高聳的森林，英雄所出：
但有時我不免也會仰慕
意大利的晴空，內心私唔，
登阿爾卑斯應如登王位，
渾忘世間凡夫的禮俗。
快哉英倫，少女無邪又溫柔，
如此單純可愛不應更奢求，
臂膀絕白垂肩夠嫻靜；
我卻時常渴望能一見
美目盼兮更深，一聆伊歌吟，
且相與浮沉在夏日的波間。

艾爾金大理石雕觀後

我的心神脆弱不堪；大限
重壓著我，像被迫沉睡不醒，
而每件幻想的峭壁，尖頂，
神工艱鉅，都說我必死不免，
像一隻病鷹仰望著蒼天。
但流淚又未免柔弱而縱情，
只為挽不住長風遠雲，
見不到清新的曙光睜眼。
腦際想像的光輝，如此恍惚，
為心頭帶來難言的惆悵；
像這些奇觀也帶來眩暈
之苦，將希臘的壯麗盡付
遠古去消磨──付與怒浪，
付與落日，付與宏大的陰影。

詠滄海

耳語切切永遠不休息，
繞著荒涼的岩岸，而高潮
會饕餮千巖萬穴，直到
月神的魔咒只留下歔欷。
往往你見他如此好脾氣，
連上次天風撒野所狂拋
的一片貝殼，那怕是最小，
也幾天留在原地不稍移。
哦，誰要是眼球不安又疲勞，
不妨飽享大海的洪量；
哦，誰要是耳鼓受不了喧囂，
或是脹滿了膩人的音樂，
也不妨坐在古洞口冥想，
到恍聞眾水靈合唱才驚覺！

重讀莎翁《李爾王》

哦，金腔的傳奇，琴韻琤琤！
華羽的海妖，遠古的仙后！
莫在這冬日不斷地演奏，
合上你的殘卷，莫要出聲：
別了！又一次劇烈的爭論，
天譴與人欲對立在兩頭，
我必須蹈火而過，再試一口
莎翁的奇果，甘苦難分：
宗師啊！你與古英倫的雲天
將深永的主題一路傳來！
當我穿過古橡的林間，
讓我莫在殘夢裏徘徊，
可是當我在烈焰中耗亡，
請給我新鳳翼飛向願望。

當我擔憂

當我擔憂自己會太早逝去，
筆還未拾盡豐盛的心田，
厚疊的詩卷，按字母順序，
還未像穀倉將熟麥儲滿；
當我在夜之星相上見到
雲態昭示著高調的傳奇，
念及我此生永難追描
其幽影，靠手到神來的運氣；
當我感慨，千載一遇的佳人，
今世只怕我無緣再睹，
再也無福能消受神恩，
一享不計得失的愛慕；
於是人海茫茫岸邊我獨立，
苦思到愛情，聲名都沉底。

有　贈

自從落網於你的美貌，
被俘於你未戴手套的纖指，
時間之海已五年低潮，
悠久的光陰沙漏何遲遲。
每次凝望午夜的星空，
總會見你難忘的眸光；
每次凝望玫瑰多豔紅，
此心就向你臉頰飛翔；
每次凝望著一苞花蕾，
我的癡耳就像在你唇際，
指望能聽到愛語，竟誤會
能飽餐其香澤──記起你
的甜蜜，令一切喜悅都失色，
令窩心的歡愉摻入悽惻。

致尼羅河

非洲亙古的月山，你是後裔！
鱷魚和金字塔，你是母河！
都稱譽你肥沃，話才剛說，
沙漠就展現在我們心底。
渾沌初開，黎民養育就仗你，
你果眞是肥沃？還是你誘惑
群氓崇拜你，從德崁到開羅，
黎民勞困，因你而暫得休息？
哦，但願亂想是錯誤！當眞；
只有無知，才以爲凡是異邦
必然是荒漠。你當然也滋潤
藺草，如我們的河水，並樂享
愉悅的曙光。也有翠嶼繽紛，
當然也欣欣地奔向海洋。

致 J.R.

願一週啊是一年，每週就
感受分手再握有多溫馨，
一年之窮就變爲千載悠悠，
臉上永帶著泛紅的相迎：
於是片刻就可以安享長生，
而時光自己也不免消殞，
渺茫若忘時，一日之行程
也可以放寬，延長以助興。
哦，但願每週一都歸自印度！
週二都登陸，自富麗的東方！
歡樂豐收可以用剎那繫住，
而靈魂也能夠永保昂揚！
今天早晨，吾友啊，加上昨夕，
我悟出該如何心存這快意。

致荷馬

困於渾然的無知而孤立，
只聽說有你和連環群島，
就像岸上人或許有意
探深海海豚的珊瑚紅礁。
原來你是盲人！唯視障已開，
宙父掀帷幕讓你住天庭，
海神的波蓬為你而蓋，
牧神教群蜂為你共吟；
哎，黑暗的邊緣總有光線，
懸崖之上有未踐的草地，
子夜總懷著待綻的曙天，
敏銳的盲人有三重視力；
這種靈視就屬你，正如往古，
戴安娜君臨人間、天國、地府。

詠艾爾沙危岩

我說，海上危岩的金字塔！
應我吧，以海鳥的啼叫！
何年你肩頭披掛著狂濤？
何年太陽照不到你額下？
何年開始，博大的造化
命你將海底的夢舉上天空，
睡在雷霆或陽光的懷中，
或是由陰雲覆蓋你冷榻？
你不應我，因為你已睡寂；
你一生兼雙重寂滅的永恆——
後身在空中，前身在海底；
前身侶鯨鯊，後身伴鷹隼——
你淹沒到地震才湧起險峻，
更有誰能將你這魁梧撼醒。

附註：Ailsa Rock乃蘇格蘭南部的蕞爾離島，因火山爆發而形成。穆旦未細
看題目，竟譯成〈詠阿麗沙巉岩〉，有時又稱為〈訪阿麗沙巉岩〉，未免
大意。

寫于彭斯降世茅舍

只有一千天陽壽的此身
彭斯啊，竟占你房中一席地，
在此你曾經寄夢於桂芬，
天眞得不顧大限是何期！
你的麥酒能令我血暖，
向偉人敬酒，我頭飄飄，
眼神已渙散，什麼都不見，
幻想已沉寂，在終站醉倒；
你的地板我可以躞步，
撐開你窗框我可以遙睹
當日你來去踏過的野徑，
我念你，直到思路都迷糊，
只能豪飲一杯敬你的盛名，
願你能笑傲眾魂，享譽千古！

致睡眠

哦，爲午夜靜悄悄沐上香膏，
用細心而體貼的手指安撫
尋幽的眼眸，不容光來侵擾，
用神奇的渾忘爲我守護：
哦，溺愛的睡眠！肯否相助，
趁你頌歌未完就讓我欣然
合眼，莫等到阿門才將罌粟
催眠的慈悲撒遍我床畔。
救救我吧，白天雖然已逝去，
仍會照來我枕上，招來禍端——
救我，莫讓多事的俗念繼續
主控著幽冥，像穿洞的鼴鼠；
油滑的鎖孔，鑰匙要輕轉，
將魂魄的寶盒悄然封住。

如果英語

如果英語得用乏味的韻律
綑綁，而商籟甘美，苦中有歡，
像安綽美妲，也不能無羈絆，
再怎麼受限，我們都必須
尋到織得更整齊的便履，
讓詩神赤腳穿來夠輕盈：
我們要檢查豎琴，要校定
每根絃的張力，要聆聽仔細
並聚精會神，爲收穫而試驗；
我們要惜用聲調和音節，
像邁達司國王吝嗇金錢，
編織桂冠要戒用枯葉；
如此，就算還不能解放繆思，
她的花環至少她可以自織。

名　氣

名氣像一個少女，眞難纏，
羞於讓人奴顏來跪拜，
卻甘心順從粗魯的少年，
而對爛漫的心靈更寵愛；
她是個吉普賽，不愛答理
不得她就不快的妄人；
無情浪女，不許人貼耳密語，
認爲議論她就是損她品行；
十足的吉普賽，尼羅河所產，
善妒的波提瓦是她姻親；
苦情詩人，她傲慢你就傲慢，
失戀的藝術家啊，全是神經！
向她深深鞠躬吧，然後告退，
如果她在乎，就會來追隨。

亮星啊，願我能

亮星啊，願我能如你堅定，
不是孤光高耀在夜空，
永不閉目，像造化的大隱，
耐心而無眠，看海波流動，
神父一般在主持洗禮，
要滌清下界人間的海岸；
不是俯望新飄落的面具，
降雪籠罩著山頂與荒原；
都不是──只求穩定又堅貞，
能枕著俏情人成熟的胸脯，
永遠感受她溫柔的起伏，
在甜蜜的不安中長保清醒，
不斷，不斷聽她輕輕地噓息，
就此享永生──不然就暈斃。

輯二

抒情詩

抒情詩綜述

　　抒情詩的範圍很廣，其實濟慈的十四行和五大頌廣義上也是抒情的，但因便於分類而且各屬特殊詩體，所以剩下來的這兩首只好分別介紹。

　　〈無情的豔女〉（La Belle Dame sans Merci）取材自中世紀的法文詩，題目也借用夏悌耶（Alain Chartier）作品的原題。其實從希臘的海妖賽倫（Siren）到德國的河妖洛麗萊（Lorelei），長髮善歌的女妖都在岩岸上用迷人的吟唱誘水手迷途而送命。濟慈最早仰慕的史賓塞（Edmund Spenser），在代表作《仙后》裏也屢有這種致命的美女：杜艾莎色誘紅十字騎士即為一例。學者多認為詩中的豔女應指濟慈的情人芬妮，我也覺得濟慈的愛情並不順利，非但成名無望，而且肺病惡化，不能結婚，心情當然是黯淡的。據說芬妮用情也不專注，使病困的詩人更增疑慮，情急之餘，更求斷然的獨占。在〈苦求你給我慈悲、憐憫、愛情〉那首十四行中，濟慈的聲調幾近哭訴：

> 請給我慈悲、憐憫、愛情，唉，愛情！
> 慈悲的愛情，不害人徒然苦等
> 專心而毫不游移，率性的愛情，
> 除掉假面，見不到一點污痕！

　　詩中豔女既然指芬妮，則憔悴的騎士當爲濟慈自況，因
爲他自知必將死於肺病，狀況將如洞中的鬼魂。這種預感也
見於〈夜鶯頌〉第三段。

　　〈無情的豔女〉用的詩體是歌謠體（ballad），頗受當
時華茲華斯及柯立基的影響。中國民俗的歌謠往往只是抒
情，西方的歌謠卻往往是一首極短的敘事詩。濟慈的這首
在格式上卻是一種變調：前三行較長，都是「抑揚四步格」
（iambic tetrameter）；末行則縮短而抑爲低調，變成「抑
揚二步格」（iambic dimeter），有長放短收之效，我的譯
文裏末行一律減成五字，但是穆旦的中譯卻不加分別，任其
與第二行等長，實在是一大失誤。

　　穆譯第二段次行：「這般憔悴和悲傷」，其中「和」
乃and之直譯，其實道地的中文應說「又」或「而」。五四
以來的新文學漸漸棄守中文靈活的「而」與「又」，反而
只會用比較機械的連接詞「和」，十分可惜。同一段的the
squirrel's granary穆譯爲「松鼠的小巢」，卻把可以直譯的
諧趣落實爲寫實。第三段中百合與玫瑰的隱喻變成了明喻，
減色不少。第四段把lady逕呼爲妖女，十分不妥。Lady無論
如何應該尊稱「淑女」、「佳人」或者「閨媛」。剛一初
遇，還不知她的底細，怎麼能叫人「妖女」？說話的人是中
世紀的騎士，對女性本應多禮才是。何況同一行中，前面剛
叫人「妖女」，緊接又譽人「天仙」，太矛盾了。而「美似
天仙」也嫌俗氣。

　　第六段說「帶她」騎馬，失之含糊，set應指「扶她」

坐在騎士前面。第七段的manna dew乃指天降甘露，穆譯卻變成了兩樣東西。第八段shut her eyes with kisses，穆譯只是「四次吻眼」，並未交代吻眼的效果，是為漏譯，失之粗率。第九、第十兩段，譯得十分混雜。原文的The latest dream I ever dreamt / On the cold hill side，一連兩行竟然都未譯出；第十段的前兩行，在穆譯中竟放大為四行，內容和形式，都亂成一團！Pale warriors為何譯成「無數的騎士」？

　　〈詠美人魚酒店〉用的是節奏明快而韻腳呼應緊密的雙行體，又稱偶句（couplet）；此體濟慈在《蕾米亞》中更用得具有氣勢。美人魚酒店在倫敦的廉宜區（Cheapside），古時因文人雅聚而聞名：莎士比亞、班江森、鮑芒、佛萊契、海立克與洛禮爵士等皆座上常客。濟慈認為伊麗莎白朝之文學渾然無為，勝於他當時的「現代」詩人。在伊麗莎白朝，班江森的盛名與霸氣蓋過莎士比亞，他的弟子海立克乃稱美人魚酒店的眾詩人與劇作家為「班子班孫」（The Tribe of Ben）。

詠美人魚酒店

年淹又代遠的詩人靈魂
棲過怎樣的旖旎仙境，
怎樣的樂土，或野苔洞天
能夠勝過美人魚酒店？
你們常飲的美酒難道
勝過店主的加納利葡萄？
還是天國的瓜果能誇
比店裏的鹿肉餅更加
美味？哦，如此的盛餐！
調配得像在等羅賓漢
和他的戀人瑪麗安
要一飲而乾的鹿角和酒罐。

我聽說後來啊有一天
店主的招牌給吹不見，
誰也不知道下落，要等
占星家的鵝毛筆一橫，
在羊皮紙上記載了下來，
說他見你多麼有光采，
掛上新製的老招牌，
從容品味神仙的酒茱，

而且嘖嘖得意地祝賀
向黃道十二宮的人魚座。

年淹又代遠的詩人靈魂
棲過怎樣的旖旎仙境,
怎樣的樂土,或野苔洞天
能夠勝過美人魚酒店?

無情的豔女

有何煩惱啊，戎裝的騎士，
臉色蒼白地獨自逡巡？
湖上的莎草已經枯萎，
　　也不聞鳥鳴。

有何煩惱啊，戎裝的騎士，
如此憔悴又如此愁苦？
松鼠的倉庫已經儲滿，
　　秋收已結束。

看你額上有一朵百合，
沁著痛苦，滲透著高燒；
頰上有一朵褪色的玫瑰，
　　很快就枯掉。

草原上我遇見一位淑女，
十分美麗，像精靈所生，
修長的披髮，輕盈的步態，
　　狂放的眼神。

我編了花冠，好讓她戴頭，
又有香帶好束腰，花鐲佩腕；
她睇我的姿態像是愛我，
　　又柔聲長歎。

我扶她騎上緩步的駿馬，
整天只看她，什麼也不要；
她喜歡側過身來吟唱
　　精靈的歌謠。

她爲我採來美味的草根，
還有野蜂蜜，和天降露滴，
對啊，她用奇妙的語調訴說：
　　「我眞心愛你。」

她帶我回精靈的洞裏，
就哭了起來，又悲歎連連；
爲撫合她狂而又野的眼睛，
　　我吻她四遍。

就在洞裏她催我入眠，
在洞裏我夢見，唉，眞糟糕！
我一生的夢裏最後一夢，
　　在寒山半腰。

我見到慘白的君王、王子，
慘白的武士，全白如枯骨
全都呼號：「無情的豔女
　　已將你囚住！」

我見到他們的飢唇在暗中
大張著，含著恐怖的警告，
醒來卻發現自己在此地，
　　在寒山半腰。

這就是何以我逗留在此，
臉色蒼白地獨自逡巡，
雖然湖上的莎草已枯，
　　也不聞鳥鳴。

輯三

頌　體

頌體綜述

1

　　1819年4、5月間，還未滿二十四歲的濟慈詩興潮湧，一口氣寫了五首頌歌，後之論者稱之為「五大頌歌」（The Five Great Odes），並且認為濟慈之為大詩人，一半賴此。也有不少學者認為，稍後完成的〈秋之頌〉（To Autumn）無懈可擊，足與五大頌歌並列。其中〈希臘古甕頌〉（Ode on a Grecian Urn）與〈夜鶯頌〉（Ode to a Nightingale）最享盛名，評論甚多，譯者也不少。〈希臘古甕頌〉的主題，該是藝術之完美與永恆，生命之憂煩與短暫，其間形成的矛盾。藝術雖美，未必能一勞永逸，解除生命之苦。藝術誠高，卻高不可攀，而且冷不可即。希臘古甕終究只是「冷面的牧歌」，可解一時之憂，為美之直覺而渾然忘憂而已。年輕的濟慈為肺病所苦，此病在十九世紀初乃不治之症，他身為藥劑科的學生，當然清楚自己不久人世。他嚮往愛情而不可得，渴求繆思而詩名不起，因此更向美之永恆尋求寄託。也就難怪，這些縈心之念（preoccupations）貫串在他的詩中，時隱時現，成為意象與比喻背後的主題。也正因此，他常向希臘神話及其載體的古代文物，例如艾爾金石雕之中去探討美之意義，成為超越哲學卻不寫論文的美學家。在〈憂

鬱頌〉（Ode on Melancholy）中，濟慈說戴面紗的憂鬱女
神，寶座其實是設在喜悅之神的殿上，與美同在，可惜美並
非長在（Beauty that must die）。《恩迪米安》開篇有這麼
三行：「美之爲物乃永恆之歡欣，／其可親可愛日日滋長，
一定／不會消失於無形。」致友人班傑明・貝禮的信中，濟
慈又說：「我所能掌握的，只有心中感情的聖潔和想像的眞
實——想像據以爲美者，定必爲眞。」這種信念正是〈希臘
古甕頌〉的前導。1976年國際筆會在倫敦召開，就以「想
像之眞」（The Truth of Imagination）爲論題；我也曾提出
一篇長文，參加研討。

　　這首詩歌詠的古甕，評論家無法確認究竟是哪一件雕
品，只能說其印象是幾件石雕或陶品綜合而成。其實甕上的
景物有兩個畫面：前三段描寫的是婚禮，第四段所見卻是祭
祀的行列。母犢仰天哀呻或云是艾爾金石雕上所見；整段的
祭神場面或云是見於洛漢（Claude Lorraine）的畫作。濟慈
應該也只是把不同的形象加以重組，自己也未必全然了解畫
面的用意，所以一直在問無言的古甕，第一段竟問了七次，
第四段也問了兩次。

　　英文好用抽象名詞，並加以擬人修詞，對於（從英文觀
點看來）文法身分不易確定的中文，很難翻譯。例如首段前
兩行：

Thou still unravished bride of quietness,
Thou foster-child of silence and slow time,

就有三個這樣的人格化抽象名詞。Quietness指的是無聲的婚禮畫面，still unravished是指尚未經初夜行房，猶保童真，foster-child是指當初做甕的師傅已死，此物從此由悠悠的歲月來領養。穆旦的譯文是：

> 你委身「寂靜」的、完美的處子，
> 受過了「沉默」和「悠久」的撫育，

卞之琳的譯文是：

> 你是「平靜」的還未曾失身的新娘，
> 你是「沉默」和「悠久」抱養的女孩，

兩人處理抽象名詞的方式都是加上引號，這當然是無可奈何的下策，懂是可懂，卻頗掃「詩興」，引號入詩尤其礙眼。卞之琳譯格瑞的〈墓畔哀歌〉（Elegy Written in a Country Churchyard），裏面的人格化抽象名詞多達十五個，也就是如此處理。積譯詩半世紀的經驗，我深信類此困境大可再加「漢化」，把無助詩意卻不礙文法的代名詞也一併掃開。同樣的兩行，我的譯文是：

> 嫁給嫻靜的新娘，尚未破身，
> 沉默與湮遠共育的養女，

我的譯文用動詞來顯示三個抽象名詞的擬人格身分
（personification），就把掃興的引號擺脫了。同時原文的
兩個thou都略去，可以把句長結束在十一個字以內，以免句
法拖沓。

　　我的譯文，句子比穆、卞二位都短，自限在九字與十一
字之間；穆譯在十字與十三字之間；卞譯更在十與十五之
間。因此我的句法有時顯得稍緊，不過省去的字多半是英文
必用而中文可免的「虛字」。卞譯的句法往往太鬆，甚至是
在「填字」。卞之琳寫詩，以白話甚至口語為基調，這風格
也用於譯詩，有時就不免太淺白了。例如第二段的這兩行：

Bold Lover, never, never canst thou kiss,

Though winning near the goal–yet, do not grieve;

語氣並不很淺白，甚至還用了canst thou的文言，但卞譯卻
是：

勇敢的鍾情漢，你永遠親不了嘴，

雖然離目標不遠了——可也用不著悲哀；

「勇敢的鍾情漢」失之重複，至於「親不了嘴」又失之太
白，甚至俗了，只怕濟慈會不贊成。我的譯文是：

莽情人，你永遠，永遠吻不成，

眼看要得手──你且莫悲；

我只用二十個字，卞譯卻用了二十八字。不同的語言風格，決定了譯文的長短。同樣的這首〈希臘古甕頌〉，濟慈的原文為五十行，動用了500個音節；我和穆旦、卞之琳也各譯成了五十行，但是我只用了503字，穆旦用了572字，卞之琳卻用了638字！讀者如真有興趣一探其中虛實，不妨再統計一下，三人各用了多少「的」、多少代名詞。這簡直是翻譯研究所博士論文，至少是碩士論文的好題目，一笑。

　　第一段第八行的What maidens loth?穆譯「在樂舞前」，實為不妥；儘管loth的意思可接到下一行的struggle to escape，但也不能用這四個字在填充。卞譯「什麼樣小女人不願意」有些勉強，「小女人」除了可以押韻，卻不合maidens的風格。

　　第二段not to the sensual ear，明明合於中文現成的「肉耳」，穆譯卻只說「不是奏給耳朵聽」，而卞譯更說成「不對官能而更動人愛憐的／對靈魂吹你們有調無聲的仙曲」，短處過簡，長處又過冗，憑空還加上代名詞「你們」來填空，no tone譯「有調無聲」也費詞。

　　第三段前三行穆譯不如卞譯精確：把boughs譯成「樹木」，leaves譯成「枝葉」，都未對準原文。最易誤解的是倒裝的第八行，濟慈為了押韻，把above置於行末，其實文法的順序該是far above all breathing human passion。其後的兩行that leaves a heart...a burning forehead, and a parching

tongue則形成一個形容子句，形容passion。穆譯第八行「幸
福的是這一切超凡的情態」，用意含糊，令人不解。這整段
卞譯雖稍嫌長，卻明白可解，只是末二行首的兩個「並」字
不如刪去。

　　第四段的heifer是「母犢」，亦即小母牛，更稱之爲
her，不知爲什麼穆且僅稱她「小牛」，而且是「它」？Not
a soul乃成語，例如There wasn't a soul to be seen，只是指
「一個人影也不見」，不必指靈魂。卞譯把末兩行說成「也
沒有哪一位能講得頭頭是道／何以你從此荒蕪的，能重新回
來」，不太易解，同時句法太長，語氣太白，更嫌冗贅，
「從此」一詞也不合原意。

　　第五段濟慈仍然對著大理石古甕凝神驚豔，遐想聯翩，
卻又看不明白，想不透徹。其實此詩開篇首段，詩人就已連
發七問，到了第四段，又問了三次。終於詩人悟出：眞相難
求，眞理就在美中，深感其美，於願已足。古甕無言，捫之
又冷，天機莫測。一代人有一代人的煩惱，到了下一代，面
對又一批觀眾，古甕仍然會說，美就是眞，不必殫精竭慮，
想入非非。最後五行尤需注意：主句是Thou shalt remain a
friend to man；至於in midst of other woe than ours則爲副詞
片語，穆且譯成「在另外的一些憂傷中」，含義欠清，乃一
大失誤。卞之琳譯成「看人家受到另一些苦惱的時候，作爲
朋友來申說」，也含混而生硬，「人家」是誰？「另一些苦
惱」又是誰的苦惱？「作爲朋友」尤其直譯得生硬。

　　最後二行的詮釋，歷來最多爭議，對譯者也是莫大的

考驗。最後五行的thou當然是指古甕。古甕既爲人類之友，
to whom thou say'st的whom當然是人類，「美即是眞，眞即
是美」當然是古甕對人類（亦即下一代又一代的觀眾）的叮
嚀、啓示。即美即眞，無美不眞：古甕正是美學的傳人，
以身見證的美學家，自給自足的唯美信徒。愛默森就宣稱：
「美，即其自身存在之依據。」（Beauty is its own excuse
for being.）至於最後的一行半，是對ye說的，ye是複數，在
本詩第二段就有ye soft pipes之例，所以末行的兩個ye，不可
能是詩人對古甕所稱，因爲古甕一直是單數的thou，更不可
能是詩人對甕上人物的稱呼，或古甕反身對婚禮與祭典的自
稱。古甕對一代代的觀眾正以朋友的身分說：「美即是眞，
眞即是美」，緊接下來自然是對人類囑咐：這道理，你們在
人間知之已足。古甕既是古物，濟慈的詩句又用古雅的thou,
ye, thy, canst, say'st, midst等語，穆旦和卞之琳的白話其實未
盡相配。所以我的譯文在詩末調得文些，如此終篇：

　　「美者真，真者美」──此即爾等
　　在人世所共知，所應共知。

2

　　〈夜鶯頌〉是濟慈最有名的詩作，歷來與雪萊的〈雲雀
歌〉齊名。拜倫生前比他們聲譽高出許多，但是主要以長詩
見稱，短篇的抒情詩卻未見如何出色，所以盛名之下竟然沒

有與〈夜鶯頌〉、〈雲雀歌〉相當的代表作。雪萊的詩比較剛直，以氣取勝；濟慈的詩比較委婉，以韻見長。雪萊富使命感，以先知與革命家自任；濟慈具耽美癖，以愛神與賽姬之祭師自許。雪萊的詩以自我的意志爲動力，像一個性格演員；濟慈的詩以深入萬物爲能事，務求演什麼要像什麼，所以最強調「無我之功」（negative capability），主張不可以主觀強加於萬物。濟慈固然寫不出、也無意去寫〈雲雀歌〉、〈西風歌〉那樣志高氣盛的力作；反之，雪萊也絕對寫不出〈無情的豔女〉那樣幽渺迷茫的歌謠，或是〈秋之頌〉那樣感性飽滿、寓想像於寫實的傑作。

　　中國的詩藝、畫藝常在虛實之間遊走，幾度出入，終於虛實相濟，而達於高妙的統一。濟慈詩藝也深諳此道，每能在虛實、正反之間進出探索，修成妙悟，而不致入虛而迷，或務實而拘。長篇的《蕾米亞》（Lamia）、短篇的〈無情的豔女〉、〈憂鬱頌〉，和這首〈夜鶯頌〉，多少都如此。〈夜鶯頌〉前兩段寫迷人的鳴禽把詩人誘引去多姿多采的南國，去享受浪漫的中世紀傳統，和可以療養肺病的地中海氣候。相對地，留在北國就只有困守人世的現實，一任青春被疾病摧毀，所以第三段是一殘酷的對比，和〈希臘古甕頌〉的第三段遙相呼應。第四段詩人果然擺脫了現實，魂隨歌去，與夜鶯同在，但靠的不是酒醉或藥力，而是詩情的神往。第五段營造林間的嗅覺，花香雖濃而可分辨。第六段又回到聽覺，但此時夜長林深，詩人身心安詳，音樂也已昇華成聖樂，可以安魂，死亡也變成莊嚴的典禮了。第七段進入

想像的高潮，詩人一念自由，神遊於《聖經》的遠古和傳說的中世紀。終於「寂寞」一字忽然破咒解魔，詩人一驚而起，回到人間的現實，發現詩翼翩翩，又何曾足以遁世：所謂fancy，其實只是騙人的妖精。虛實之際，寤寐之間，其界何在？七百多行的《蕾米亞》，問的也是這問題。

　　穆旦譯文的第一段，細節不夠精確：「毒芹」譯成「毒鴆」，「鴉片酊」譯成「鴉片」，都失之籠統。在濟慈的時代，習於將少量鴉片溶於酒中，給病人服藥，謂之鴉片酊（laudanum）。Dryad of the trees譯成仙靈，而不譯「樹精」也嫌泛泛。Of beechen green, and shadows numberless在文法上乃上接plot，卻被穆譯截斷，憑空加上「你躲進」，未能緊隨原文。

　　第二段在tasting後有五個受詞，穆譯顛倒太甚，而且country green譯倒了，而sunburnt mirth又譯得不足。

　　第三段here之後一共用了四個where，乃英文文法所必需，但在中文裏一再譯出，卻有掃詩興：這是許多譯者還參不透的「譯障」。末二行的Beauty和Love標出大寫，變成抽象的本質，最令譯者爲難。解決之道，一爲加上括弧，表示架空，但是礙眼不美；另一則遷就中文語境，還以血肉之軀，歸於具體。這兩行穆旦似乎誤解了，因爲「新生的愛情活不到明天就枯凋」雖然動員了十三個字，卻漏掉了at them兩字。Them是指上一行的her lustrous eyes，漏譯了，前後兩行就失去呼應了。

　　第四段的the dull brain，就是this dull brain of mine，也

就是此詩一開頭就說明的drowsy numbness；但譯成「這頭腦」卻意思欠明，也不如「此心」渾成而有詩意。也就是我所說的：只拘泥以白話譯詩，而未想到文言能及時救急。

第四段的already with thee，不知何故穆且要用足一行來譯。因爲林深葉密，外面夜色只能猜想，所以說haply the Queen-Moon is on her throne；穆譯忽略此點，倒似乎在林中可以舉頭見月了。又starry Fays的意思穆譯不全；我譯成「仙扈星妃」，比較周全，仍然是仗了四字成語的對仗之力，比起穆譯「周圍是侍衛她的一群星星」來，不但省去了英文文法需要而中文文法可免的「她的」，句法也穩健得多。

第五段次行的incense爲免與flowers重複，而換了一種說法，穆譯竟重用「花」字。至於embalmèd darkness，姜夔早有「暗香」一詞，大可倒過來譯，還渾成得多。本段末行「它成了夏夜蚊蚋的嗡嘤的港灣」，十三個字拖拖沓沓，連用兩個「的」字，又憑空添上一個代名詞「它」，全無需要。此外，「嗡嘤」搭配得勉強，「港灣」也欠妥貼。

第六段穆譯大致平穩，不過mused rhyme譯成「好的言辭」，太欠文采了。To take into the air my quiet breath，譯成「把我的一息散入空茫」，雖然未能照顧到quiet的意思，仍不失爲佳句。To cease upon the midnight with no pain譯成「在午夜裏溘然魂離人間」，卻失職了。「裏」純然多餘；「魂離人間」要配cease，也太花，太俗，而下一行眞正的soul卻降級爲「心懷」，說不過去。也許是爲了遷就押

韻，就應在用韻上多下工夫，不能如此以韻害情。同時，「溘然」是突然的意思，跟cease...with no pain不合。譯文中看不出有什麼with no pain，實為漏譯。

　　第七段前四行自成一個quatrain，穆旦繞了一個大圈子的句法，把原文所無的「喜悅」放在第四行末，仍無法與「蹀躞」押韻，詞窮一至於此。此段末二行失誤最多：charm'd magic casements竟譯成「引動窗扉」，既不貼合原文，也太平淡。原文有景無人，但人自在景中，不外是中世紀的古堡囚著公主或情人，大海橫阻，救援不至。穆旦卻憑空加上「一個美女望著……」破了氣氛，還有點俗。原文用同一個字forlorn分置在第七段末、第八段首，把變調呼應得天衣無縫。穆譯卻把兩字分隔到兩行之遠，失職了。My sole self用sole加強forlorn的感覺，穆譯不予理會，卻說成「我站腳的地方」，全不相干。顯然，他把sole理解成「腳底」了。末二行用was和is對照幻想與現實，一迷一悟，更用that來推開夜鶯的魔歌。所以我強調「剛才」之幻；穆旦卻把它拉近，說成「這是個幻覺」，不妥。

　　〈夜鶯頌〉原文一共八段，每段十行，除第八行縮為六音節外，均為十音節，所以全詩八十行，共為768音節。我的譯文共用了771字，穆旦卻用了848字，比我多出七十七個字。難怪他往往一行長達十三個字，而我絕不超過十一個字。翻譯小說或散文還不打緊，譯詩家寸土寸金，卻揮霍不得。

3

　　〈賽姬頌〉是五頌第一首，在詩體上是他寫過許多十四行詩後有意試驗較爲延伸而又繁複的形式。Psyche來自Psycho，希臘文「元氣」之意，亦可喻靈魂、生命、心靈。雪萊〈西風歌〉首句就是O wild West Wind, thou breath of Autumn's being，正爲此意。古希臘人相信人死後靈魂會化蝶從口中飛出，所以濟慈的〈憂鬱頌〉更有「莫讓甲蟲或飛蛾來充你／哀傷的賽姬」之句。在古典文學裏，賽姬進入奧林匹斯之神仙譜很晚：她的故事直到公元二世紀才在阿普留斯的《金驢》（Apuleius: The Golden Ass）中出現。說是人間美女賽姬爲小愛神愛若斯所戀，夜夜來會，日出即去。愛若斯嚴禁她查問其身分，但某夜她點燈相窺，一滴熱油落在他肩頭，他一驚醒便逃遁不回。她甘願淪爲維納斯之奴，受盡折磨，終於得與愛若斯結合，成了神靈。

　　濟慈憐其登仙太晚，無廟可歸，無香可禱，無祭司也無唱詩班來供奉，乃自告奮勇要爲她立廟上香，植松養花，擔任她的祭司。但這一切都不必形而下地落實，卻可形而上地在詩人的靈思妙想裏無中生有，燦然大備。本詩共爲四大段：首段最長，竟達二十三行，寫的正是賽姬與愛若斯之戀情，純屬形而下之情慾。愛若斯（亦即邱比特）之名Eros，就是形容詞erotic之所本。其後的三段，一段比一段懇切，詩人對女神表明自己的心願，到了末段，場景越加生動逼眞，其實都已內化，成了內景（inscape）。全詩末二行就

以夜不關窗，只等愛若斯回來作結。

　　有一些評家看得更深，認爲詩中的情愛也大可視爲對詩神的崇拜，所以冥想槎枒（branchèd thoughts）可比松林，意匠經營（working brain）可比玫瑰院落，妙思無窮（gardener Fancy）可比園藝高手。總之，拱奉賽姬即所以拱奉繆思。

<h2 style="text-align:center">4</h2>

　　〈憂鬱頌〉是五大頌裏最短的一首，但其主題之發展與呈現卻緊湊而生動。主題是「憂鬱」，濟慈並不感情用事，不僅以表現此一情緒之抒情爲滿足。在第一段中，他指出要應付憂鬱，不可避重就輕，遁入負面的絕望，遺忘或輕生，因爲「陰影加陰影未免太昏瞶，／會吞沒靈魂清醒的痛苦。」。

　　到了次段，濟慈強調要對付憂鬱應該回身面對，用美好的東西來相迎，例如用甘霖、濃霧、玫瑰、彩虹、芍藥、熱情等等。末三行對待戀人發嗔之道，尤爲生動而詼諧。也就是說，憂鬱之來，不可漠視，而要全神迎接，做足禮貌，加以享受。

　　到了末段，憂鬱更從戀人升等爲女神，並與「美麗、歡樂、喜悅」等分庭抗禮，一齊登壇升龕，接受膜拜。Melancholy、Beauty、Joy、Pleasure這些人格化了的抽象名詞，在譯成中文時最不討好，因爲在西方文法裏其身分十

分明確，不像在中文裏，同一「憂」字有時是名詞（憂從
中來），有時是動詞（仁者不憂），有時是狀詞（憂心忡
忡）。但是在濟慈的原詩裏，這些擬人抽象名詞，卻能形成
生動可觀的關係。本詩在修辭上巧妙地完成了美學的辯證：
首段說明，負面的毒藥與死亡對似乎是負面的憂鬱，並無互
補之功，反有蒙蔽之弊。次段暗示，憂鬱之為物，當與美好
之物對立並比更為鮮明。末段更進一步，用擬人與隱喻來暗
示，憂鬱與美、喜、樂等等似乎對立，其實相剋相生，相得
益彰，因為憂能持久，而美不能，喜更短暫，樂不可求，求
則引禍。

　　末段的節奏，流暢而有力，第五、第六兩行臻於高潮，
成了結論：「哎，就在歡悅之殿堂內，／戴紗的憂鬱坐她的
神龕。」其後的四行似乎只能漸鬆，以遞減（diminuendo）
終場，因為第五、第六兩行太強了，而第七行又以though引
進一個附屬子句。結果竟然力道不衰，終於再掀起一個高
潮，而以一個單音節的主動詞hung斬釘截鐵煞住。

　　末段的代名詞，在性別上也有講究。為首的she和其後
的三個her都是指憂鬱女神。其他的代名詞一律是陽性的
him、his。為了區別與對立，末段末四行的文法結構必須
看清楚。這四行用平易的英文來說，應該是：Although she
（Melancholy）is seen by none except such a man whose
strenuous tongue can burst Joy's grape against his fine palate;
His（such a man's）soul shall taste the sadness of her
（Melancholy's）might and be hung among her cloudy trophies.

5

〈懶散頌〉當然是五大頌裏較弱的一首；一般英詩選都沒挑到，評論家也少爭論。在其他四頌裏，濟慈在純情與美感之外尚有知性的冥想與探索，所以那些詩不僅是lyrical，也可稱meditative，探索的對象介乎美學與哲學之間。但〈懶散頌〉的主題似乎不那麼形而上，比較關切他自身的三個問題：愛情、野心（名氣）、詩藝。年輕、多病、默默無聞的濟慈，對愛情與名氣都不敢奢望，只有對自己的詩藝，得失寸心知，尚存有幾分自許、自信。另一方面，他對自己的詩風也不無自省、自覺，感到自己的筆調偏於「陰柔」，耽於「甜美」。所以他一方面不勝人間現實之煩惱，直歎「哦，只求一生能免於煩惱，／無需知曉月亮的變幻，／或聽從人情世故的喧囂！」這些話在〈希臘古甕頌〉、〈夜鶯頌〉、〈憂鬱頌〉裏他早已再三歎訴過。好在另一方面，他又毫不含糊地宣稱：「我可不甘被甜言飼養，／做一頭羔羊演自憐的鬧劇！」

6

〈秋之頌〉本來不在「五大頌」之列，而且原題也不稱Ode to Autumn，但是後來的評論家都很推崇此詩，強調文本分析的新批評家尤其強調此詩為「完美而均衡之作」。〈秋之頌〉雖然分成三段，但彼此呼應緊湊，發展得非常有

機。三段描繪的都是秋季，但在感官經驗上，首段著重觸
覺，中段著重視覺，末段則強調聽覺。論者與史家常讚美濟
慈乃十足感性（sensuous）的詩人：此詩正是佳例。就這一
點來比，雪萊的詩藝情感激越，音調強烈，卻不太能落實於
感官經驗，有時會顯得空洞。其次，此詩意象豐富，但一以
貫之的意象是擬人格（personification）：首段把秋季寫成
太陽的密友同謀，合力催使瓜盈果飽；中段把秋季寫成收割
的農夫；末段則把秋季寫成大地的合唱隊。第三，在季節的
時序上，首段是寫初秋的成熟，中段寫秋收的農忙，末段以
刈後的平野來寫收割之餘的「秋聲」。第四，在朝夕的推移
下，三段的進展也有自朝至夕的描寫或暗示。

　　就文法的結構觀之，年輕的濟慈也開闔有度，呼應
得體。例如首段，前二行並非文句，只是兩個名詞片語
（noun phrase），亦即修辭學所謂的綽號（epithet）。其後
的九行只是一長串的分詞片語（participial phrase）：其骨
架是conspiring with him how to load and bless...to bend and
fill...to swell and plump...to set later flowers budding...until
they think。一連串的排比句法，這麼多的動詞原形（to＋
verb），造成了流暢的節奏。其實，中段和末段也以句法流
暢取勝。中段的文法骨架是Sometimes whoever seeks abroad
may find thee sitting...or asleep...and sometimes thou dost
keep thy head steady...or thou watchest。末段也一樣，骨架
是While barrèd clouds bloom the day and touch the plains,
then gnats mourn...and lumbs bleat, crickets sing...red-breast

whistles...and swallows twitter。年輕的濟慈在句法的安排上兼顧均衡與流暢，十分穩當，令人佩服。這種才華，在他對十四行詩的布局上，已流露可觀。

我教英詩半世紀，每次講授到這首〈秋之頌〉，都非常享受，因爲它的天籟直接來自造化，並不依賴神話、宗教、歷史、文化等等背景，簡直不掉書袋，沒有典故的核殼要敲開，對中國的讀者，除了賞析的美感之外，可謂一無障礙。所以我也認爲此詩大可代取〈懶散頌〉而列於「五大頌」之中，或加上五頌而成六頌。

賽姬頌

女神啊！聽我唱無調之歌，
憑甜蜜的壓力，貼心的記憶，
並請原諒，你的祕密竟然我
要唱進你軟貝殼的耳裏：
我今天真的夢見，或是親睹
用清醒的眼睛，帶翼的賽姬？
當時我無意間在林中漫步，
忽然，被嚇得簡直要昏迷，
只見有兩個俏身影，並臥
在芳草深處，頭頂窸窣，
而有顫動的花和樹葉做窩，
　　遮住一小溪流過：
四周寂靜，冷花的眼色芬芳，
或藍，或白，或泰紫初綻，
人影喘息已定，躺在草床上；
四臂相擁，四翼也交纏；
四唇雖不接，但也未分開，
像剛被睡夢輕輕拆散，
還準備再吻，更密於剛才，
只等柔眸破曉再交歡：
　　我認得這少年有翼；

但幸福的白鴿啊，誰又是你？
　竟是他忠貞的賽姬！

哦，在神山黯淡的天庭，
生得最晚，風姿最婀娜，
美貌勝過藍空的月神，勝過
黃昏星，天上多情的流螢；
比眾神都美，卻無廟可拜，
　無祭壇可供鮮花；
無處女合唱隊在午夜前來，
　吟誦得如此高雅；
無歌，無琴，無笛，無氤氳
　從懸吊的香爐升起；
無龕，無林，無神諭，無熱情
　鼓動先知素口的夢囈。

哦，至豔之神！古誓已過時，
太晚，太晚是癡迷的琴聲，
曾經，聖潔長佑林中的花枝，
天風，海水，火焰都神聖；
而即使在今日，復古已遲，
敬神的歡愉已遠，你的雙翼
在失色的眾神間仍在拍動，

仍召我凡眼，來見證，歌頌。
且容我充你的合唱隊，子時
　　長為你虔誠吟詠；
充歌，充琴，充笛，充氤氳
　　從懸吊的銀爐升起；
充龕，充林，充神諭，充熱情
　　鼓動先知素口的夢囈。

真的，我願充你的祭司，此心
在無人之境建一座神廟，
讓槎枒的冥思，苦樂相生，
代替松林在風中起潮：
在空曠的四周讓樹影重重
掩映一脊脊高峻的野嶺；
加上西風，流泉，鳴禽和鬧蜂，
當可催眠苔居的樹精；
而在曠野岑寂的地點，
一座玫瑰院且容我闢建，
意匠經營的窗格錯綜，
用花蕾，鐘鈴，無名的星斗，
一任名為妙思的園丁虛構，
培育的百花絕不雷同：
其間幽思之遐想都盡量
為了你高興無不備足，

火炬長明，夜間不關窗，
讓多情的愛神飛入。

希臘古甕頌

嫁給嫻靜的新娘，尚未破身，
沉默與湮遠共育的養女，
山林野史，你講的軼聞
多采多姿，更勝過我的詩句；
花邊的傳說繚繞你一身，
說的是神，是人，或兼有神人，
在丹陂或是阿凱迪谷地？
何來的人或神，不服的村女？
何來的狂追？何來的逃拒？
何來的笛與鼓？何來的歡騰？

樂曲而可聞雖美，但不聞
卻更美；所以柔笛莫住口，
不是對肉耳，而更加動人，
是無聲之調對心神吹奏：
樹下的美少年，你的歌聲
不會停，而樹也永不枯萎；
莽情人，你永遠，永遠吻不成，
眼看要得手——你且莫悲；
縱你無緣，她也難抽身，
你的情不休，她的美不褪！

啊，幸福，幸福的花枝，永不
落葉，永不對春天說再會；
幸福的樂師，不覺得辛苦，
不老的樂曲不停在吹；
更幸福，更加幸福的愛情，
永遠熱烈，永遠有指望，
永遠在苦盼，永遠不怕老；
超脫了人間的六欲七情，
不害此心厭煩又哀傷，
不害額頭發燒，舌頭發燥。

來此祭祀的又是何人？
神祕的祭司，這青春祭壇，
你牽來的母犢仰天哀呻，
光滑的兩脅都戴著花環。
何來小鎮在河畔或海邊，
或依山而建，安寧的城寨，
在拜神的早上，居民全出門？
小鎮啊，你的街巷將永遠
寂靜，而為何你如此淒冷，
能說明的人，誰也回不來。

希臘的典型啊，優美的神態！
大理石精雕細琢的男女，

有茂林繁枝，草地任踩；
你的靜態逗得人苦思竭慮，
如永恆逗人。冷面的牧歌！
當老邁將我們這一代耗損，
你仍會流傳，去面對來世
新的煩惱，與人為友，且說
「美者眞，眞者美」——此即爾等
在人世所共知，所應共知。

夜鶯頌

我眞心痛，催眠的麻痺，折磨
著我，好像剛剛服了毒芹，
或乾了鴉片酊，連渣吞沒，
才一會，竟已向忘川沉浸：
不是爲妒嫉你好運氣，
是見你幸福而深感幸福——
只爲你，輕飛的樹精，在林間，
　　　在載歌的空地，
山毛櫸青青，樹影密布，
你飽滿的歌喉頌揚夏天。

哦，多想喝一口葡萄的醇醪，
在深邃的地窖歷久冷藏，
其味如花，如鄉野的芳草，
如舞，如南國之歌，如享豔陽！
哦，多想滿杯溫潤的南方，
斟滿眞正害羞的仙泉，
有泡如珠，在杯邊眨眼，
　　　把嘴唇染得多豔紫；
讓我飲罷能告別人世，
隨你遁入朦朧的林間。

遠遁吧，羽化吧，渾然忘掉
你在密葉間未經的世情，
未經的疲勞，高燒，煩惱，
不聞世人向彼此呻吟；
麻痺得留不住慘白的髮莖，
少年無顏色，憔悴而成鬼；
每一起念就滿懷傷情，
　　　和眼神沉重的心灰；
美人的明眸不能長保，
也難盼新歡苦戀過明朝。

遠遁，遠遁，讓我飛向你，
不是搭乘酒神的豹輦，
而是駕著詩神的隱翼，
儘管此心已困頓而不前；
真到你處了？夜色猶未央，
也許月后已高就寶位，
四周簇擁著仙扈星妃；
　　　但林間卻不見透光，
除非由微風吹來，自天庭；
穿過綠蔭，順著蜿蜒的苔徑。

看不見腳下是什麼芳馨，
或是枝頭懸什麼香料，

但只憑暗香就能夠猜到
是什麼花譜值月正當令，
正開在草地，荊叢與果林——
白山楂，還有薔薇花野生；
速謝的紫羅蘭掩葉待朽；
　　五月中旬要生頭胎：
將綻的麝香玫瑰，帶露如酒，
夏暮把嗡嗡的飛蟲引來。

在暗中我傾聽，有好幾次
幾乎要愛上安逸的死神，
冥想用詩韻暱喚他名字，
將我平靜的呼吸融入夜氛；
此刻就死去似乎更豐富，
歸化於子夜，不覺痛苦，
乘你正滔滔傾瀉魂魄，
　　以如此的狂歡極樂！
你一面唱吧，我充耳不聞——
輓歌雖莊嚴，我已成土。

你並非生而為死，不朽之禽，
非饑荒的世代所能作踐；
今夕匆匆我聆聽的鳴聲
帝王和村夫古來早聽見：

或許相同的歌聲曾經
也傷了露絲的心，只因念家，
她在異國的麥田裡泣下；
　　同樣的歌聲頻頻
迷住了魔窗，開向海上，
向驚波駭浪，在寂寞仙鄉。

寂寞啊！這字眼像一記鐘聲，
敲醒我回到自身的孤影！
別了！幻想其實騙不了人，
儘管她騙出了名，騙子妖精。
別了！別了！你的哀歌飄過
附近的牧場，飄過平溪，
飄上了山坡，終於埋沒
　　在另一邊的谷地：
剛才是幻境，是半寤半寐？
那音樂已沉──我是醒是睡？

憂鬱頌

莫，莫，莫去忘川，也莫要揪扭
根深的烏頭來取毒漿；
也莫讓龍葵，陰間的紅酒，
留吻在你蒼白的額上；
莫用水松子串你的念珠，
莫讓甲蟲或飛蛾來充你
哀傷的賽姬，更莫讓梟類
來分擔你無歡的神祕；
陰影加陰影未免太昏瞶，
會吞沒靈魂清醒的痛苦。

可是當憂鬱一陣子發作，
突然像天降淚雨潸潸，
來養那許多垂頭的花朵，
且用四月的濃霧遮住青山；
何妨用早晨的玫瑰來餵愁，
或是用沙岸的彩虹來止憂，
或是用一簇簇飽滿的芍藥；
或是當戀人正大發癡嗔，
就緊握她嬌腕，任她吼叫，
並深深地飲她至美的眼神。

她與美共存——而美必亡；
也與喜同在——喜常掩嘴角，
作勢道別；傷人的樂，在一旁，
只要蜂來吮，就化成毒藥：
哎，就在歡悅之殿堂內，
戴紗的憂鬱坐她的神龕，
誰也看不見，有一人卻舌健，
嚼欣喜之葡萄而能辨味，
唯其魂能品出憂鬱之神功，
並高懸在她的戰利品中。

懶散頌
——人影不費力也不轉動

某天早晨眼前出現三人影，
垂著頭，疊著手，只見側面；
一個跟一個，步態輕盈
閒踩涼鞋，披著白袍翩翩；
走過去，像大理石雕的人物，
當你把石甕轉向背面；
又走過來，當你把古甕再度
旋轉，先見的身影就重現；
看來真奇怪，凡菲迪雅文物
的行家，看古瓶都有同感。

為什麼，陰影啊，我不識你？
怎麼用噤聲的面具偷躲？
難道是沉默密謀的鬼計，
要盜我閒散的時光，害我
一事無成？正逢慵睏的時辰，
幸福的雲彩當昏昏長夏，
麻痺我眼神，脈搏愈加低沉；
痛已無刺，樂的花圈花已枯：
你們為何不化掉啊，讓我心神

把一切都擺脫，除了空無？

第三度又走過，且過且轉，
一個接一個，暫把臉朝我；
然後又隱沒，而為了追趕，
我焦急得想飛，認出這三個；
第一個是嬌娃，名叫愛情；
第二個是野心，臉色慘白，
疲倦的眼神總監視著我；
我更愛的是最後一位，內心
怨她也更深，此妹最不乖──
我認出原來是我的詩魔。

人影漸淡，其實，我只要雙翅：
愚哉！何為愛情！而今又何在？
至於可憐的野心！開始
無非是人心狹小的癡愛；
為詩憔悴！不，她毫無歡騰，
至少我無份──甜蜜得像午睏，
像黃昏浸在甘美的慵懶；
哦，只求一生能免於煩惱，
無需知曉月亮的變幻，
或聽從人情世故的喧囂！

第三度又走來——唉，爲何
睡眠繡滿了淡遠的夢？
靈魂的草地綴滿了花朵，
還有抖動的樹影，光線朦朧。
晨空多雲，但陣雨不降落，
雖然雲睫含五月的甘霖；
窗扇敞著，壓著爬藤的新葉，
卻迎入暖芽和畫眉之歌；
人影啊！此刻正應該揮別！
我並未淚沾你們的衣裙。

別了，三鬼魂！花間的冷枕上，
休想叫我把倦頭昂舉；
我可不甘被甜言飼養，
做一頭羔羊演自憐的鬧劇！
從我眼前悄悄地隱去，重回
夢幻的甕上做假面模型；
別了！我有的是對夜的嚮往，
白晝的玄思也有一大堆；
散掉吧，幻象！從我的閒情
沒入雲間，永莫再來訪！

秋之頌

多霧的季節，瓜盈果飽，
和成熟的太陽交情最深，
與他共謀該如何用葡萄
來加重並祝福茅簷的爬藤；
把屋邊的果樹用蘋果壓彎，
教所有的果子熟透內心，
把葫蘆鼓脹，榛殼撐滿，
用甜蜜的果仁；更為蜂群
催晚開的花樹越發越豔，
害群蜂以為永遠會溫暖，
因夏季把蜂巢已填得濕黏。

誰不常見你自守著庫藏？
有時只要去巡視就見你
逍遙地坐在穀倉的地上，
長髮隨簸穀的風勢飄起；
或是在半割的畦間睡著，
被罌粟的濃香薰倒，而鐮刀
暫且放過了雜花的麥疇；
有時又像是拾穗人，垂頭
沉沉地俯臨在小溪之上；

或是在榨汁架邊耐心守候
好幾個時辰，凝望著稠漿。

春日之歌在何處，哎，在何處？
別管它了，你自己也有歌詠——
當橫霞燎豔將逝的薄暮，
把刈後的平野染成玫紅；
溪邊的柳叢就有小蚊群
哼成哀怨的合唱隊，時高
時低，要看是風起，風停；
肥壯的羊群在山上叫喊；
蟋蟀在籬下低吟；女高音
是知更在花園裏吹口哨；
成群的燕子在空際呢喃。

輯四

長　詩

《聖安妮節前夕》簡析

濟慈的傳奇長詩《聖安妮節前夕》（*The Eve of St Agnes*）近則取材於包敦的雜記《百憂探源》（*The Anatomy of Melancholy*），遠則可上溯薄伽丘的傳奇《十日譚》（*Decameron*）。聖安妮乃公元四世紀初的基督徒，因堅守信仰且拒嫁非基督徒之羅馬人而被判有罪，倖免於強暴，卻遭火刑成仁。她的忌日一月二十一日成了聖安妮節：其前夕相傳為一年最寒，童真少女若齋戒仰臥，午夜當能瞥見未來丈夫的幻象。Agnes本應譯為阿格妮絲，但嫌太長，不便入句，譯文縮為安妮。

詩中一對情人Porphyro與Madeline，兩家有宿仇，波飛羅夜闖敵營，浪漫而驚險，令人聯想《羅密歐與茱麗葉》。主題充滿對照，其場景外則嚴寒與老病，內則節慶與囂鬧，介於其間則為年輕的愛情。但是濟慈更著意處理的，是情人相處時虛實相生的情境。梅德琳安頓身心，準備一睹情郎的幻象，見到的確是波飛羅的真身。香煙嫋嫋，月色迷離，情韻悠悠，波飛羅以真就假，入了紗帳。第三十六節處理得十分巧妙：

> 他化入她的夢，像玫瑰清芬
> 與紫羅蘭融合為一體——

交流美滿。

如此遣詞，比《西廂記》已經更含蓄了，但是當年他的編輯仍嫌不妥。其實這正是濟慈詩風的特色，於此詩尤其爲然。他的詩意、詩境每能落實於具體的感性（sensuousness），似乎得了莎士比亞的眞傳，因而在唯情是縱的浪漫派之中勝過拜倫與雪萊一籌。除莎翁外，濟慈之詩藝亦得益於前輩史賓塞與米爾頓。但是在史賓塞的意象生動與米爾頓的音調鏗鏘之外，濟慈還善於營造觸覺與質感：〈秋之頌〉便是佳例。《聖安妮節前夕》二十六節也有此特色：

> 她摘去髮上纏繞的珍珠，
> 把戴暖的寶石一一解下，
> 又鬆開溫香的胸兜，讓華服
> 滑退到膝下，窸窸窣窣
> 像藻間的人魚，半顯半蔽，

浪漫派詩人熱中於探索古代與異國，以超脫平庸的現實。濟慈此詩的背景正是中世紀的豪門，所以遣詞用語每有擬古（archaism），有點像柯立基的《古舟子詠》。此外，在器皿與食品上，爲營造富貴氣象並促進細節的實感，也引了不少中東的事物；從西歐人的角度來看，便是所謂「東方情調」（orientalism）了。濟慈小小的年紀，又非出身富貴，實在難爲了他。當然也就難免向前人（例如莎翁）作品中去

學藝了。

　　至於詩體，此詩也就襲用史賓塞的《仙后》，號稱「史賓塞體」（Spenserian stanza）。那就是每段九行，前八行均爲「抑揚五步格」：每行十音節，其中五個重音落在雙數音節上。第九行，亦即末行，則延伸爲十二音節六重音的「抑揚六步格」（又稱「亞歷山大體」Alexandrine）；前六個音節與後六個音節之間往往小頓（pause or caesura）一下。至於韻序（rhyme scheme），則十分嚴格，必須排成abab / bcbcc，所以對譯者要求頗苛。凡此種種規定，我皆盡量遵守；在韻序上至少做到abab，至於bcbcc五個韻，則彈性處理，有時幸運，福至心靈，也會九韻全部對齊，教濟慈自己看了，如果他通中文，也會點頭吧。

聖安妮節前夕

1

聖安妮節的前夕——苦寒啊難熬！
夜梟空擁羽衣，也不敵寒意；
野兔顫顫跛跳過凍草，
欄裏的羊群也一片噤寂：
誦經人手指凍僵，一面默計
著念珠，一面呵氣成霧，
像虔敬的香煙，生於古爐，
不經死亡，就升向天國迢迢，
掠過聖母的畫像，他一面默禱。

2

念罷禱詞，這耐心的僧侶
便提起燈來，站直了身體，
瘦小而蒼白，赤腳走回去，
沿著教堂的過道，緩緩地：
兩旁，死者的雕像似已凍住，
被煉獄一般的黑柵囚困：
騎士和淑女都默默跪訴，

他走過去，心神太虛，不能
想像他們披甲戴巾，凍得有多疼。

3

轉北出小門，還不到三步，
忽然音樂金色的舌頭
將可憐老人的熱淚引出；
免了吧──他的喪鐘已敲奏，
一生的歡樂已說夠、唱夠，
聖安妮前夕，他得深深懺悔。
他改向而行，沒有多久，
就坐在骨灰間為本心贖罪，
也為眾人悲禱，一整夜都不寐。

4

老經僧聽到柔美的前奏，
正巧許多門戶都大開，
讓人進人出。不久，從高頭，
咆哮的銀喇叭開始責怪：
平整的房間燈火好氣派，
正準備接待上千的貴賓；
天使的雕像，眼神不稍怠，
齊都灼灼，把飛簷撐在頭頂，

長髮都向後飄，雙翼在胸口交併。

5

終於燦銀的慶宴一擁而入，
戴翎毛，插冠冕，盛裝富麗，
擁擠如幻影在夢中進出，
少年的心靈，充滿古傳奇
熱烈的勝利。這些不用管，
且轉頭專說有一位女郎，
嚴冬一整天滿心只苦盼
愛情，和天使聖安妮的幫忙，
只因她曾聽老嫗們再三宣講。

6

老嫗們總說過節的前宵，
只要一切都行禮如儀，
等待甜蜜的午夜一到，
凡閨女就能看到大吉
的形相，聽到情郎的傾慕；
規定上床前不准晚餐，
白如百合的玉體仰天而宿；
不准後顧或旁眄，只能抬眼，
向上天祈禱，望一切都天從人願。

7

梅德琳爲此心事重重：
音樂急切如天神在哀吟，
她卻聽不見；純稚的眼瞳
注視著地板，只瞥見衣裙
紛紛曳過──她全不在意：不少
多情的郎君踮腳來跟前，
卻徒勞而退，並非阻於高傲，
而是她未見，她心不在焉，
只渴望聖安妮之夢，一年最甘甜。

8

她隨眾舞踊，目光淡漠而茫然，
嘴唇焦燥，呼息短促而緊急；
神聖的時辰將臨：她哀歎，
四面是鼓聲，人潮正擁擠，
耳語有的是不滿，有的是淘氣，
表情有愛有恨，不屑，或反抗，
蔽於胡思亂想；一切都沉寂，
只剩下聖安妮和她的羔羊，
和天亮之前有幸福自天而降。

9

就這麼，存心隨時要抽身，
她姑且徘徊。此際馳過荒原，
年輕的波飛羅，心急如焚，
來會梅德琳。他站在門邊，
躲在背月的牆下，祈願
眾聖徒讓他一睹梅德琳，
漫漫的長夜只為這一眼，
只求探望與膜拜，不露蹤影；
或傾訴，下跪，握手，接吻，有例可循。

10

他鼓勇潛進：細語不許密告，
一切眼睛要蒙好，否則百劍
會直搗心窩，愛情的碉堡。
對他，蠻軍埋伏在門後面，
宿敵如豺狼，堡主多凶險，
連惡犬都會猙猙地狂吠，
詛咒他家族：沒有人會可憐，
饒了他，在那醜陋的莊內，
只除了一個老嫗，身心都已衰萎。

11

　真巧啊，來的人正是老嫗，
　蹣跚地，扶著象牙頭拐杖，
　到他的站處，火光照不到，
　巨大的廳柱正好阻擋，
　嬉鬧和合唱都隔在遠方。
　她嚇了一跳，但立刻認出他，
　握他的手在風癱的手掌，
　說道：「天哪，波飛羅！快逃命吧！
今晚全在此，這一大夥惡賊凶煞！」

12

　「逃吧！逃吧！矮子西伯連
　剛發過燒，時歇又時發，
　他咒你全家，咒你的家園；
　還有莫禮斯老爺，一頭白髮，
　卻一點不心軟──天哪，逃吧！
　連鬼影都別留。」──「哦，好婆婆，
　此地很安全；扶手椅可坐下，
　跟我說」──「天哪！別坐了，別坐；
跟我來，孩子，否則這石雕就是你墓座。」

13

他隨她穿過矮矮的廊道，
高插的帽羽掃開了蛛網，
她一路叨唸著「糟了——糟糕！」
終於走進小房間，有月光
映窗格，蒼白，淒冷，靜若墳場。
他說，「快說吧，梅德琳在何處，
快說，看在神聖紡機的面上，
那紡機唯特准的修女目睹，
爲了把聖安妮羊毛敬紡成絨布。」

14

「聖安妮啊這是聖安妮前夕——
但是在佳節仍有人殺人：
除非你能叫篩裏水不滴
或是能號令鬼怪和妖精，
否則怎敢闖進來：見你現身，
眞嚇人，波飛羅！——聖安妮前宵！
天可憐！小姐今晚要求神：
天使們行行好，把她哄著！
讓我笑一笑，有的是時間尋煩惱。」

15

淡淡的月色裏，她淺淺地笑；
波飛羅打量著她的皺臉，
就如頑童端詳著老嫗，
戴著眼鏡，坐在壁爐邊，
拿一本神祕的奇書，卻不掀。
但他的眼神驟亮，聽她講
小姐的心意，他簡直難掩
熱淚，想到夢幻無非是淒涼，
梅德琳也無非睡在傳說的膝上。

16

突然有一念，像玫瑰盛開，
令他的額角泛紅，他的苦心
掀起了豔潮：他提出來
一個巧計，令老嫗吃驚：
「無情的傢伙，你不安好心；
讓小姐去求神，安眠，作夢，
只容好天使相陪，卻要當心
你這種壞人。走吧，走！我懂，
以前你裝得好，其實你完全不同。」

17

「我不會冒犯她，神明見證，」
波飛羅說：「願神不接納，
一息尚存，我臨終的祈請，
只要我敢動她一絡捲髮，
或是好色地窺她臉頰。
安吉拉，我的淚水你該相信，
否則啊哪怕是一剎那，
我就會狂叫把仇人驚醒，
管他比狼兒或熊狠，都跟他拚命。」

18

「唉！你何苦嚇唬我這龍鍾，
這風癱可憐蟲，快要入土，
不到夜半或許就敲起喪鐘；
為你祈禱，朝朝又暮暮，
從沒有誤過。」—— 一番怨言，她才
教火燥的波飛羅語氣變軟；
看到他這麼傷感，這麼悲哀，
安吉拉答應他，說她情願，
管它是凶是吉，決心要為他成全。

19

那便是，把他悄悄地領去，
直接去梅德琳的閨房，
就躲在壁櫥裏，十分隱祕，
好讓他獨窺秀色，不露行藏，
或許當夜就贏得無雙
的新娘，乘精靈群舞於被單，
而幽幽的魔法將她蔽障。
自從墨靈將一切魔債償還，
戀人就不曾在如此的夜裏會面。

20

老嫗說，「一切都照你所願，
奇珍異果都很快會供好，
今晚得過節；在刺繡架邊
她的琴你會看見。時間不早，
我遲緩又虛弱，怎麼敢草草
在這件事上亂擺茶點。
耐心等一會，孩子，先跪禱
一陣吧。你啊可要娶她為眷，
否則我死後在墓裏永升不了天。」

21

說著，她跛行而去，滿心憂懼。
情人的佳期漫長又遲緩；
老嫗踱回來，向耳畔低語，
叫他跟她去；老眼驚轉，
怕有人偵探。終於平安，
兩人才穿越暗廊，走到
少女的閨房，柔美，寂靜，貞婉；
波飛羅心滿意足地躲好。
他可憐的嚮導便退出，寒顫難熬。

22

安吉拉婆婆伸顫抖的手，
扶著欄杆，摸索著樓梯；
梅德琳，中了佳節的魔咒，
正上來，恍惚像天遣靈異，
端著銀燭的幽光，小心翼翼，
她轉身扶老婆婆向下走
到安穩的平蓆。現在要留意，
少年波飛羅，要看好那床頭；
她來了，又來了，像斑鳩受驚又逃走。

23

她匆匆入房，燭光熄掉，
輕煙散入了淡白的月光；
她關門，喘息，似乎感到
精靈和幻象就近在身旁：
一聲都別響，怕禍從天降！
但可對心說，心事千言萬語，
沐香的玉體有苦難講，
像斷舌的夜鶯徒有歌曲
梗在喉頭，悶在心頭，在谷底死去。

24

三層弧形拱櫺的高窗
都有精雕裝飾的圖案，
雕成水果、花朵、萹蓄的形狀，
更用各式的玻璃鑲嵌，
用繽紛璀璨的色彩點染，
有如燈蛾深紅的粉翅；
而中央，在千百徽章之間，
圍以幽淡的聖像，朦朧的紋飾，
有一面盾牌，用帝后的鮮血浸漬。

25

冬夜的月光照在窗上，
投緋紅的條紋在她胸口，
她此刻正跪禱神恩天降；
玫瑰落影在她交疊的雙手，
紫水晶落在她銀十字上頭，
光輪戴在她髮上，如聖徒，
她真像新妝的天使，等候
　升天，只欠翅膀──看得他恍惚
她跪著，如此純淨，如此超越污俗。

26

不久他心又跳起：晚禱既罷，
她摘去髮上纏繞的珍珠，
把戴暖的寶石一一解下，
又鬆開溫香的胸兜，讓華服
滑退到膝下，窸窸窣窣；
像藻間的人魚，半顯半蔽，
她心事重重，假寐片刻，恍惚
　目睹她床上是聖安妮，
卻不敢向後看，怕魔咒全會褪去。

27

在又軟又寒的窩裏微顫，
她半醒半寐，迷惘地仰臥，
等到睡夢像罌粟的燠暖，
來撫慰四肢，將倦魂解脫；
像一念有福，悲喜都難縛，
高飛遠颺，一直到明朝；
像不理異教徒把禱卷緊握，
像日出或下雨一概都不瞧，
像玫瑰應該收瓣，重新做花苞。

28

潛入了天堂，滿心狂歡，
波飛羅注視她卸下的衣裝，
更細聽她的噓息，看看
她是否已進入溫柔的睡鄉；
果然聽到了，真是福從天降，
他鬆了一口氣，便爬出壁櫥，
像曠野中的恐怖，一聲不響，
在沉默的地毯上，無聲舉步，
向紗帳裏窺望，啊，她睡得好熟。

29

在她床邊，有淡淡的月色，
撒落朦朧的銀輝，他輕放
一張小桌，半帶慌張，又擺設
繡花桌巾，腥紅，墨黑，又金黃——
哦，但願夢神的符咒能幫忙！
午夜節慶，小喇叭的噪音，
還有銅鼓，和豎笛的遠揚，
雖然是餘響，也使他不寧——
大堂門又關上，一切喧囂歸清靜。

30

蓋著白淨、平滑、薰香的被褥，
她正酣然於藍瞼的睡眠，
而他正從壁櫥裏搬出
蘋果、 桲、青梅、甜瓜等蜜餞；
還有果醬比乳酪更好嚥，
透明的糖漿，像肉桂香醇，
仙味和蜜棗，由費茲的海船
運來，異香的珍羞，無美不臻，
來自絲路的撒馬干，杉香的黎巴嫩。

31

諸般珍羞他用熱情的手
堆在金盤和纏繞的銀絲
編成的籃裏：豪貴的珍羞
累累，對著夜色寧靜的隱私，
清香溢滿了寒冽的閨室。
「好了，吾愛，美麗的天使，醒醒！
你是我的樂園，我是你的隱士。
莫辜負聖安妮，快睜開眼睛，
否則我就睡你身旁，因我太傷心。」

32

他喃喃自語，暖而無力的手臂
伸入她枕底。她的美夢
隱約在帳裏——這午夜的魔力
像凍溪一般不可能消融：
亮盤在月色中晶晶閃動，
地毯鑲著寬闊的金邊；
他似乎永遠，永遠不能從
如此的密咒中使她睜眼，
只能沉思片刻，陷入虛幻的綺念。

33

他恢復清醒，拿起她的空琴，
錚錚琮琮，用最柔的旋律
奏一首古調，今人卻少聽，
在普羅旺斯叫〈無情的豔女〉。
樂聲就近在她的耳際
將她驚醒，發出一聲輕吟。
他住手——她急喘——而突地
她驚定的藍眼睜開豔明；
他雙膝跪下，蒼白如平雕的石品。

34

她雙眼大睜，已完全清醒，
但眼中所見仍是夢裏幻象：
這變相太難受，幾乎失盡
夢中又純又深的吉祥。
梅德琳不禁淚水滿眶，
囈語喃喃，不斷地歎息，
一直緊盯著波飛羅不放；
他跪著，雙手握著，滿眼憐惜，
不敢動或開口，她似乎仍在夢裏。

35

「波飛羅啊！」她說，「你的聲音
剛才我覺得還如此甜蜜，
更因甜蜜的誓言而動聽，
憂愁的眼神也空靈而清晰；
怎麼都變了！多蒼白又冷寂！
再恢復那口吻吧，波飛羅，
那不倦的眼神，可親的怨氣！
莫留我一人啊終生難過，
萬一你死去，吾愛，我不知歸宿爲何。」

36

聽到迷魂的情話，他的激情
遠非凡人所能忍，便起身，
飄然而興奮，悸動如一閃星，
顯現於青空寧靜的深沉；
他化入她的夢，像玫瑰清芬
與紫羅蘭融合爲一體——
交流美滿：此時霜風陣陣
警告戀人，用凜冽的冰雨
拍打寒窗；聖安妮的月亮已下去。

37

天色昏暗，風雪拍窗正交加：
「你不是做夢，梅德琳，好新娘！」
天昏地暗，冰風咆哮又敲打：
「不是做夢，唉！唉！我眞悲傷！
波飛羅要丟下我，憔悴，絕望——
太絕情！你帶來什麼負心漢？
不怨你，我心已失給你心腸，
不管你將我遺棄又欺騙——
像失群的鴿子，羽毛披散病懨懨。」

38

「我的梅德琳，好新娘！愛作夢！
說吧，我能否做你的寵臣？
爲你的美充盾牌，心狀而朱紅，
銀色的殿堂啊，讓我安身，
像飢餓的香客，歷經苦尋
而有獲——因奇蹟而得救贖。
儘管我尋到你香閨，卻無心
掠奪，除了女閨主；如你肯託付，
美人梅德琳，就付我，斯文的異教徒。

39

「聽啊！這是仙鄉吹來的風暴，
看似狂野，其實是福氣。
起來吧，起來！天就快破曉，
飽脹的酒鬼沒人會注意——
走吧，吾愛，腳步要緊急；
誰也聽不到，誰也看不見——
全都不勝醉意和睡意。
醒來吧！起來吧！吾愛，勇敢點，
在南方的荒野我為你已建好家園。」

40

她聽罷匆匆起身，滿心害怕，
只因四周睡滿了龍旗禁軍，
或許正持矛眈眈地視察——
兩人沿樓梯在暗中逃命，
整棟華邸聽不到動靜。
門上的掛燈都閃閃爍爍；
那掛氈，織滿騎士、獵犬和鷹，
被咆哮的旋風吹得抖索，
長幅的地毯在風掃的地板起落。

41

兩人像幽靈，潛躡到大廳，
像幽靈一般，躡到鐵門前；
有闇卒仰臥，手腳不平衡，
喝空的大酒壺倒在身邊；
驚動了抖擻的大獵犬，
機警的眼睛認出是主人。
閂閂——輕抽出膛沿——
腳印斑斑的石上鐵鍊寂冷，
鑰匙一轉動，鉸鏈嘰嘰便開了重門。

42

他們一去不返：啊，年淹代遠，
一對戀人逃入了風雪之中。
許多事故那一夜堡主夢見，
赴宴的武士也久做惡夢，
撲朔迷離，龐然的蛆蟲，
還有巫婆和妖怪。安吉拉婆婆
癱蜷地死去，縮歪了面容；
而誦經老僧，千遍念珠數過，
也在骨灰中長眠，無人來問下落。

《蕾米亞》簡析

蕾米亞（lamia）一詞來自希臘神話，意為蛇妖，相傳上身為女軀，下身為蛇體，原為利比亞皇后，天帝宙斯所戀，生子遭天后Hera所害，遂因遷怒而吞食一切孩童以為復仇。濟慈此詩取材於包敦之《百憂探源》（Robert Burton：*The Anatomy of Melancholy*），其實本事應回溯三世紀希臘作家費洛崔托之《阿波羅涅》（*Apollonius of Tyana*）。

濟慈的故事循希臘傳統而益之以中世紀傳說。大意是蛇妖暗戀科林斯書生萊歐斯，不得親近，適逢宙斯（羅馬神話稱宙父Jove）之使者──報神墨赴立（Mercury，希臘稱赫米斯，Hermes），愛戀一林泉小仙卻遍尋而不見，乃為墨赴立破解小仙隱身之咒，並求墨赴立施術化己身為美女，以便親近書生。萊歐斯果然為蕾米亞所誘，墮其妖術而不自知。兩情相悅，深居蕾米亞虛設之宮中，萊歐斯終於不甘惜福而思炫耀於親友。蕾米亞恐萊歐斯老師阿波羅涅會識破幻象，求他莫邀老師來赴婚宴。阿波羅涅不速自來，果然當眾揭發真相。頓時蕾米亞與她張設的幻境煙消而滅，萊歐斯亦悲駭而死。

這故事令人想起《白蛇傳》，只是中國的故事多了一個小青。兩個愛情悲劇似有正邪之分，卻又不全如此。正方有理，可是得理不饒人，反而以理害情，造成傷害。反方有

情，但徒情不足恃，反而犧牲了。濟慈在詩中是說書人的身
分，本來應該是同情一對戀人的，不過口吻有些曖昧。於是
評論家乃有歧見。《蕾米亞》當然是幽明跨界神人（至少是
人妖）相歡的故事，當不得眞。可是當作寓言來看，其暗喻
可施於情與理、想像與現實、藝術與科學、美與眞。

　　濟慈的好友海頓（Benjamin Haydon）在自傳中記述：
某次雅聚，酒酣神馳，濟慈表示同意蘭姆的看法，即牛頓的
《光學》淪彩虹爲三稜鏡，簡直毀了虹的詩意。難怪《蕾米
亞》下篇一開頭，說書人就這麼說：

　　　　愛情住陋屋，靠水和麵包屑
　　　　只算是——愛神別見怪——灰飛煙滅；
　　　　愛情住皇宮，也許到頭來
　　　　下場更慘於隱士的戒齋：
　　　　那是仙境可疑的傳奇，
　　　　凡人要領略確是不易。
　　　　萊歐斯若長命把故事傳後，
　　　　對這教訓或許能改皺眉頭，
　　　　或更握緊：但他們幸福太短，
　　　　還不足起疑生恨，以嘶嘶繼嬌喘。

「嘶嘶」指蛇，「嬌喘」指美人：一時還不會拆穿。到了下
篇接近尾聲，說書人就說得更明了：

　　　　　　　　　一切魔咒，

　　　哲學的冷指下豈不都飛走？

　　　曾經，天上有莊嚴的虹帶：

　　　什麼材料，如何織成，現在

　　　已公開，一五一十，毫不稀奇。

　　　哲學會剪掉天使的雙翼，

　　　用界尺與繩墨來收拾虛玄，

　　　把天神和地怪都清除不見，

　　　把彩虹拆散，就像曾經

　　　把嬌柔的蕾米亞化成陰影。

有評論家認為，蕾米亞乃暗喻濟慈的女友芬妮（Fanny Brawne）：濟慈愛她，卻也隱隱覷到她一些缺陷，不過又不肯向自己坦承。所以書生萊歐斯該是詩人自喻了。至於阿波羅涅，竟有評論家疑是蘇格蘭惡意的書評家，那就扯得太遠了吧？

　　詩無達詁，本非科學。西方在古代，科學尚未定稱，所以philosophy即指科學，而natural philosophy即指自然科學，natural history即指博物學。說得玄些，《蕾米亞》隱喻的也可以是藝術與科學。我倒覺得科學未必會敗壞詩興，反之，有時還有助詩興，可以提供新的感性。我的近作Arco Iris，對彩虹就有新的感悟。

　　《蕾米亞》的詩體採用韻感單純而呼應直接的英雄式的偶句（heroic couplet），取法的對象是十七世紀的朱艾

敦，尤其是他的《寓言》。偶句的韻式久之會嫌單調，所以濟慈不時用十二音節的長句，「抑揚六步格」（iambic hexameter or Alexandrine），來調劑。有時爲了加強語氣，一連三行都會連韻，就變成三連句（triplet）。凡此變體，我都劍及履及，緊緊跟隨。一般的「抑揚五步格」詩行，我都在譯文中用十個方塊字來對應英文的十音節；爲求自然與彈性，有時我也會在九字與十一字之間伸縮。希望讀者在譯文中偶見一行竟有十二、三個字，不要誤會是我失檢、失控。不過原文的專有名詞，有時音節太多，失之於長，譯文一行負擔不起，我只好稍加簡化，或另用稱呼。例如 Apollonius，如果譯全，就成了「阿波羅尼厄斯」，太難入句了。又如名城科林斯，有時便簡稱科城。

蕾米亞

上　篇

話說從前，精靈家族還未將
仙子和妖怪趕出了林莽，
而奧伯隆王燦燦的金冠，
權杖、披風、露水爲扣的亮鑽，
尚未將林仙和牧神都一起
趕出草叢，樹叢，野櫻草地，
久害相思的赫米斯只記掛
著偷情，竟把金寶座丟下，
從奧林帕斯山他借光盜彩，
在天帝宙父的雲下，避開
他主神的監視，並且躲進
克里特島海邊的森林。
只因那仙島上住著一位
水神，兩蹄妖獸都向她下跪；
憔悴的海神在她趾前獻珠，

但是登陸後只徒然仰慕。
靠近她常去沐浴的溪旁
和她不時出沒的牧場，
堆滿了供品，詩神所未見，
但幻想的寶盒卻任你自選。
啊，愛情的世界向她拜倒！
赫米斯想著，仙體的熱潮
便由腳跟延燒到雙耳，
從一片白皙，皎若百合，
在他的金髮下赧成玫瑰，
金髮成捲，可羨在兩肩披垂。

多少山谷，多少森林他飛遍，
不減的激情吹拂在花間，
沿多少河流向源頭迴溯，
要尋俏水仙把床藏何處，
卻不見；俏水仙無處可覓，
他歇下，落在寂寞的野地，
心事重重，滿懷難堪的嫉妒，
妒那些林神，甚至所有的樹。
他正站著，忽聽見有聲淒苦，
善心人聽了，會百痛盡除，
只剩憐憫：寂寞的聲音哀吟：
「從委曲的墓中我何時能醒，

何時命好此身行動得自由，
有愛情，有歡樂，有熱血追求
貼心和親吻！唉，我真命苦！」
赫米斯舉足如鴿，悄悄移步，
繞過雜樹叢，輕快地掠掃
高草萋萋和花繁的野草，
終於發現有一條蛇在發顫，
蛇身明豔，在暗蕨中盤旋。

她雖亮麗，卻糾纏成一團，
硃砂點點，又金，又綠，又藍；
多帶如斑馬，多斑如猛豹，
多眼如孔雀，還有腥紅成條；
滿身是銀月，每當她換氣，
月色忽隱忽現，其明麗
就和較暗的圖案交替──
腰身七彩，染上了一些悲淒，
她似乎又像悔罪的精靈，
又像是妖婆，又像妖魔自身。
她頭頂有黯淡一團火焰，
濺出火星，像阿蓮尼的后冕：
她的頭是蛇頭，但苦中帶甘！
嘴像女人，編貝都齊全：
眼睛呢，如此美目又何用，

除了哭罷再哭，歎天生美容？
像冥后哭念西西里的天空。
雖是蛇喉，她吐的口音
卻似流蜜，全由於愛情。
就這麼，赫米斯歛羽暫駐，
像獵鷹俯衝向他的獵物。

「俊美的赫米斯，戴羽而閃光，
昨夜我見你，只美夢一場：
見你坐在金色的寶座上，
與眾神並列，在古神山崗，
唯獨你不樂，只因你不聞
九繆思輕弄的淙淙琴聲，
甚至也不聞阿波羅獨唱，
渾不聞他放喉的長歌悠揚。
夢中我見你披著紫霞，
多麼風流地穿朝雲而下，
迅如太陽神燦爛的飛鏢，
直射克里特島；你竟已飛到！
斯文的赫米斯，可尋著那美女？」
聽她此言，忘川之星不猶豫，
赧然口快便向她問起：
「你這條伶嘴蛇，真有主意！
你這俏花捲，滿眼哀愁，

你要的什麼幸福我都有，
只要告訴我，那水仙遁何處——
住在何方？」「明星啊，空說無助，」
蛇回話，「且發個誓吧，俊仙郎！」
「我保證，」赫米斯說，「憑這蛇杖，
憑你的俏眼，你戴星的頭顱！」
在花間吹送，他的重話飄舞。
於是再展陰柔的聰明：
「癡心郎！你失去的仙靈，
自在如風，無影無蹤，她漫遊
這一片無憂的原野；歲月清幽，
由得她獨享，無人見她捷腳
留下蹤跡在香花與野草；
從疲乏的藤蔓，壓低的枝條，
無人見到她摘果，或浴澡：
她的妖嬈靠我的法力遮護，
不容人來冒犯或來輕侮，
不容大小牧神的俗眼
來窺色，醉眼的老妖徒歡惋。
她的仙身變得虛弱，受害
於這一批求歡客，她的悲哀
令我同情，就教她用魔漿
來浸潤長髮，如此可經常
保她的婀娜隱形，卻不礙

她到處漫遊，自由自在。
只要你肯守諾言，賞我神恩，
就能見她，赫米斯，就你一人！」
於是著迷的神再度發誓言，
那良言，聽進她蛇耳裏面，
溫馨，微顫，虔誠，如詩篇。
她不禁狂悅，昂頭如色嬉，
面泛桃色，輕快的唇音細細：
「我前生是女人，讓我恢復
女身吧，而且要動人如故。
我愛科林斯一少年——真天幸！
請還我女兒身，放在他附近。
下來吧，赫米斯，我一吹你前額，
你的俏水仙就出現，此刻。」
天神半斂翼，輕輕落地，
她在他眼上吹口氣，驀地，
隱身的水仙竟現身，含笑，在草地。
不是在做夢，也可說正是夢，
眾神做夢都成真，其樂無窮，
在不醒的長夢裏享受平靜。
熱烈而害羞的一刻，盤旋不定，
像因水仙之美所激，他如焚；
不落足印地降在草地，轉身
來昏去的蛇前，懶懶伸臂，

輕巧地，用他的魔杖發揮神力。
事成，他轉眼眷顧著水仙，
滿面愛羨的淚水與慰勉，
向她步去；而她，像缺月一彎，
當著他轉暗，畏縮，難按
恐懼的飲泣，像朵合瓣的花，
到黃昏就暈厥，不支而塌垮：
但天神撫慰她冰涼的手，
使她轉暖，眼神也轉柔，
於是像蓓蕾迎晨頌的蜜蜂
而盛放，且將蜜漿全貢奉。
一對情人飛入了綠陰深處，
卻不像俗世情侶般淡出。

剩下她自己，蛇妖開始蛻變；
妖精的血液劇烈地流轉，
口吐白沫，草地濺到都枯槁，
這樣的露珠，再甜，也是毒藥；
蛇眼痛得直瞪，苦惱又悽慘，
發燙，發白，放大，睫毛全燒乾，
閃磷光，射火星，無涼淚可沾。
七彩迤邐，全身都已熊熊，
她扭來轉去，不勝其灼痛：
深沉的火山黃取代她身上

比較典雅而低調的月光；
正如熔漿摧毀了草原，
她的銀鎧和金錦也不免
任所有的斑點和線條遮暗：
新月蝕盡，群星也吞完；
剎那之間她只剩裸赤，
再不見寶藍、翠綠，和晶紫，
還有絳銀：一切都烏有，
除了痛苦和醜陋，一切不留。
她的頭頂還閃現，旋即消隱，
她自己也突然化於無形；
空際傳來她如琴的新聲，
「萊歐斯，斯文的萊歐斯！」一併
隨明霧飛繞蒼山才消掉，
克里特島的林中再聽不到。

蕾米亞去了何處？她已變淑女，
十足的美人，年輕而秀麗。
從森克烈海濱去科林斯城，
她遁世的谷地是行人必經。
她在那一帶荒山腳歇下，
皮連河的源頭由此出發，
另一邊是迤邐的野嶺，籠雲
罩霧一直向西南延伸

去克雷奧內。她便佇立，
約當幼鳥可撲飛的距離，
有座茂林，草坡上有道苔徑，
在一泓清池邊她大發豪情，
自照竟已逃出了難關，
衣裙像水仙花一般翩然。

萊歐斯有幸了！——有女如斯，
誰能夠比美，縱然都有辮子，
都嘆氣，害羞，在春花的牧場
向遊唱詩人擺動綠裳：
如斯處女，清唇無邪，卻熟諳
愛情之道，能深入人心坎：
降世不到一時辰，但論世故，
卻能分辨幸福與近鄰痛苦，
辨禍福之窄界，析禍福
之交際，與旦夕之反覆；
能用亂真之偽境而明察
惑人之毫末，屢試不差；
似乎在愛神學府她早已
逍遙地卒業，仍純真不移，
懶懶散散修完了玫紅的學期。

這位俏佳人何以像精靈

在路邊徘徊，我會說明；
但首先該解釋，雖身在蛇獄，
當初她卻能隨心所欲，
冥思又夢想，離奇或者輝煌，
只要起念，她何處都能往，
無論渺茫的旖旎仙境，
或下潛漂髮的海浪，乘波靈
的順風，沿珠梯入海神私寢；
或酒神飲盡了瓊漿，悠然
在黏脂的松樹下睡酣；
或在冥王的宮苑之中
戰神的巨柱圍廣場而炯炯。
有時她會送夢魂入城，
追逐宴樂與騷響相混；
有一次她混入凡夫俗子，
見到科城的少年萊歐斯
在爭路的賽車場一馬領先，
像青春的宙父神定氣閒，
當時就情迷愛上了人家。
而此刻正薄暮，蛾影上下，
她知道，從海邊回科城，
萊歐斯會路過；東風陣陣
剛吹起，此刻他的帆船，
銅首磨著石墩，在森克烈灣，

從艾吉納嶼來停靠泊岸：
他去艾吉納祭罷宙父神廟，
大理石廟門久等血祭與香料。
宙父許他誓願，卻償過於求，
也是正巧有緣分，跟朋友
說了再見，他踏上了歸途，
也許對科城的清談不滿足；
他越過了寂寥的山徑，
漫不經心，尚未見到黃昏星，
心已不清，遐思幻想乃迷途，
在柏拉圖玄虛的幽靜薄霧。
蕾米亞見他越走越近身——
毫不注目，幾乎要錯身，
涼鞋無聲地踏過苔蘚，
如此靠攏，卻視而不見，
她站住：他過路，自閉於玄境，
頭腦密裏如披風；她的眼睛
追隨他腳步，白頸多高貴，
也在轉——吐音清晰，「萊歇斯，喂，
你難道要留我一人在山間？
萊歇斯，轉過來，人家要愛憐。」
他回身；不是冷峻的疑問，
而是奧菲斯對亡妻般溫存；
她的話真是悅耳的歌吟，

似乎一整個長夏他都愛聽：
立刻，他雙眼已飲盡她嬌美，
不留一滴在迷人的酒杯，
但杯中仍酒滿──他深恐
她會消失，害他來不及貢奉
應獻的頌詞，便開口讚揚；
她的柔情轉羞，見他已落網：
「留下你一人！回頭看！啊，女神，
看我的眼神能否離你一瞬！
憐憫掩不住我的傷心──
如果失去你，我就會送命。
站住！雖然你只是小小水仙，
溪流都順從你的心願；
別走！雖然綠林都由你掌管，
綠林也自願把朝雨喝乾；
雖然生屬七姊妹星譜，難道
沒有一位，善奏的姊妹淘，
能調順你的星空，代閃銀輝？
你的呼喚是如此甜美，
令我耳醉，若是你化爲烏有，
對你的相思也令我消瘦──
憐憫永不磨滅！」──「眞要我留下，」
蕾米亞說，「踩著人世的泥沙，
在這崎嶇的花叢走得腳痛，

你能說能做的有何神功
來慰解我細膩的鄉愁？
你總不能要我跟你奔走
在這些荒山野谷，無人喜歡，
跟長生和幸福都毫不相干！
你是個書生，萊歇斯，該知道
精緻的仙靈必定受不了
人世的風塵，活不了：唉癡少年，
你豈有清純的滋味能慰勉
我的麗質？何處有更安寧
的宮苑，可娛我六欲七情，
用什麼妙計能解我無盡的渴心？
不行的──再見吧！」說罷，她立起
踮起腳尖，攤開白臂。他深懼
與她自艾自怨的愛約相錯，
一時情迷，喃喃而訴，難過
得憔悴。淑女心狠，全不露出
疼惜她少年情郎的悲楚，
反而，似乎嫌明眸還不夠豔，
用更豔的眼神，從容的歡顏，
用新唇吻他的唇，獻出自己
久久蟠蜿在曲身的活力；
而當他一陣情迷後又一陣
情迷，她便揚起了歌聲

為美貌、新生、愛情，為一切歡騰，
唱一首情歌，非凡琴能盡演，
當星群屏息，斂起抖動的火焰。
然後她低語成輕輕顫動，
像戀人苦等後首次相逢，
終於放心地單獨一聚，
情話不需用目傳；她叫他抬起
頭來，把心底的疑慮掃開，
因為她已成了女人，不再
有玄奧的仙液流過血管，
只有熱血，而且如他的一般，
脆弱的心中懷著痛楚。
她又說奇怪為何他未睹
她一面，在科城多年，說自己
在該地半隱居，說在該地
好日子要靠金幣來安排，
不是靠愛情；過得還自在，
直到見他之前，走過他身邊，
他正悠然出神，倚在一柱前，
在愛神廟的長廊，四下都是
滿籃催情的藥草與花，摘自
初夜，那正是阿當尼斯盛宴
之前夕，後來就無緣再見面，
她只能獨泣，泣何以要暗戀？

萊歐斯死而復甦，滿心奇異，
見她還在，唱得正甜蜜；
聽她低訴女人經如此內行，
他又從驚異轉為歡暢；
她每講一句他就更著迷，
滿心踏實的欣悅與歡喜。
讓輕狂的詩人隨意誇說，
說仙子、精靈、女神多灑脫，
洞裏，湖畔，瀑布下來去，
仙班之中有什麼豔遇
比得上人間女子，無論出身
是琵拉的卵石，亞當的後人。
蕾米亞想了又想，終於想通：
萊歐斯愛她，不能半帶驚恐，
要令他傾心，傾得更深，
就不能做女神，要扮女人；
他不能受驚，只能驚豔，
豔色雖可驚，卻有驚無險。
萊歐斯的回應十分流利，
每句話都配上一聲歡氣，
終於指著科林斯，問得殷勤：
夜深了，她的嬌足可否遠行。
其實不遠，只因蕾米亞心急，
略施法術，就教十里八里

縮成了短程；萊歐斯目迷，
只對她關注，卻全不懷疑。
怎麼就進了城，他全不明白，
太靜了，他根本沒有去猜。

人常在夢中囈語，科城亦然，
不僅它金碧輝煌的宮殿，
還有繁華的街道，放蕩的神廟，
像風雨起自遠方，都在嘈嘈。
對著塔上的夜色茫茫，
不論男女或貧富，乘著晚涼，
都穿著便鞋在街頭閒步，
或同行，或獨步；豪奢的慶祝
此起彼落，有火光明晃，
將抖動的人影投在牆上，
或映出人影被簷影掩護，
或聚在拱門下，或出沒廊柱。

他蒙起臉，怕跟熟人會面，
緊握住她手指，正有人近前，
捲髮灰白，眼神銳利，又禿頂，
披著哲人的長袍，緩步而行
走過身邊時，萊歐斯的身體
在篷斗裏更瑟縮，步伐更急，

蕾米亞趄得發抖：他說「唉，
你為何抖得這麼厲害，吾愛？
你的柔掌為何竟濕透？」
「我累了，」蕾米亞說，「那老頭
究竟是誰？我實在記不起
他的面容──萊歇斯，為何你
要躲避他的銳眼？」萊歇斯道：
「那是阿波羅涅，我的指導，
良師，但今晚他無異是蠢鬼，
竟來我的美夢裏作祟。」

這麼說著，他們已來到
一道柱廊，有一扇拱門高挑，
銀燈懸著，曉星的光芒
倒映在下面的石板階上，
柔如水中星光，大理石
的光澤這麼新，這麼純澈，
這麼通透的晶瑩，流暢，
布著黑紋，只有神仙的腳掌
才可以觸摩。風鈴叮噹，
由鉸鍊帶響，每當拱門寬敞，
有時開出無名的天地，
誰也不知，除了兩人自己，
和幾個波斯啞僕，就在那年

有人見啞僕在市場出現，
但住在何處誰也不知，好奇
的人無法追蹤他們去宮裏。
此外則有待飛揚的詩句
來坦述，後來是什麼悲劇，
讓大家開心，就此放下他們，
避開不肯輕信的凡塵。

下　篇

愛情住陋屋，靠水和麵包屑
只算是——愛神別見怪——灰飛煙滅；
愛情住皇宮，也許到頭來
下場更慘於隱士的戒齋：
那是仙境可疑的傳奇，
凡人要領略確是不易。
萊歐斯若長命把故事傳後，
對這教訓或許能改皺眉頭，
或更握緊：但他們幸福太短，
還不足起疑生恨，以嘶嘶繼嬌喘。
何況，夜夜光輝太耀眼，
愛情，妒忌如此的一對美眷，
在他們寢宮的門楣上，
聲浪可驚，盤旋並磨響翅膀，

向走道盡頭的地板投下豔光。

這一切卻終於毀滅：並枕，
兩人一同就位於黃昏，
躺在御榻上，身旁的紗帳，
輕鬆透風，用一條金絲懸盪，
飄曳進房來，卻遮不住
夏日的晚空，藍得多清楚，
兩邊是大理石柱——兩人憩著，
慣於如此溫馨，眼睛閉著，
只留一條縫，為愛情而開，
好瞇著對方，在半寐狀態；
這時從郊外的山坡傳來
喇叭的亢揚，把燕語遮蓋，
萊歇斯一驚——其聲雖沉寂，
卻留下一念擾人於腦際。
自從在甘於犯罪的華宮內
他窩藏以來，這還是頭回
他神遊越過金色的界外，
到幾乎已棄絕的塵世裏來。
那美眷，始終警覺，已看出
這點，很難過：這顯示不滿足，
還奢求更多，非她的狂歡
天地所能供應，便長吁短歎，

他一念竟越過了她：她也懂
一念之短能敲響癡情的喪鐘。
「你為何歎氣呢，美人？」他低問。
「那你又為何分心？」她應聲：
「你不要我了——丟我在何方？
你煩惱壓眉頭，就沒我在心上
對，對，你趕走了我，我不在
你心上，無家可歸：就這樣，唉。」
他俯身向她睜開的眼睛
照出天國的小倒影，並回應：
「我的明星，照黃昏也照早晨！
說得為什麼如此哀沉？
倒是我一直怕用情不足，
要更耗心血，倍加受苦，
一心想把你的靈魂纏住，
縛住，囚進我靈魂，把你困住，
像未綻的玫瑰含著幽香。
唉，像一個蜜吻——看你多憂傷。
我分心！要我交心嗎？聽好！
凡人得了寶，而別人得不到，
因此不安，又不知該怎麼辦，
誰能不偶然拿出來展覽，
自鳴得意，就像我因你自豪，
那管科林斯流言的警告？

讓敵人都哽住，朋友遠遠呼喝，
熱鬧的大街上你的新娘車
輪軸卻閃閃而過。」美人
面容顫動，無言，蒼白而柔順，
起身跪在他面前，淚如雨滴，
爲他的話傷心，終於痛苦地
哀求他，將他的手撑了又撑，
求他改變主意。他感到傷心，
脾氣變強，益發奇想，要收服
她又野又馴的個性，由他作主：
何況，強要克己，不管愛得多深，
也昧著自己良心，反而放任
自己，以她此刻的傷心爲樂。
他的激情變殘酷，露出慍色，
兇狠而又暴躁，就像額上
沒爆青筋的人也會的那樣。
盛怒得控才好，就如當年
亞波羅鎮定地張弓搭箭
要射死巨蟒——哈，巨蟒！當然
她不是。她動情，愛上專斷，
終於完全臣服，答應在良辰
被他領去婚禮做新人。
子夜寂寂，那少年耳語細細：
「你當然有個俏名，但不瞞你，

我一直沒問，總是不把你
當凡人，而是神仙的後裔，
此刻我還是一樣。有何俗名，
有何稱呼配得上你的麗影？
或是有什麼親友在世間，
可以來道喜，參加婚宴？」
「我毫無朋友，毫無，」蕾米亞說，
「科林斯雖大，誰也不識我：
父母的遺體都收在骨灰罈
葬掉，沒有香為他們點燃，
後人無福，除了我都已亡故，
而我，連和你的婚儀也疏忽。
廣邀來賓吧，隨你的便，
只要你的心意還有一點點
為我著想，就千萬莫請來
阿波羅涅那老頭，讓我避開。」
萊歇斯不解她如此的妄語，
便詳加追問；她一直閃避，
假裝睡著；而他，片刻的工夫，
已陷入了酣眠的糊塗。

當時風俗是要把新娘
在紅霞的黃昏帶出閨房，
面罩輕紗，坐上馬車，途中

有撒花與火炬前導，奏著婚頌，
和其他排場；但這陌生麗人
沒有熟人，只剩下自己一身
（萊歇斯正出門去招親戚），
她深知自己絕對無力
勸他別癡心冤枉鋪張，
便盡心竭力，親自來設想
如何將災難妝扮得光彩。
大功告成；但如何又從何而來，
卻教人難猜，何來伶俐的僕從。
在大堂走動，又出入於門中，
只聽見翅膀騷響，片刻時光，
輝煌的宴客廳便拱門大敞。
音樂祟人，也許竟是虛屋頂
獨一無二的支柱，始終不停
在歌吟，像擔心符咒會退去。
新雕的香柏，像林間的空地，
兩側是棕櫚和芭蕉，靠向中間，
高供在廳堂，獻給新娘：
兩棵棕櫚接兩棵芭蕉，等等，
從兩側的幹上枝柯交伸，
形成跨廳的長巷；在樹底，
燈火如溪流從近牆到遠壁。
上有帳幔，下有待嘗的酒宴，

異香四溢。蕾米亞盛妝莊嚴，
默默地巡行，且巡且觀，
在不滿之中有淡淡的自滿，
命隱形的僕從務必鋪張
轉彎抹角所有華飾的輝煌。
樹幹之間，先鋪著大理石板，
然後是碧玉鑲嵌；接著不斷
蔓延的是小樹叢的形影，
與大樹交纏成小巧的繽紛。
一切都稱心後，她褪去色相，
把私房關上，不聲，不響，
停停當當，只等鬧宴開始，
讓成群惡客來糟蹋她的隱私。

白晝來臨，也帶來多嘴的人群。
傻郎君啊！瘋子！你為何挑釁
寧靜的福氣，溫馨隱居的時光，
讓俗眼來窺私密的閨房？
眾人來到；每個人都不閒，
來到門口，更四處看遍，
詫異地擁進：街道本就熟悉，
從小對這一切都有記憶，
不該有遺漏，但從未瞻仰
這堂堂宮廊，這崇高的氣象；

一擁而入，迷惘，好奇而渴望，
除了一人，顧盼的眼神嚴厲，
緩緩舉足的步態有威儀：
正是阿波羅涅：他也在發笑，
似有難解的問題，一直困擾
他耐心的思考，此刻正解凍，
正在消融——果然被他料中。

他在竊竊私語的玄關裏
遇見這少年弟子。「照常理，
萊歇斯，」他說，「不速之客
不可以擅自闖門，也不可
妄自插進晚輩活潑的同伴，
可是這規矩我不得不犯，
要請你原諒。」萊歇斯赧赧，
把長者領進了重門寬坦，
不斷地陪罪，加謙恭執禮，
才勸笑了夫子的壞脾氣。

富麗堂皇是盛宴的廳堂，
處處洋溢著光彩和異香：
每一面鑲板前都冉冉供著
一座香爐，焚沒藥和香料，
下面用祭鼎高高地托起，

鼎足細長分跨在質地
毛料的氈上：五十縷香煙
從五十座爐中輕颺翩翩，
升向高穹，一面更被壁鏡
反映出孿生的對對香雲。
十二張圓桌用銀椅圍繞，
高及成人的胸部，都用豹爪
在下面撐住，桌上堆著重金
打造的各式酒杯，豐盛的食品
三倍於穀神之角，大號酒具
從暗木桶裏倒酒，酒色可喜。
盛宴堆滿所有的桌面，
神像供在每一桌中間。

等所有的賀客在前一間，
由奴僕擠壓整塊的海綿
在手上和腳上，感到涼爽，
又按儀式把精油芳香
倒在髮上，便披白袍順序入場，
圍坐在銀椅上，全部納罕，
如此的揮霍與排場誰來負擔。

輕柔的音樂沿輕柔的氣氛，
先是希臘語流利，母音低哼，

在賓客間交傳，一開頭
耳語喃喃，只因酒尚未入口；
等喜氣的醇醪抵達頭腦，
話就轉吵，音樂就越加高調，
樂器的力道——色彩繁富，
廳堂開啟，亮麗的帳幕，
莊嚴華美的高穹，酒酣的歡暢，
俏女僕，和蕾米亞又上場；
等美酒發揮了紅香的力道，
每人的心靈都解脫了煩惱，
一切就不再新奇；酒酣，酒甘，
仙境飄渺也不覺太神奇，美滿。
不久巴克思酒神高高在上，
眾客已酡顏，眼神更明亮：
花環由每一片草野，眾芳
由每一片谷地，或是向樹上
新摘來織金的籃裏，正堆得
高與籃柄看齊，只爲了配合
貴賓的心願，按各人的念頭，
或戴在額頭，或逍遙做枕頭。

什麼花環給蕾米亞？給萊歇斯？
什麼花環給哲人，阿波羅涅師？
在她痛苦的額頭該懸吊

小蛇藤和柳樹的長條；
至於那少年，趕快，且爲他剝光
酒神的手杖，讓他注視的眼光
能游入忘境；至於那長老，
就讓羽茅和惡毒的薊草
向他的鬢角宣戰。一切魔咒，
哲學的冷指下豈不都飛走？
曾經，天上有莊嚴的虹帶：
什麼材料，如何織成，現在
已公開，一五一十，毫不稀奇。
哲學會剪掉天使的雙翼，
用界尺與繩墨來收拾虛玄，
把天神和地怪都清除不見，
把彩虹拆散，就像曾經
把嬌柔的蕾米亞化成陰影。

她旁邊，萊歇斯欣然坐主位，
這廳上別的臉都不在眼內，
終於收斂起迷情，高舉
一滿杯酒，向對桌投去
遙遙的一瞥，求尋老師
皺紋的臉上有一瞥回視，
好向他敬酒。禿頭的哲人
不閃也不眨，凝定的眼神

專注在驚惶而美豔的新娘，
威脅她的綽約，擾亂她的端莊。
萊歇斯緊握她手，深情撫慰，
她的手蒼白，襯出長榻的豔緋，
而且冰冷，寒意傳入他血管；
忽然又發燙，十分不自然，
燥熱的痛感刺進他心房。
「蕾米亞，怎麼啦？怎麼如此慌張？
你認得哪人嗎？」可憐她不應。
他緊盯她眼睛，她的眼睛
對他的哀求完全沒響應；
他盯得更緊，簡直要亂性，
那嫵媚正被魔法所渴吞，
一對眼珠已經認不出人。
「蕾米亞！」他喊──沒嬌聲應他。
眾人全聽到了，震耳的喧譁
頓時無聲，莊嚴的音樂已悄悄；
千百花圈的桃金孃都病倒。
人聲，琴聲，宴樂漸平息，
逐步擴張著一片死寂，
終於死寂像悚然已降臨，
沒有人不感到髮豎可驚。
「蕾米亞！」他尖叫；只有叫聲
和回聲能打破死氣沉沉。

「滾你的，惡夢！」他大吼，再細審
新娘的臉龐，此刻已無青筋
遊走開朗的鬢旁，沒有光彩
來滋潤她臉頰，沒有熱愛
來照豔深陷的憧憬——只有敗壞；
蕾米亞美貌不再，枯坐著死白。
「閉上，閉上魔球的眼睛，狠心人，
轉過眼去，惡賊！否則遭眾神
正義的詛咒，威武的神像
在廳上代表眾神冥冥在場，
會突然用荊棘刺你雙目，
因痛而盲；只留你單獨
顫抖而老弱，去面對良心
微弱的驚駭，只為神力久失敬，
只為你瀆神而狂妄的詭辯，
非法的巫術，蠱惑的謊言。
科林斯人！看這白鬚的老妖
看他，中了邪，眼皮都掉了睫毛，
卻仍包著妖眼！科城人，且看！
我的好新娘被妖術摧殘。」
「笨蛋！」詭辯師說，語雖低沉，
粗魯中卻帶輕蔑，萊歇斯應聲，
像臨終呻吟，痛心而迷惘，
最後仰面倒在苦鬼的身旁。

「笨蛋！笨蛋！」他又說，眼神仍然
不放鬆，動也不動，「命中有難，
哪一次我沒救你，直到現在，
難道會讓你被蛇妖毒害？」
蕾米亞終於嚥氣，詭辯師眈眈
像一枝銳矛，將她刺個對穿，
鋒利，冷酷，通透，尖刻：而她
已手軟，雖有心竭力要傳話，
作勢要叫他住口，根本不靈。
他直瞪著！直瞪著不停——不行！
「是蛇呀！」他回應，話沒說完，
她一聲慘叫已煙消影散。
萊歐斯的懷中再無歡娛，
從那夜起，他四肢再無生趣。
他躺在高榻上！——朋友都圍集，
將他扶起——已無脈搏或呼吸，
穿著喜袍，蜷著沉重的屍體。

　　　　　　　　　　——2009年7月31日譯畢

《亥貢亮之敗亡》簡析

　　濟慈的夙慧早熟一直令我們驚奇：他短暫的一生連二十六歲都不滿，竟然寫下了七首長詩，依次是《恩迪米安》、《蕾米亞》、《伊莎貝拉：紫蘇盆花》、《聖安妮節前夕》、《亥貢亮》、《奧陀大帝》、《小丑的帽與鈴》。其中最長的是取材希臘神話的寓言詩《恩迪米安》（Endymion），長達4050行，而最短的一首《聖安妮節前夕》也有378行。就算他沒有寫過這些長篇，僅憑其他的詩作，包括六十一首十四行詩與所謂的「五大頌」，他也足以列於英國浪漫詩派重要詩人。

　　《恩迪米安》與《亥貢亮》是少年濟慈自許的雄圖，簡直有意直追米爾頓的史詩，然而兩者都沒有成功。米爾頓寫《失樂園》時，已經五十九歲，而寫《復樂園》更晚了四年。濟慈寫《恩迪米安》與《亥貢亮》，才二十三歲，不但古文與古典文學的修養遠不及米爾頓，「詩齡」也才四年，十分之淺，簡直尚未脫學徒時期。要處理這麼高古博大的主題，他只能仰懸米爾頓為典範，不但風格如此，連句法、遣詞也不免。幸而濟慈品味能力不弱，頗有自知之明，不久就發現這篇少作「傷感」而又「草率」，有了警覺。不久果然引來保守黨背景的《黑森林季刊》惡評。同時濟慈又開始寫規模龐大的《亥貢亮》，仍然掙不開米爾頓的磁場。次年他

寫信給瑞諾茲說：「我已經放棄了《亥貢亮》——學米爾頓
的倒裝句法太多了。英文的本位還是該守住的。」所以到了
1819年4月，他便爲之擱筆了。但是該年七月中旬，他不甘
心，又另寫這篇《亥貢亮之敗亡》，原意是想重整失敗了的
《亥貢亮》，但仍困於米爾頓的陰影，對於神人之間的對應
難以掌握，同時病情也不利於工作。因此《敗亡》篇只寫到
第二章的六十一行，就無以爲繼，此詩直到濟慈身後，才於
1856年出版。

　　《亥貢亮之敗亡》也頗受但丁《神曲》的啓發，敘事的
過程也呈上升之勢：始於花園，再進廟堂，終抵神龕。此詩
之全名是：*The Fall of Hyperion——A Dream*。敘述始於作者
夢見在林中有神仙宴罷，剩下許多仙果。他飲了果汁陶然醉
倒，醒來不見了園林與涼亭，只見有一座古老的神殿，雖然
崇高而莊嚴，卻歷經滄桑，十分荒涼。向西望時，遠處祭壇
旁有一雕像，巍然而大，但要去朝拜，卻要循石階多級，先
下後上。作者辛苦下階，幾乎衰竭，幸好及時踏到底級，頓
覺元氣恢復，輕易上攀，有如死而再生。原來這是一場考
驗，印證詩人要成大器就必須歷經苦難。這才發現雕像旁
有一祭司，面紗低垂，語音溫婉，原來是莫妮妲，亦即記
憶之神尼姆西妮（Mnemosyne）。她告示作者：寂如雕像
之神，正是農神，亦即巨人朝代（the Titans）之主神薩騰
（Saturn）。此時又來了一人，綽約而高眺，來安慰戰敗而
失位、頹喪而失神的薩騰，正是其妹后娣雅（Thea）。

　　薩騰在絕望之中也向他妻子吉貝蕾（Cybele）訴苦，怪

她生下那些凶兒（thy pernicious babes），竟把生父趕下寶座，篡了王位，推翻了巨人朝代，而由奧林帕斯諸神取而代之。其實薩騰要怪自己相信命運的預言：說是他的兒輩會將他推翻；於是他先發制人，將剛生的孩子一一吞噬。這種食子自保的可怕惡行，在西班牙畫家戈耶的作品中描述得觸目驚心。不過第六個孩子出世後，做母親的娣雅救了他，改以石塊裝入襁褓，讓薩騰吞下。逃脫大劫的兒子正是奧林帕斯的主神宙斯（Zeus）。

　　第二章開始的四十八行半，應該是接上第一章末莫妮姐對作者濟慈的陳述，所以才會說：「凡人啊，為了免你誤解，／我要對你的耳朵說人話，／用人間的事情來比喻……」接著又說到「我鷹族尚有一位保有／其君權、其疆土、其氣象：／光燦的亥賁亮駕其火球，／仍在位，仍嗅著爐香不斷／從凡人升到日神……」亥賁亮乃巨人族之要角，傳說他是日、月、黎明之父，他的兒子赫毅留斯（Helios）就是日神。希臘神話的族譜非常複雜，在眾多古典作家的筆下很不一致，所以亥賁亮常會和亞波羅混為一談，令人莫知所從。其實亥賁亮父子是巨人族的世家，而亞波羅是宙斯之子，已屬巨人族之後的王朝了。莫妮姐之言到四十九行為止；其後的十一行半，說話的人卻是作者自己了。

　　薩騰，巨人族的主神，其實是暴君兼惡父，難怪其子宙斯要掀起革命，不惜以子弒父，並建立新的天庭，亦即奧林帕斯王朝。不過革命者當權後也會變成反革命：例如普羅米修斯原為巨人族艾耶批塔司之子，曾助宙斯反抗巨人族，後

因同情人類而盜天火予凡人，乃被宙斯重懲，囚於高加索山上，並遣天鷹日噬其肝。這故事後來成爲雪萊詩劇《普羅米修斯之被釋》的主題。濟慈處理這題材卻用了翻案觀點，反而似乎同情薩騰。第一章412行到438行之間，薩騰不斷埋怨：「歎吧，同伴啊，歎吧，我們／已被吞，已無緣再行神道，／向星辰黯澹去施展仁功，／在人間收成上維持太平，／至高的神明爲求心安的／一切仁政，都無緣……歎吧，歎吧，我仍在此—不然助我／把孽子們扔下來，讓我得勝。／我要聽別人呻吟，號角齊鳴，／爲寧靜的勝利，節慶的讚歌，／傳自天國雲層的金色峰頂，／柔婉宣布的聲音，空貝殼張弦／的清脆震顫；還要加上／美事翻新，給高空的孩子／感到驚喜。」巨人族不但體格魁梧，孔武有力，而且是以力服人，薩騰卻自命是行仁政，以懷柔制勝。在米爾頓的典範面前，《亥貢亮之敗亡》不但詩體效法《失樂園》，抑且情節也近於後者：淪落的眾神頗似淪落的天使，連敗軍之帥，Saturn和Satan，不也在發音上若相呼應嗎？

　　也有論者爲濟慈辯護，說他此詩另有象徵：他不僅效法米爾頓，同時也向但丁取經；作者在夢中從林間到神殿，從廟宇到神龕，其實是朝聖之旅，而台階之下而復上，信徒之死而重生，也可聯想煉獄向天國的考驗。而這一切，豈不是也可象徵詩人對藝術至善之境的追求？

　　第一章從140行到202行，濟慈借神人之間的對話再三探求詩人的本分，認識到詩藝之大成當先受盡苦難、歷經滄桑，而此苦難不僅屬於自我，更要深入人間，與眾生同擔。

至少有兩段值得引證：「爾所稱同儔皆非空想家，／又答：此等絕非逐夢之弱者，／所逐者乃人面，而非奇蹟，／乃喜悅之人聲，而非音樂，／彼等未來此，也無意來──／爾則來此，爾遜於彼等──」（162行至166行）「詩人與夢者絕非同類，／兩者不類，而又對立，互爲正反。／一邊爲人世敷上香膏，／另一邊刺激傷口。」（199行至202行）

年輕的濟慈雖然是浪漫詩人，但在品味上卻很能自省，不甘縱情濫感，遁世自閉。他的詩學通於美學，已經悟出虛實互補，悲喜相生相剋之道。如果他得聞中國哲學的陰陽共存，一定更有益於他的認知。〈憂鬱頌〉所探討的正是憂喜相鄰相彰之道。〈懶散頌〉中的兩行也爲一般論者所注目：「我可不甘被甜言飼養，／做一頭羔羊演自憐的鬧劇！」

《亥貢亮》既受米爾頓的影響，所用的詩體自然也就近取材，採用米爾頓最擅長的無韻體（blank verse），文法上的一整句往往跨越多行，不免常出現倒裝句法，更加上附屬子句或插入片語。好處當然是開闊吞吐，格局宏大，頓挫多姿；壞處則是顯得做作，遠離口語，失之空洞，架子大於眞情。Blank verse直譯就是「白詩」：「白」就是沒有用韻，卻仍然是「詩」，因爲仍保留了詩的某種節奏，也就是習用的每行十個音節、逢雙重讀的所謂「抑揚五步格」（iambic pentameter）。這種節奏的句法不但常用來寫敘事詩或冥想詩（meditative verse），更常用來寫詩劇的對話，例如莎士比亞的詩劇。中國古典詩中從未出現過這種無韻體，所以中國感性的耳朵聽不慣這種句法。照說詩而無韻，應該較易翻

譯，其實不然，因爲譯文掌握不妥就會顯得散文化，不是太鬆散就是太油滑。無韻體另一特色，就是一連數十行不分段落，而且詩行往往是在句末迴行，成爲「待續句」（run-on line or enjambment）；這也不是中國耳朵所慣聽，因爲中國的古典詩中也罕見這種句式。西方的無韻體不像有韻的詩體（例如雙行體、十四行詩、皇家體或史賓塞體）那麼聲調鏗鏘，節奏流暢，呼應明快；但是句法伸縮較富彈性，節奏較緩，風格也較古樸剛勁。因此無韻體對譯者更是一項考驗。英國詩的無韻體，雖以每行十音節爲常態，但也偶有甚至屢見十一音節者。我在譯文中把握的彈性，是每行不短於九個字，也絕少長逾十一個字。

亥賁亮之敗亡

第一章

狂熱的信徒有自己的夢
可編教派的天國,而蠻族
也可從睡眠中精織對天堂
崇高的臆想;可惜他們未能
用上好皮紙或印地安草葉,
把悅耳的故事捕光捉影,
就那麼缺詩而活著、夢著、死去。
因為這種夢只有詩能訴說,
只有著魔的美文能保妙想,
不讓它隨著黑咒和啞術
一起消逝。時人誰敢說
「爾非詩人——不足以述夢」?
無論是誰,只要靈魂非頑土,
都有其夢想可說,只要他愛過
而且對母語有深厚的修養。

我眼前準備詳述的夢，究竟
說來像詩人或狂徒，要等待
我熱血的活手入土後才知。

記得我好像站在雜樹林裏，
棕櫚、桃金孃、橡樹、槭樹、椈樹，
還有車前草、香料，遮陰如屏風；
附近有泉水（柔和又充沛，
水聲盈耳），更有（香味觸鼻）
玫瑰叢不遠。我回身看見
有屋頂傾斜的涼亭，下面
藤架攀著爬藤、鐘形花、大花，
像插花的香爐，在風中搖晃；
而飾花的門口，苔蘚滿丘，
攤開了一席夏果的盛宴，
走近看時，倒像是餐後狼藉，
天使或夏娃媽媽剛吃過；
空殼剩皮散落在草地，
葡萄莖只摘了一半，餘下不少，
芳香可聞，我不識究竟何名。
剩果之多，比傳說中的羊角
倒三次還有餘：那是冥后回鄉
之宴，有小白犢吼叫。我感到
一生未有的食欲正大開，

便津津有味地大嚼起來。
不久又感到口渴，一旁
正有瓶清涼透明的果汁，
過路的群蜂吮著，我取來，
祝罷現世的芸芸眾生，
敬罷名留後世的一切古人，
才飲下。一飲而盡乃起詩興。
頃刻便陶然：多疑的回教主，
用所有東方鴉片及仙丹，
在僧舍密室調製的毒藥，
來解決紅衣祕會的眾老，
都不像我喝的能解脫苦命。
遍地鮮果皮與嚼餘的漿果，
在草地上我竭力地抗拒
蠻橫的酒力，終告不敵：
渾茫的沉醉襲人，令我傾倒，
像古瓶上所繪的酒神。
酣睡有多久，實在難說。
等知覺恢復，我忽然驚起，
簡直要飛；但嘉陰已不見，
也不見苔丘青翠與涼亭。
四顧只見一古老的神殿，
有雕刻的牆壁，屋頂莊嚴，
體勢高峻，似乎聳出於

浮雲之表，俯臨於星辰之上。
古老的情狀我想不起人間
何處有如此滄桑：我見過
暗澹的大教堂、扶牆、頹塔，
淪落故國的朽敗與殘餘，
也見過野岩頑抗風波，
但比這圓穹的永恆神廟，
卻似乎只是朽物的棄場。
我腳下的大理石地上布著
許多奇異的瓶罐，帳幔成堆，
一定是石綿染色後織成，
或是蠹蟲也蝕不了的地方，
織品如許白皙，有些可見
圖案縱橫，出自憂鬱的紡機。
卻雜沓堆疊，混合在一起：
衣袍、金鉗、香爐，與火鍋，
腰帶、鍊條，與敬神的珠寶。

從此情此景，肅然，我舉目
向四面八方打量這現場；
浮雕的屋頂，有闃然而宏偉的
成排石柱南北延伸；沒入
虛無，然後朝東，有黑色重門
把晨光永遠關在外面。

然後朝西望，只見遠處
有一雕像，其貌博大若雲，
腳邊有一座沉睡的祭壇，
通道要靠兩側的石階，
和大理石欄杆，要耐下心來，
辛苦地不斷拾級而上。
朝著那祭壇我肅然而行，
不敢急促，怕冒犯了神明；
到了近處，才看見神龕邊
有人在供奉，有聖火升騰。
正是五月中旬，懶懶的東風
突然向南吹，溫暖的細雨
將百花的芬芳一起解凍，
使空中充滿了喜悅的活力，
連垂斃的人都忘了殮衣。
所以啊那昂揚的聖火
發出春神的香氣，散播
對一切的釋念，只留祝福，
讓整個祭壇籠著軟煙，
而從清香的白帳中我聽見
傳出語音：「爾若是登不上
這石階，當死在大理石地。
爾肉身不脫芸芸之凡塵，
當失養而枯竭──爾筋骨

不數載當萎盡，悉皆無存，
任誰明察秋毫亦不見絲毫
眼下，爾立足冷石之身。
短壽如沙漏，爾頃刻即殞，
乾坤之大任誰出手亦無力
教沙漏倒流，除非膠葉猶燃，
而萬古此高階爾已攀登。」
如是我聞，我見，兩感一致，
如此細緻，如此微妙，深感
威脅之嚴峻與苦功之難成。
下階正覺其艱鉅；膠葉
燃猶未盡——突感麻痺的寒慄
從地面襲上了我四肢，
更迅速上升，凜然扼住
咽喉一側血管的暖流；
我尖叫，伴之而來的劇痛
猛刺我雙耳——我竭力擺脫
麻痺感；掙扎到最低一級。
步伐遲緩、沉重而力竭：寒意
在心頭扼住我，窒息著我，
我欲握雙手，卻毫無感覺。
正要斷氣，凍腳卻觸到
最低一級；只一觸，活力就
覺得湧進十趾：我向上攀，

有如昔日梯上美麗的天使
從青青草地飛向天國──「尊神，」
我大呼，走近角飾的神龕，
「我憑什麼，竟能免一死？
我算什麼，又逃過了一劫，
瀆神的妄言竟未遭扼止？」
蒙面的影像說──「爾已體會
死亡之眞相，且死而復生，
竟不逾大限，乃以身有大才，
是以無害；與自身之末日
爾已錯過。」──我說，「大祭司慈悲，
全憑作主，濯清我心中迷霧。」
「無人能奪此高位，」幽影答我，
「除非以世間一切痛苦
爲己任，不甘掉頭而弗顧。
他人若遁世已自有樂園，
可高枕而無憂，空度暇日，
即使無心誤闖入此殿，亦當
殞于爾曾半殞之石地。」
在陰影的柔聲鼓勵下，
我說，「世人豈無千千萬萬，
愛同伴愛到可共生死，
深心感受人世之巨痛，
甚至甘爲苦者做奴隸，

爲世人之福盡力？但願此地
我能見同儔，卻唯我獨來。」
「爾所稱同儔皆非空想家，」
又答：「此等絕非逐夢之弱者，
所逐者乃人面，而非奇蹟，
乃喜悅之人聲，而非音樂，
彼等未來此，也無意來──
爾則來此，爾遜于彼等──
爾于朗朗世界究竟有何益？
爾曹有何益？爾但解作夢，
但解自戀──盍多念人間，
爾心所寄有何福可言？
何港可依？眾生莫不有家，
每一人一生皆有樂有苦，
出力無論高尚或卑微，
苦樂皆獨當，兩者不相淆；
僅有夢者一生盡毒恨，
受苦之重非其罪所應當。
因此歡樂若與人同享，
如爾之徒亦有緣可入
適才爾所經歷之園林，
並且准入此廟堂：因此
即立于雕像膝下亦無妨。」
「我無德無能竟然蒙寵，

如此慈祥的垂詢爲我療養
不算可恥的疾病，令我歡欣，
哎，如此重賞令人喜極欲哭。」
我答罷，又說，「可否請問，
莊嚴的巨影，請明示，向世人
眾耳所唱之樂曲美音
當不至一無是處：詩人乃智者，
人文學家，全人類之仁醫。
非我所能，我自知，正如鷹群
在場，兀鷹當自知非同禽。
我又算什麼：尊神提到我同儔，
誰是同儔？」面紗垂白的高影
再發言，語氣更認眞，噓息
吹動了薄紗皺摺，垂拂
手鍊吊著的金香爐四周。
「爾非耽夢者之儔侶乎？
詩人與夢者絕非同類，
兩者不類，而又對立，互爲正反。
一邊爲人世敷上香膏，
另一邊刺激傷口。」我不禁
大叫，暴躁如日神的女祭司，
「亞波羅！過氣了！遠飛的日神！
一切騙人的詞客，自大的妄人，
信口狂呼專寫劣詩的傲徒，

亞波羅含混的瘟疫爬進
你們住宅與門縫，現在何方？
縱然我和他們死氣共吞吐，
見他們先我入土才是活路。
莊嚴的陰影，請問我在何處，
這是誰的祭壇，香爲誰嬝嬝；
神像是誰的面容，我看不清，
大理石的巨膝遮住；尊神是誰，
柔婉的談吐是如此高雅？」

　於是面紗低垂那高影
吐露眞言，語氣更認眞，噓息
吹動了薄紗摺疊，垂拂
手鍊吊著的金香爐四周；
聽她聲音我知道她流下
久不輕彈的淚珠。「這哀愁的
孤廟是一場鏖戰所殘留，
遠古之戰火，因巨人族王朝
鎭亂而起：現場這古像，
雕刻的面目因傾頹而皺蹙，
正是農神；我是莫妮妲，留守
廢墟，至高唯一的祭司。」
我無言以對，無用的鈍舌
在口腔內難找得體的字眼

來回稟莫妮姐的悲哀。
一時沉寂，祭壇的火光
因甜食而減弱；我望著祭壇
又俯視石地，附近就堆著
成束的肉桂，還有許多綑
其他的酥脆香料——然後我
又回顧祭壇與其上的鹿角，
已蒙灰塵，燭火已低沉，
然後再審視奉獻的祭品；
如此巡視——直到莫妮姐叫道，
「獻祭已禮成，但因你好意，
我好心待你不會稍減。
我的力量，對自己雖是天譴，
對你卻不失為奇蹟；一幕幕
仍生動醉人的場面貫穿
我的圓顱，痛苦如變電，
你就用凡人的鈍眼也可見，
不會痛苦，只要你不畏奇蹟。」
神明天降之諭，若能溫柔
像慈母，上面的話正如此；
我卻仍然畏她的衣裙，
尤其是面紗，從她的額上
蒼白垂下，將她籠罩于神祕，
使我自恨心狹，盛不住心血。

女神會吾意，自舉聖手
揭開了面紗。我乃見臉色蒼白，
非人間哀傷之憔悴，其燦素
乃千古大病卻又不會死；
其素皙恆在變易，非死之樂
所能了結；以死爲終站，
而永不抵達，那臉色；已越過
百合與雪花；更進一步，我
此刻不能推想，就算已見面──
若非因她慈目，我早應逃走。
她卻留住我，用親切的眼光，
更加柔婉是靈性的眼瞼，
半開半閉，一若全然無視
於外在之物；視我而不見，
只有透空的光采，如月色清柔，
安慰萬物，卻不知是誰舉目
在仰望。正如我在半山腰
找到了一粒金砂，激起
貪心，竟然睜大了眼睛，
更搜索深山鬱鬱的金礦，
窺見莫妮妲的愁顏，我也
急於探看她空寂的心頭
祕藏了什麼，有什麼大悲劇
正在她深邃的心房上演，

竟然在她冰唇上施加
恁重的負擔，在她星眸中
注入如此的光芒，使她語音
勾起如此哀傷──「記憶的身影！」
跪在她足前，我叫起來，
「憑破廟四周全然的黑暗，
憑這末代殿堂，憑黃金時代，
憑大神亞波羅，您的好養子，
憑您自己，無依的神明，
沒落世家黯淡的嫡傳，
照您親口所說，讓我眼見
您心中究竟為什麼激動！」
我的祈求剛恭敬出口，
神人竟然就並肩而立
（像矮灌木靠在嚴松身邊），
在谷中濃陰蔽愁的深處，
遠在勃勃的朝氣下方，
遠隔著燥午和傍晚的孤星。
在幽暗的樹枝下我前瞻，
看到最初我誤認的巨像，
似高高供在農神的殿上
一尊神。於是莫妮妲的聲音
簡短地入我耳內──「當初
農神下台即如此坐姿」──於是

我心生活力，眼界大開，
能見神所見，並深入萬物，
靈巧毫不遜肉眼，能知
物之體積與形狀。一聞此言，
主題崇高即湧現在我心底，
思網半開。我即採取了
雄鷹的守姿，好高瞻遠矚，
且過目而不忘。閉塞的谷地
生命毫無動靜，就像夏日
之經天，也無多大的風
從茸草地上吹走輕盈的種子，
枯葉落下，著地就歇止；
小溪無聲地流過，更加死寂，
只因頹敗的神明展開
更濃的樹陰；水精在蘆葦中，
冷冷的手指更緊按嘴唇。

在沙岸邊有巨大的足印，
止於當年農神歇腳的
地方，農神一眠，至今還未醒！
低貶了，冷落了，泡了水，
老朽的右手衰弱而報廢，
失去權杖，閉上失權的眼神，
似乎垂首在俯聽大地，

他的老母，向她祈求慰藉。

　似乎什麼力量都撼他不醒，
卻來了一人，伸出親切的手
恭敬地俯身，撫他寬闊的
肩頭，儘管受者已不知。
傳來尼姆西妮的哀吟，
哀哉我聞。「適才自荒林
踽踽而來之神明，舉步遲疑，
來朝見我殿失位之君者，
乃是娣雅，吾朝伊最溫婉。」
我發現女神身姿綽約，
較白皙的莫妮妲高出一頭，
含哀更似帶淚的女子。
她的凝睇像矍然在傾聽，
似乎大難才剛要開始，
似乎惡歲前面的雨雲
雖已施盡其邪毒，但後方
更陰沉，雷霆來勢正倍增。
她一手按住的痛苦焦點
正是凡人心跳的部位，似乎
她儘管是神，該處卻最苦；
另一手她按住農神的垂頸，
並朝向他空耳的部位

俯身啓唇，說了一句話，
音色莊重而語調深沉；
哀傷之言，憑凡人的鈍舌
當會有如此口吻；多脆弱啊
怎能比前朝眾神的洪音！

　「農神啊！抬頭吧──可憐的廢王，
爲什麼？我不能安慰你，不能；
我不能哭，你爲何如此沉睡？
天國已經離開你，而人間
不識你，如此不堪，怎算神；
海洋也一樣，潮音再莊嚴，
也不理你權杖，至於大氣，
也掃清了你老邁的君威；
你的雷霆，不服新的指揮，
只勉強在我們棄屋上隆隆；
你的利電，在新手的掌中
只燒烤我們舊有的寧境。
新災無情，又如此匆匆降臨，
教疑惑簡直無暇喘息。
農神啊！別醒來：無知如我，
又怎能犯冒你的獨眠？
我怎可叫你的愁目睜開？農神，
別醒來，讓我哭在你腳旁。」

正如在一個出神的夏夜，
枝柯被蠱於熱切的星群，
森林入了夢，整夜靜靜夢著，
只有突發的一陣驟風
吹脹了沉默，然後消逝，
似乎退潮的大氣只有一波，
那句話的起落也一樣；同時，
她優美的寬額貼著大地，
正好讓垂髮成捲地鋪開，
成柔軟的綢墊給農神墊腳。
兩位神明的身姿久久不動，
有如雕塑，以自己的神力
在墓上建成。歷時漫長得可怕，
我凝望著他們：一無變化。
凍結之神仍俯身向大地，
哀傷之女神哭倒他腳下，
莫妮妲無言。無人扶持，
只有靠自己的凡軀，我承擔
這沉默無盡無止的重負，
不變的陰暗，三神凝定的
身影壓在我心頭，加一輪滿月。
我火熱的神智泰然自忖，
她銀白的時光灑著月色，
而日復一日我感覺自己

越變越�艦瘦——我再三祈禱，
認眞地，求死亡救我逃出
這幽谷全部的重負——因求變
無望而喘氣，我不斷地自咒。
終於老農神舉起了衰目，
四顧發現故國已不存，
只留下遍地的陰沉，哀傷，
綽約的女神跪倒他腳下。
正如花草樹葉潮潤的芬芳
使林中的谷地瀰漫香氣，
林棲者的鼻孔所熟悉，農神
之言也充溢這一帶苔陰，
更傳遍老朽橡樹的空洞，
還有曲折迂迴的狐穴，
音調哀沉，他一開口就把
奇思遐想傳給孤獨的牧神。
「歎吧，同伴啊，歎吧，我們
已被吞，已無緣再行神道，
向星辰黯澹去施展仁功，
在人間收成上維持太平，
至高的神明爲求心安的
一切仁政，都無緣。歎吧，哭吧，
歎吧，同伴啊，歎吧；看，叛變的
太空在旋轉，眾星仍運行，

雲層陰濕仍不放大地，
仍然向日月飽吸光輝，
樹仍在抽葉，海岸仍在私語；
宇宙之大，何來死氣沉沉，
嗅不到死亡──應有死亡──歡吧，歡，
歡吧，吉貝蕾，歡吧；你的凶兒們
已將一尊神變成痛風癱。
歡吧，同伴們，歡吧，我已力盡，
弱似蘆葦──軟弱──虛疲得沙啞──
啊啊，痛啊，虛疲得痛苦。
歡吧，歡吧，我仍在此──不然助我
把孽子們扔下來，讓我得勝。
我要聽別人呻吟，號聲齊鳴，
為寧靜的勝利，節慶的讚歌，
傳自天國雲層的金色峰頂，
柔婉宣布的聲音，空貝殼張弦
的清脆震顫；還要加上
美事翻新，給高空的孩子
感到驚喜。」他疲極住口，
止住微弱而病態的腔調，
我覺得聽到了世間老者
在哭訴世間的喪亡；我的
耳目也無力配合得恰好，
將美聲與雅態兼顧，也無力

把悲劇豎琴的哀愁腔調
結合魁梧的身姿。我再細看，
他仍僵坐在黑樹影下，
枝柯如臂散亂成蛇形，
叢葉噤聲；他駭人的顯身，
（萬籟齊暗）無可救藥，拆穿了
我剛才所聽聞──只有他雙唇
還在捲曲的白鬚裏顫動。
不過他真話婉說，白髮
高貴地垂著，像天顏之上
飄著正午的卷雲。娣雅起身，
在洞黑深處伸出她白臂，
遙指一方向：於是他也起身，
像龐然的巨人，舟子海上所見，
陰沉的午夜蒼白地升自波間。
我望著他們沒入了林中，
正要轉身，莫妮妲叫道：「他倆
急急要逃去憂傷之家，
在黑岩的屋頂下虛耗，痛苦
而陰暗，希望全無。」她說下去，
說什麼，只要高興從此夢的
前堂進來的讀者，自會讀到；
不過在敞開的門口，我卻要
耽誤一下，好向記憶去撿拾

她的高調——或許不敢更深入。

第二章

凡人啊，爲了免你誤解，
我要對你的耳朵說人話，
用人間的事情來比喻；
否則你大可去聽風聲，
風聲對你是空洞的噪音，
雖然風過樹間充滿了傳說。
在憂愁的國度卻令人痛哭，
更有類此的哀傷，類此苦惱，
非凡人之舌，文人之筆能盡述。
勇猛的巨人族，逃遁或入獄，
都渴望恢復前朝的忠貞，
淪亡之餘苦等農神能揚聲。
幸好我鷹族有一位佝保有
其君權，其疆土，其氣象：
光燦的亥賁亮駕其火球，
仍在位，仍嗅著爐香不斷
從凡人升到日神：其位卻不穩。
只因在人間悲慘的事變
令人恐慌又困惑，他照樣發抖，
不是爲狗叫或怪鳥傍晚尖鳴，

或是一個人的喪鐘初敲，
感受到十分熟悉的天譴；
而是恐懼，巨人神經所擔當，
教亥賁亮大神傷心。他的明宮
用燦金的金字塔來保衛，
旁接青銅的方尖塔投影，
一片血紅照遍上千的庭院，
拱門，穹頂，火豔的走廊；
所有的帷幕如曙光朝霞
一般怒放；他會品味一圈圈
香氣，自聖山冉冉上升；
他不要甜食，宏大的胃口
最嗜有毒的黃銅，脆薄的五金。
因此靜躺在沉夢的西天，
過了一整天晴朗的佳日，
只等仙憩在高架的榻上，
安眠在樂曲悠揚的懷裏，
他踱過逍遙適意的暇時
闊步穿越高廳與大堂；
而在每一側廊與暗角深處，
簇立著他有翼的寵僕諂臣，
驚惶失色；有如焦慮的群眾
在廣野擠成悲哀的隊伍，
當地震搖撼雉堞與城樓。

此刻農神自冰夢中醒來，
緩步帶娣雅，由林間出走，
亥賁亮把暮色留在後方，
正下坡馳向西天的關口——
且往那邊去。」——此刻我立在亮處，
已擺脫幽谷。尼姆西妮
坐在磨光的四方石上，
通透的深處純淨地映出
她的祭司女袍——我一眼掃過
盛哉縱堂又縱堂，地窖又地窖，
掃過芬芳而繁花的涼亭，
與鑽石嵌板悠長的光燦拱廊。
轉瞬急馳過耀眼的亥賁亮，
戰袍熊熊飄拂著腳踵，
發吼洪亮，宛如大地起火，
驚潰了溫馴、縹緲的時辰，
使其鴿翼顫動。他朝前飛躍。

——2011年1月2日改定

輯五

書　信

濟慈的書信

　　濟慈的生命雖然短促，卻留下不少書信，有的是寫給弟妹，有的是寫給好友，也有一些是給其他作家。這些書信可以印證他對生命、思想、閱讀與寫作等等的態度，增加我們對他的了解。其中他對自己寫作的進展，與對於詩藝的獨特見解，尤為後世的評論家所重視。濟慈命短而志高，早已敏感自己在有生之年恐怕來不及盡展所長，將佳作一一寫出，因此在靈魂的重負之下他的詩藝竟然加速地成熟。他的十四行詩〈當我擔憂〉，即以此為主題。

　　英國文學史上，頗有一些重要的評論家本身原是大詩人，例如朱艾敦、頗普、柯立基、安諾德、艾略特。甚至雪萊，並不以評論家見稱，但也寫過分量很重的論文《詩辯》。濟慈比他更短命，連創作都忙不過來了，遑及評論。但是他天生夙慧，在感性之美與知性之真之間反覆探索，有意在想像之自由與現實之困境之間求得平衡，所以他的作品不但滿足了我們的美感，抑且激發了我們的哲思。在浪漫的詩人之中，濟慈尤其是一位高超的美學家，前則可追柯立基，後則堪比史蒂芬斯（Wallace Stevens）。

　　儘管如此，濟慈並沒有像布雷克或葉慈一般發展出一整套的象徵體系來。他只就希臘神話與中世紀傳說去找主題並加以變奏。所以他在書信裏談論詩藝，往往吉光片羽，

點到爲止，倒近於中國古代的詩話了。那些眞知灼見，諸如「想像之眞」（the truth of imagination），「無爲之功」（negative capability）都已深入人心，成爲詩藝、詩學的術語。至於他在信中不時推出的比喻，生動而又巧妙，也予人難忘的印象。「想像有如亞當之夢，醒來發現夢已成眞。」「我的想像是修道院，而我是院中之僧。」都是佳例。

　　本書選了濟慈的五封信。收信人之中，班傑明・貝禮是濟慈的知己，收信時還是牛津大學的在校生，濟慈曾去牛津會他，並和他同遊莎翁故鄉，愛芳河畔之斯屈德福。喬治和湯瑪斯都是濟慈的弟弟，前者小濟慈兩歲，後者小四歲。約翰・泰勒是正爲濟慈長詩《恩迪米安》排版的出版社店東。里查・伍德豪斯是年輕的律師，也是濟慈的知音，保留了濟慈不少的手稿和書信。至於第五封信的收信人雪萊，就不必介紹了。

　　這許多信都是寫給朋友或家人，顯然也都匆匆寫成，不遑斟酌詞句，有時不免筆誤。至於標點，也不暇細究，所以破折號用得很多，而句點用得很少。

致班傑明・貝禮

1817年11月22日

　　……哦,但願我能確定你的煩惱都已結束,正如確定你對想像之真正開始思考。我所能把握的,只有心中感情的聖潔和想像的純真——想像據以為美者,定必為真——不管它以前是否存在過——因為我對於一切激情,例如愛情,都一視同仁,認為凡激情皆壯麗,皆能創造至上之美——簡言之,我最得意的看法,從我的第一本書和我上一本書中寄你的小詩你可以得知——處理這些東西的可採方式,這正是邅思的表現——想像有如亞當之夢——醒來發現夢已成真。這件事我尤其認真,因為迄今我一直無法感受:凡事要求真,竟能只靠逐步的推理——但是實情一定如此——難道最偉大的哲人能夠不排除千萬的異議就抵達自己的目標嗎——不管如何,哦,此生所求是「感覺」,不是「思想」!所求的是以青春造形的遠景,是未來現實的投影——這看法進一步給我信心,因為它依附的是我另一個得意的理念,就是我們身後將享受的,該是將此生所謂的幸福會再嘗一遍,不過滋

味更精純，所以一嘗再嘗——只有喜歡感覺而非如你一般渴求真理的人，才會交到這種好運——亞當的夢正可說明，其信念似乎在於：想像與其高天的倒影，等於人生與其靈性的輪迴。剛才我是說，單純的想像之心，其報酬在於本身的默默操作，不斷施於精神，其來也忽然，卻很精緻——大事與細節對比——難道你，被一曲舊調所驚醒——在一個好去處——被一個好嗓子——從未重溫過當初它首次激發你靈魂的那種思考與臆測？——你可記得，當時你留下那歌者的面貌，美得不近情理，可是一時超逸，你並不在意——當時你乘著想像之翼如此高舉——所以其典範就一直留下了——你一直會見到那張動人的臉——多妙的一刻！我一直在遠離話題——這當然不盡是複雜心靈的情況——複雜的心靈不但想像豐富，而且注意效果——這種人過的日子會半重感覺、半重思考——歲月一定會帶給他智者的心懷——我認為你正是這種心懷，所以為了你的永久幸福，你不但必須飲下這天國的古酒（我是指把人間最空靈的冥想加以反芻），還得增進知識，臻於全知。聽你說你會順利過復活節，很感欣慰——你很快就會把討厭的功課苦讀完畢，於是！——可是人間仍充滿煩惱，而我沒理由自認為不勝煩惱——簡茵或瑪蓮對我的好評，實在不敢當——真話實說，我認為自己的病情和我的弟弟們的病沒有關連——真正的「原因」你比她們清楚——我也絕對沒有像你這麼受苦過——也許你曾經相信真有「福滿人間」這回事有一天會到來，可算出是在某朝某代——你的天性註定有此傾向——我幾乎記不起什麼時候指

望過幸福——如果不是當下，我可不會去找幸福——除了此
刻，我才不怕虛驚呢。落日總會教我自在——如果一隻麻雀
來我窗前，我會加入牠的生命，陪牠在碎石地上啄食。每當
聽到別人的遭遇不幸，首先觸動我的便是：唉，有什麼辦法
呢——好在他可以考驗自己精神有多少本錢，現在要請求我
的摯友貝禮，今後你如果發現我有些冷漠，不要歸因於無
情，其實是心不在焉——相信我，有時一整個星期我都會感
應不到激情或柔情——這情況有時拖得很長，我就會懷疑起
自己和自己在別的時候感情是否純眞——會認爲那些心情不
過是幾滴無聊的悲劇之淚。

摯友約翰・濟慈

致喬治與湯瑪斯・濟慈

1817年12月21日

　　未能更早寫信，十分抱歉……星期五晚上我去了威爾斯家，次晨又去看了〈死在蒼白的馬上〉。這幅畫真是不凡，想想看，魏斯特都這麼老了；可是毫不令人興奮；畫的女人都不令人渴求一吻；沒有一張臉栩栩如生。藝術之高明全在其張力，全在逼近了美與真，始能趕走一切討厭的東西——細讀《李爾王》，從頭到尾都足以印證；可是這張畫絕無撼人的深度足以啓人深思，消人厭煩，這幅畫大於遭退件的〈基督〉——星期天你們去後，我跟海登同餐，整天歡聚，我還跟霍瑞斯・史密斯同餐（近日我出門太頻了），並會見了他的兩兄弟，加上希爾、金斯敦，還有一人姓杜布瓦，這幫人只教我確信，爲求消遣，幽默比伶牙俐齒高尚多了——這幫人話一出口總令人吃驚，卻不令人會心，全都一樣；舉止也都一樣；時尚都無所不知；吃相跟喝相，甚至拿酒瓶的手勢，都有一定功架——他們談到寇音和他的低級伙伴——我倒寧可跟他的伙伴混，也不希罕跟你們這幫人呢，

我心裡想！我知道這樣的淺交對自己毫無益處，可是星期三我還要去看雷諾茲──布朗和迪爾克還陪我去看聖誕節的默劇，又走回來。我跟狄爾克並未爭論，只是研討若干論題；好幾件事情融會在我心中，我猛然想起，究竟是什麼才華能造就有爲的俊傑，尤其是文學家：莎士比亞在這方面稟賦特厚──我是指「無爲之功」，有此才者身處無定、神祕、疑惑之境，不會急躁地追究事實與理由──例如柯立基，從神祕的至玄之境探得一精妙而孤立的逼眞之景，由於無法安於一知半解，就會放過不究。這問題無論寫多少書來追究也難解決，還不如這麼說吧：就大詩人而言，美感勝過其他的考慮，甚至掃開了一切考慮。雪萊的詩集已出版，聽說遭受的壞評不下於《小仙后》。可憐的雪萊啊，他也有天賦的某些長處，老實說！！盼早來信，你們的摯友兼大哥。

約翰

致約翰·泰勒

1818年2月27日

　　我覺得你的更動眞是一大改進──書頁的編排美觀多
了……有人居然得先克服「偏見」才能讀我的「詩」，實在
令我遺憾──這件事比起苛評某一段詩來，更加令我難受。
在《恩迪米安》一詩中，我最多只是扶著護繩爬進學步車而
已。針對詩藝我有幾條守則，你該看出我離其三昧還有多
遠。首先我認爲，詩要驚人，該憑美妙的盡情，而不是憑怪
誕──詩應該讓讀者覺得，其詞句有如出自他自己最高明的
意念，幾乎像是回憶所得。其次，詩的美感絕對不能半途而
止，只讓讀者屛息以待而不得滿足：意象之崛起、發展與收
束，該像太陽升降那麼自然──照著讀者然後寧靜地落下，
仍不失其壯麗，仍浴他於奢華的餘暉──不過空想詩該如何
總比眞寫出來要容易──這就引到我的第三守則了。那就
是：如果詩寫出來不能像樹生葉子那麼自然，就不如不寫出
來。不過對我而言，我不會見識到新的天地而不大呼「但願
有狂熱的繆思飛騰！」如果《恩迪米安》能爲我開道，也許

我就該滿足了。我有充分的理由應該知足，因爲謝天謝地，
我能夠飽讀莎士比亞，說不定還能了解莎翁的深意；此外，
我敢說自己還有不少朋友，萬一我失敗了，生命和脾氣都變
了，他們會歸因於自謙而非自傲——歸因於尋求大詩人的翼
庇而非世無知音的憤嫉。我現在急於出版《恩迪米安》，爲
了好把它忘掉，續繼前進……

　　　　　　　　　　　　　　　　摯友約翰・濟慈
又及：《恩》集短序當及時奉上。

致里查‧伍德豪斯

1818年10月27日

　　閱來信十分快慰，主要是因為信中的友情，而不是因為
喜歡其中的論題，儘管「易怒的一族」已將它解釋得可以接
近。我盡可能給你的答覆，是像學者一樣，根據兩點原則，
略做評論，這樣便可像索引一般，直指天才論述之正反雙
方，加上觀點、成就、雄心等等。首先，說到詩人的本性
（特指當行的詩人，如果我算數，則我正是一位；此與華茲
華斯式的或自我中心式的崇高觀不同，已是另一回事，宜分
別處理）其實詩無本性，原非自我──它是萬物，也是空無
──它沒有性格──它耽於光影；無論陰晴，高低，貧富，
貴賤──無論是塑造伊牙哥或伊慕庚，它都津津樂道。道學
家所怪者，善變的詩人樂之。萬事萬物，它對於陰暗面的興
趣，不會比對於光明面的嗜好為害更大，因為反正都止於觀
察。詩人是萬物之中最無詩意的，因為他不執著於自我──
他只是不斷在尋求──在進入其他的軀體──太陽、月亮、
男男女女，一切活生生的動物才有詩意，具有不變的本性

——詩人卻沒有；不具自我——詩人在神造的眾生之中是最
無詩意的。如果他沒有自我，而我又是詩人，那麼我說我不
再寫詩了，有什麼稀奇呢？話一出口，我豈不是正在思考
薩騰和奧普斯的性格嗎？從實招來真是難堪；不過真相是，
凡我說出的話，沒有一句可以理所當然認定是出於我的本性
——我既無本性了，怎麼會出於本性呢？如果我跟一房間的
人在一起而又無須在腦中經管自己的創意，則回去家中的不
是我自身，而是房中每個人對我的壓力，所以我很快就消失
了——也不是只在成人之間才這樣；在育嬰室中也一樣：不
曉得我這話你是否全懂了：希望已經夠讓你明白，我那天所
說的全不可靠。

　　其次，我要說說我的看法，說說我此生目的何在——我
有志為世界效一分勞：如果我能倖免，此事當可留待壯年
——其間我將努力攀爬，只要我的肌腱受得了，就會登上詩
國的峰頂。我對未來詩歌的淺見，常會令我血湧額頭——只
盼我對世事不致於全不關心——但願我孤身對掌聲的冷漠以
待，就算掌聲是精英人士所拍響，也不致於磨鈍我敏銳的遠
見。我想不致於如此——我深信，就憑了單單對於美的嚮往
與喜愛，我也會寫下去，儘管夜間的辛苦次晨都燒掉而不得
任何人青睞。不過，即使此刻，我也未必是自己在發言，而
是代此刻我寄生的靈魂在說。下面的這句話，我卻深信，是
自己在說了。你的焦慮、美意和友情，令我至為感動。

　　　　　　　　　　　　　　摯友約翰・濟慈

致伯熙・畢喜・雪萊

1820年8月16日

　　你遠在異國，自顧恐已不暇，竟然寫信給我，還寫得如此懇切，真令我十分感動。要是我內心不深懷預感只恐無能為力，你的邀請我當會接受——在英國再過一冬，我一定會命終，其狀而且不爽不快，令人難過，所以無論坐船或坐車，我都得去意大利，就像戰士得奔赴敵陣。目前我的心情無比低沉，但是想到，狀況再壞，總不致於久困一地，令人痛恨任一張四柱之床，又稍得安慰。拙作新詩多謝你關心——要是我愛惜羽毛一如過往，若有可能，我恨不得努力重寫。大作《倩綺》一冊已拜收，李衡寄我等於你親寄。我能置喙的，不過是其中的詩與戲劇效果：這年頭不少人士認為戲劇效果等於財神。據說現代的作品必須有其目的，或許就是敬神——藝術家必須敬財神——必須「自我關注」，也許是唯我私利吧。我敢說，你大可收斂起天下為公的胸懷，更著重藝術，而且把你的主題「每一處礦隙都填滿」金砂。如此苦鍊的念頭，對你說來一定冷如鐵鏈，因為你從未收

翼端坐超過六個月。身爲《恩迪米安》的作者，我這麼說不是奇怪嗎？我自己的頭腦也曾像一副七零八落的紙牌——現在卻收拾得井然有序了。我的想像是修道院，而我是院中之僧——其中的道理你得自己去參。天天我都盼望能收到《普羅米修斯之被釋》。我爲此書求好心切，恨不得你尚未完稿——不然才要寫完第二幕。還記得當日在漢普斯台荒原上，你曾對我說潦草的初稿切莫付印——我現在將這勸告奉還給你。我寄給你的那本《1820詩集》裏，大半的作品都已寫了兩年以上，若非爲了版稅，絕對不會就出書；所以你該明白我這是存心接受指教。再容我多謝盛情並代向尊夫人致意；希望不久相會。

　　　　　　　　　　　　　摯友約翰・濟慈

附　錄

弔濟慈故居

余光中

豈能讓名字漂在水上
當真把警句咳在血中
「把蠟燭拿來啊，」你叫道
「這顏色，是我動脈的血色
一個藥科的學生怎會
不知道呢？我，要死了」
寫詩與吐血原本是一回事
乘一腔鮮紅還不曾咳乾
要搶救中世紀未陷的城堡
古希臘所有炎炎的神話
五呎一吋的病軀，怎經得起
冥王與繆思日夜拔河
所以咳吧，咳吧，咳咳咳
發燒的精靈，喘氣的王子
咳吧，典雅的雅典古瓶
那圓滿自足的清涼世界
終成徒然的嚮往，你註定
做那隻傳說不眠的夜鶯
在一首歌中把喉血咳盡

兩百年後，美，是你唯一的遺產
整棟空宅都靜悄悄的
水松的翠陰濕著雨氣
鬱金香和月季吐著清芬
像你身後流傳的美名
引來東方的老詩人尋弔
—— 我立在廊下傾聽
等一聲可疑的輕咳
從你樓上的臥室傳來
唯梯級寂寂，巷閭深深
屋後你常去獨探的古荒原
陰天下，被一隻滄桑老鴉
　　聒聒，嗓破

1996年8月23日

想像之真

余光中

　　前言：1976年8月23至28日，國際筆會第四十一屆大會，由英國筆會主辦，在倫敦召開。本屆大會的論題為「想像之真」（The Truth of Imagination），典出英國浪漫詩人濟慈1817年11月22日致友人班傑明・貝禮的書簡：「我所能把握的，只有心中感情的聖潔和想像的真實——想像據以為美者，定必為真。」濟慈於詩雖無長篇宏論，但在書簡之中論及詩藝，隻字片語，輒多真知灼見，為後之詩評家所珍，以為濟慈的詩識，寓繁於簡，並不遜於柯立基與雪萊。文藝創作不脫想像，英國筆會拈出「想像之真」一語為各國作家之論題，當有激發論辯的用意。

　　我忝為臺北筆會七位代表之一，八月初由香港獨自啟程，先在美國作半月之遊，再由紐約直飛倫敦，與其他六代表會合。本屆大會各國作家所發表的論文與演說，分為詩、小說、戲劇、電影等四組，依次舉行。除詩組外，在大會上致詞的各國作家之中最引人注目者，應推英國詩人也是英國筆會會長的史班德（Stephen Spender），匈牙利作家柯斯特勒（Arthur Koestler），英國小說家也是國際筆會會長的普禮契特（V. S. Pritchett），英國小說家墨兒達克（Iris

Murdoch），和美國批評家宋妲格（Susan Sontag）。無論
在組織上和活動上，國際筆會一向是白種人的天下，今年林
語堂先生逝世之後，國際筆會的十四位副會長已是清一色的
西方作家。本屆大會發表論文的東方作家，只有熊式一先生
和我兩位，日、韓等國的作家都未發言。

　　詩組討論會在第一天下午舉行，由史班德主持，發表
演說者七人，除筆者以外，為英國桂冠詩人貝吉曼（Sir
John Betjeman），美國詩人羅威爾（Robert Lowell），美
國女詩人魯凱瑟（Muriel Rukeyser），匈牙利詩人伊利耶
（Gyula Illyes），法國詩人克朗西耶（Georges Emmanuel
Clancier），希臘詩人庫佐凱拉司（Jean Coutsocheras）。
貝吉曼年已古稀，八月二十八日即為其七十大壽，那天他推
說眼疾不便，只朗誦了自己的一首小詩 Tea Shop，便退席
了。史班德在羅威爾致詞之後，也曾就「想像之真」的論題
發了一番議論。因此在臺上發言者實為八人。八人講畢，自
聽眾席上起立發言者極為踴躍，但經主席允許得握麥克風
者，不過四人。史班德主持討論會，執法甚嚴，規定臺上演
說者不得超過十分鐘，臺下發言者限五分鐘。我的論文如果
全部宣讀，近半小時，好在事先已將要點勾出，因此當時讀
來，恰為十分鐘。

　　八月二十七日在倫敦出版的《新政治家》（New
Statesman）週刊，發表了巴恩斯的〈筆的力量〉（Julian
Barnes: The Power of the PEN）一文，對本屆的大會頗多評
論。涉及我的一段是：「詩的演講會討論的是濟慈的『想像

之真』一詞，講者的作風形形色色：羅威爾的講詞是深思苦慮，魯凱瑟的是溫暖而流暢的狂想，半為慶幸，半為悲哀，余光中的則是神祕難解的隱喻（『詩人乃是走私高手，總能過關脫身』；『詩是為廚房裏那位髒女孩而揮動的那支脆弱的魔杖』）。」

　　在撰寫下面這篇短論時，我曾忖度，像國際筆會這種場合，臺下的聽眾該是作家多於學者，而真能吸引他們的，該是生動的意象，不是繁瑣的分析，也就是說，在眾多作家的面前，你應該表明自己是一位當行本色的創作者，而不僅是一位穿針引線的論述者。因此在文中我用了不少譬喻來形容想像在詩中的功用。《新政治家》的作者大概僅憑聽講印象匆匆落筆，乃稱我的隱喻「神祕難解」（inscrutable），未免斷章取義。以下特將這篇演講稿改用中文寫出，讓中文讀者看看，我的譬喻是否晦澀不明，一笑。中文自成章法，並非英文原稿的逐句翻譯，好在同出一心，也無須拘謹過甚了。

　　後人常愛設想，如果濟慈不是英年夭亡，他的成就該未可限量。也許他會超越少年時代對感官經驗的迷戀，進而展示知性的深度。也許他對丁尼生，愛倫坡，甚至法國象徵派的詩人會有更博大、更微妙的影響。也許他會拋棄希臘神話的那一套道具，用他「神來的妙手」（magic hand of chance）去把握法國大革命和工業革命之類的慘澹現實。濟慈生前確也寫過幾首像「賦於李衡先生出獄之日」一類的

國際筆會現場所備小冊

Le Deuxième Jour

Mardi le 24 aout

LE MATIN

10.15 Départ des cars pour
La Cérémonie d'Inauguration
au Queen Elizabeth Hall

Orateurs:

Stephen Spender	Arthur Koestler
Sir Victor Pritchett	A. den Doolaard
Retour des cars au Penta	

L'APRES-MIDI

14.30 **Première séance littéraire**
au Penta
La Poésie
Président: Stephen Spender

Robert Lowell ⁻	Stephen Hermlin
Sir John Betjeman	Kwang-chung Yu
Muriel Rukeyser	Georges Emmanuel
Gyula Illyés	Clancier

LE SOIR

17.30 Départ des cars pour la réception
18.00-20.00
Réception du Government
au Banqueting Hall, Whitehall
Lord Donaldson, Ministre des Arts, nous
recevra.
Complet veston
Retour des cars au Penta

The Second Day

Tuesday 24 August

MORNING
10.15   Departure of special coaches for
         The Opening Ceremony
         at the Queen Elizabeth Hall

         Speakers:
         Stephen Spender   Arthur Koestler
         Sir Victor Pritchett   A. den Doolaard
         Coaches return to the Penta

AFTERNOON
14.30   **First Literary Session**
         at the Penta
         Poetry
         Chair: Stephen Spender
         Robert Lowell   Stephen Hermlin
         Sir John Betjeman   Kwang-chung Yu
         Muriel Rukeyser   Georges Emmanuel
         Gyula Illyés   Clancier

EVENING
17.30   Coaches leave for reception
18.00-20.00
         Government Reception
         at the Banqueting Hall, Whitehall
         Lord Donaldson, Minister of Arts, will receive
         us.
         Dress: lounge suits
         Coaches return to the Penta

詩，但畢竟是例外之作，而前述之詩也天眞過分，幾與政治
無涉：

> 他邀遊史賓塞的堂上和林間，
> 採摘魔幻的花朵；他伴隨
> 無畏的米爾頓飛越天上的田園：
> 他真純的天才欣然高飛
> 向自己的天地⋯⋯

儘管如此，年輕的濟慈自己也明白，在臻於成熟之前，還有
漫漫的長途要走。他在一封信中說：「少年的想像是健康
的，成人的成熟想像也是健康的，但是兩者之間卻隔著一段
人生，在這段時期，靈魂恆在騷動，性格不穩，生活方式無
定，前途渺茫：乃有感傷之情。」他又曾說：「詩要驚人，
有賴美妙的放縱，而不賴怪誕。」這樣的區分，豈非創造
的想像與無聊的幻想之別？我想濟慈「美妙的放縱」（fine
excess）一詞，也許是從莎士比亞的「美妙的瘋狂」（fine
frenzy）得來的靈感。《仲夏夜之夢》第五幕第一景，雅典
公爵席遐思這麼說：

> 詩人之眸，在美妙的瘋狂中旋轉，
> 天堂到人間任一瞬，人間到天堂，
> 待想像栩栩勾出了
> 奇異的物象，詩人之筆

> 便賦之以形體，給空幻的虛無
> 一個固定的場所，一個名義。

這一段有名的臺詞，對於想像之爲物，形容得淋漓盡致——此地只引了其中的六行。莎士比亞借席遐思的口，說想像之爲物，乃瘋人，情人，詩人所共有，而想像的作用則遠逾理性的侷限。在前引的六行詩中，如果說「空幻的虛無」是指處於微妙狀態的某種情緒，感覺，或意念，則「固定的場所」所指，該是那種栩栩如生逼人眉睫的實感。也就是說，詩人憑藉想像的天賦，能夠捕捉難以把握的情狀，並爲無名的事物命名——這種任務，即使如雪萊那樣的大詩人，往往也未必能達成。

　　這一段臺詞似乎認爲詩的題材只是「奇異的物象」和「空幻的虛無」，這一點未免使人心有不甘。問題在於：這一段臺詞的綺思妙想，是以浪漫喜劇的迷幻世界爲背景，而莎士比亞自己的看法，與劇中人物也不必盡同。濟慈對於想像與空泛的幻想之間容易相淆的情形，並不是沒有警覺的。〈夜鶯頌〉的末段，濟慈喟歎說：

> 別了！幻想其實騙不了人，
> 儘管她騙出了名，騙子妖精。

「幻想」也好，「騙子妖精」（deceiving elf）也好，在此地所指的無非是詩。年紀輕輕的濟慈，已經有此自覺。

　　我們對一件東西的了解，可分兩種方式。理性的方式要靠觀察，調查，和資料，但是所得的結果往往是知識多於了解，現象多於眞相。直覺的方式則有賴想像，有賴詩人設身處地，想像他自己是別的人物，這樣投入萬事萬物的結果，會依次產生了解，同情，共鳴，而終於合一。我們通常所謂的同情，其實就是部分的或是短暫的合一。我們同情雪中折翼的麻雀，是因爲一刹那間，我們想像自己也是受難的小鳥。濟慈在給伍德豪斯的信中說：「道學家所怪者，善變的詩人樂之……詩人是萬物之中最無詩意的，因爲他不執著於自我。他只是不斷在尋求──在進入其他的軀體──」詩人沒有「我執」，因爲他樂於和他人他物合成一體。想像，可說是眞理的捷徑，沒有了想像，物我的交融與合一是不可能的。詩藝之中，像明喻，隱喻，換喻，象徵，誇張，擬人等等的手法，都可以視爲創造性想像的鍛鍊，因爲綜而觀之，這種種手法都是運用「同情的摹仿」（sympathetic imitation）使天南地北的兩件東西發生關係。雪萊在「詩辯」的長文裏說得好：「想像所行者乃綜合之道；理性重萬物之異，想像重萬物之同。」所以想像是一種妙變的過程，事實經想像澄清而成眞理，被動的知識經想像點醒，成爲主動的了解。想像，是啓示美的一道電光，排開一層層現象，而直擭意義。

　　如用文化傳統來區分，則詩的想像在運用上可以分成兩種方式。用典，是間接的方式，借物使力的作用有如槓桿。想像的槓桿，以宗教，神話，歷史，文藝典籍等爲支點，輕

施巧力，便把一個繁重的主題舉了起來。用典之道，正如其
他形式的創造性想像一樣，是以綜合的原理爲本的。一個民
族世世代代累積的經驗和記憶，結晶成爲一則則含義豐富聯
想無窮的故事，詩人借用過來，巧加比附，乃將現代與古
代，個例與典型，卑微與崇高，綜合在一起。當然，用典不
當也有缺點。例如以古喻今，千足一履，胡亂比附，也會流
於濫調，有礙新經驗的表達。又如用典太僻，淪爲炫學，反
而自遠於讀者，無補於溝通了。也有詩人拋卻書袋，一空依
傍，不向故紙堆中去拾取靈感，只願憑藉個人的敏悟，去建
立自己的感性世界或象徵系統。這一類詩人運用想像，可以
說是直接的方式，給人的印象似乎較爲質樸。米爾頓和惠
特曼，艾略特和威廉姆斯，李商隱和陶潛，正形成這兩種
方式的對照。習於間接想像的詩人在心態上好作回顧；對
於他們，典故的作用正如同現代汽車的防震彈簧 （shock-
absorber），在崎嶇的現實和敏感的心靈之間，有緩衝之
功。直接想像的詩人，只有赤手空拳，去和現實搏鬥。其實
兩條路都不好走：用典的詩人必須證明自己確能出經入史，
與古人同遊，而略無寒傖之色；不用典的詩人，也要有本領
「給空幻的虛無一個固定的場所，一個名義」，才能卓然自
立。

　　一位詩人，無論觀察有多犀利，經驗有多豐富，如果缺
乏想像的話，仍是難以把握現實的。想像是詩人的鍊金術，
可以把現實鍊成境界。想像如水，使現實之光折射成趣。想
像如麵粉，使經驗的酵母得以發揮。觀察止於理性的邊境，

想像則舉翼飛了過去。想像，是詩人天賦的自由之權利，如果自己不濫用，誤用，則雖暴君與審查官也不能橫加剝奪。

詩人是走私的高手，總能過關脫身。他私運入境的寶物，不但證明他走私成功，更證明他確是深入了異域再回來的。濟慈曾說，詩人是神派來刺探人間的間諜。希望我的走私隱喻和濟慈的探卒形象不至於格格不入。我相信詩人的走私手法是雙重的，因爲他爲日常的生活帶來了神光異彩，同時又賦想像的世界以逼眞的實感。且以美國女詩人狄瑾蓀的兩首詩爲例：

春的光輝

春來的時候有一種光輝，
　　爲整整的一年之間
任何其他的季節所沒有。
　　當三月尚未露臉，

有一種顏色遙遙地憩腳，
　　在荒寂無人的山頭，
科學不能夠將它捕捉，
　　但人的性靈能感受。

它慇懃伺候在草地上面；
　　它洩露遠樹的形狀
在我們熟悉的極遠山坡；

它幾乎對我有話講。

但是當地平線舉步遠行，
　或是報銷了午時，
也沒有聲音所具有的形式，
　它離去而我們留此：

一種遺失所特有的性質
　影響到我們的內心，
像市場的交易忽然侵犯
　一種神聖的幽境。

死　時

死時我聽見一蠅營營；
　室中那份沉寂
有如空中大氣的肅靜，
　當暴風雨暫歇。

四周的眼睛都全已擰乾，
　鼻息都蓄勢戒嚴，
待最終的攻擊，待那君王
　在室中赫然顯現。

　　我分遣罷紀念品，又簽罷

　　　屬我而又可遺贈

　　的東西——而就在這時候

　　　插進來一隻蒼蠅，

　　帶著莽撞的營營，青青無定，

　　　在天光和我之間；

　　然後是窗戶的消隱，然後

　　　是我的視而不見。

這兩首詩可以說明：詩是矛盾的綜合。能夠將平凡和奇異，
真實與虛幻綜合在一起。在〈春的光輝〉裏，一年一度早春
重臨大地的現象，變成了一幕神祕的啞劇，像魔幻行列在遠
方消逝。〈死時〉則是垂死之人迅將泯滅的意識裏感到的景
象。死亡固然是一種確實的經驗，卻沒有存者能加以描述；
整個崩潰的過程，只能得之於想像之間。狄瑾蓀的詩卻以
回憶的方式來處理，給人一種若有其事的實感。對於生者而
言，死亡這件事情，只能從旁觀察，不能親身體驗，所以，
要用第一人稱來描寫死亡，對於詩人的想像力確是一大考
驗。不過在詩中，也有一些情況，既不能向他人觀察，也不
能由自己體驗，只能純憑想像。例如在九世紀初的中國，是
沒有人能夠羽化登仙飛瞰茫茫九州的，但是李賀憑了他神異
的想像，卻創造了一個宏美的幻境，比之現代衛星攝得的照
片，似乎並不遜色。

夢　天

老兔寒蟾泣天色　　雲樓半開壁斜白

玉輪軋露濕團光　　鸞珮相逢桂香陌

黄塵清水三山下　　更變千年如走馬

遙望齊州九點煙　　一泓海水杯中瀉

顯然，這首詩的前四行是寫李賀登月之行，次二行是寫天
上所見人間滄桑變化之速，末二行則寫凌空下窺，九州之
大，也只餘點煙杯水，空間感非常逼人。五、六兩行的時間
意象，雖爲陳典，卻是活用，和羅賽蒂詩〈幸福的女郎〉
（The Blessed Damozel: by D. G. Rossetti）中天國俯視人間
的時間意象，可以相比：

那是上帝之居的巍巍城樓，

她立在城樓之上；

上帝樓臨無底的深淵，

清虛此下自茫茫；

那樣高，從樓頭向下看，

也難以覷見太陽。

樓倚九霄，像一座長橋，

橫跨浩浩的太虛。

下視晝來夜去如浪潮，

> 光焰與陰影交替，
> 於空際。最低處的地球
> 疾轉如侏儒生氣。

詩人憑藉同情的想像，才能了解人的內心和物的生命。他必須具有這種才賦，才能縱浪大化之中，與萬物交感共鳴。詩人之所以異於哲學家或神通家（mystic），在於他能入能出，能用令人難忘的語言把自己的經驗傳給讀者。再以走私爲喻，詩人的兩棲生命要充分發揮，就必須經常往來於想像與現實之間，而不宜滯留在海關的任一邊。人與自然的交相感應，是中國詩的一大本色。西方詩人歌詠自然之美時，常視自然爲神性的化身，表面上在歌詠自然，眞正在頌讚的卻是神造萬物的奇蹟壯觀。中國詩人所樂道的，卻是天人之間的共鳴交感。李白〈獨酌清溪江石上寄權昭夷〉詩中之句；

> 舉杯向天笑
> 天迴日西照

辛棄疾〈賀新郎〉之句：

> 我見青山多嫵媚
> 料青山見我應如是

在西洋詩中是不可思議的。中國詩人的豪放之氣，在西方人

看來，不免有自大之嫌。想像雖爲詩之本色，仍不免受文化
背景所約束。

　　如果詩人過分沉溺於自己的想像，則此種神聖的自由恐
亦會一同喪失。如果詩人不尊重現實的限制，則想像的相對
自由亦將無效。潛水人奮身一躍，便從陸上投入空中復投入
水中。這種自由當然是可羨的，但必須以回到陸上爲條件，
否則潛水的意義與溺水何異？同樣，鷹飛空中也失去意義，
如果鷹巢不建於地上。在希臘神話裏，伊卡瑞斯隨他的父親
從克里特島的迷宮裏逃了出來，伊卡瑞斯飛得忘形，不顧父
親的警告，振翅翔近太陽，結果蠟化翼脫，墜海而死。這眞
是一個奇妙的寓言題材：如果神牛迷宮象徵現實生活，則蠟
膠的翅膀就是純然的想像了。詩人在現實生活裏是沒有自由
的，他的自由在死後才開始。正如里爾克筆下的天鵝，詩人
在岸上的步態是笨拙可笑的，但是一滑上水面，看，他無聲
的泳姿又何其從容而優雅。岸是生，水是死。不然，岸是現
實，水是想像；岸是拘禁，水是自由。無論如何，沒有岸上
狼狽的步態，就襯托不出天鵝水上的逍遙之遊。再以辛黛瑞
拉的童話爲喻，南瓜變馬車，老鼠變馬，都可以憑藉想像，
但這篇童話之所以迷人，也就是結構上所以成功的關鍵，全
在午夜必歸的時限。仙人的魔杖原爲廚房裏苦役的女孩而
揮，詩，是一隻玻璃舞鞋，只適合給她穿。

　　想像，有如水上的倒影，總似乎比現實要美好，但如果
岸上原無此物，則水上何來倒影？想像之爲眞實，有一個先
決條件，就是它對於現實的意義，必須起探索，澄清，促

進，或詮釋的作用。眞正的詩人非但不逃避現實，還要拓展現實的境域，加強現實的彈性。爲想像而想像，勢必淪爲文不對題的空想和夢幻，到那時，詩便成爲一隻贋品的玻璃舞鞋，什麼腳都穿不進了。

　　十九世紀初年《黑森林雜誌》和《評論季刊》對濟慈一輩少年詩人的批評，雖然失之嚴峻，倒也不是完全不公平。有時候，評得嚴一點未始沒有健康的作用。拜倫的處女作《懶散的時光》是一本幼稚的詩集，當初也受到這些雜誌的攻擊。經此挫折，拜倫才奮筆寫出他第一首辛辣的諷刺詩〈英格蘭的詩人和蘇格蘭的書評家〉。濟慈當年在書評家筆下所吃的苦頭固然不好受，但比起現代作家在某些國度遭受的泛政治的文藝批評來，仍算是輕鬆的。《黑森林雜誌》指控濟慈對頗普一輩的新古典詩家有失尊敬，又無能區別「英國人的文字和倫敦東區的土腔」。《評論季刊》認爲濟慈的詩難懂，粗糙，荒謬，冗長，可厭，又嘲笑他連「包含一個完整思想的偶句」都寫不出來。諸如此類的批評雖然失之於苛嚴，但其基本的態度仍然是文學的。現代的作家固然不會羨慕濟慈的處境，但也不會擔心這樣的批評在政治上會招來什麼危機。因爲在現代的極權國家裏，批評家念茲在茲，樂之不疲的，不是用藝術的標準來衡量一件作品的高下，而是用正統的意識，官樣的術語，來鑑定它路線的正誤。平庸與空洞，都在所不計，戞戞獨造，卻不能容忍。對於這樣的批評家和他們背後的政權，濟慈堅信的「想像據以爲美者，定必爲眞」一語，不但是文不對題，而且是頹廢之見吧。對於

他們，濟慈的邏輯應該倒過來，變成「正統舉以爲眞者，定
必爲美」。

　　無論就濟慈的詩或信看來，這樣的邏輯，都不是他所能
接受的。雪萊認爲詩人是人間未經公認的立法者；濟慈寫
詩，顯然志不在此，其實他對於志不在美的一切詩都感到懷
疑。他曾在信中勸雪萊少馳騁先憂後樂的濟世壯志，多在詩
藝上下點工夫。他在給雷諾茲的信中論及前輩華茲華斯的載
道詩風：「對我們顯然有所企圖的詩，我們都痛恨。」濟慈
信中有名的「無爲之功」（Negative Capability），爲現代
學者所津津樂道，用他自己的話來解釋，便是「身處無定、
神祕、疑惑之境，不會急躁地追究事實與理由」。濟慈既非
革命家，也非預言家，他純然是一位藝術家。他固然也耽美
成癖，但他的唯美世界仍比王爾德所追求者爲健康。我們不
要忘了，濟慈所關懷的，不但是「想像的眞實」，還有「心
中感情的聖潔」。

　　詩人的想像，有愛心爲之導引，必然是健康而眞切的。
濟慈在詩中所愛者，是友人，家人，情人，是自然，藝術，
希臘，中世紀。固然他尚未推己及人，養成對人類和萬物深
厚的認識和博愛，但是我們不要忘記，這位夭亡的少年眞正
的「詩齡」不過六年，許多大詩人在同樣的「詩齡」時，成
就都不能和他相比。一位行將死於肺病的少年，是該有一點
「自私」的權利吧。

　　也許就是在這樣的心情下，濟慈才喟然感歎：「哦，此
生所求是感覺，不是思想！」垂死的少年對春花秋月的大

好世界當然是戀戀不捨的。詩人的世界誠然是感官的世界，但要完全放逐思想，泯滅知性，那後果卻是危險的。詩要強調感性，用意原在主題的經驗化，形象化，但如果是為感性而感性，就淪為濫感了。浪漫主義病在濫情，從象徵主義到超現實主義的現代詩，往往病在濫感。主題寓於形象化的經驗，是好的，但形象化到只看見一堆散漫的意象而不見主題時，就接近頹廢了。濟慈的這句話，早在愛倫坡之前，就已將浪漫主義擺渡到象徵主義，並種下現代詩的不少病根。這是我們在同情濟慈之餘，不能不警惕的。年輕詩人能掌握的，正是想像，感情，感覺，但是思想，正如經驗一樣，要到中年以後才深厚得起來。濟慈當年不夭亡的話，他的詩觀就不致厚彼而薄此了。

1976年9月12日

如何誦讀英詩

余光中

　　把詩讀出聲來，就是誦讀，也就是朗誦，如果聲音不大，就是唸了。誦讀也不一定要怎麼大聲，如果大得超過感情的需要，就太戲劇化了，顯得做作。但是無論如何，誦讀與默讀是不同的。默讀只要用心，全爲自己，不必擔心讀了別字或誤了音韻。誦讀卻會露出馬腳，洩漏了自己的無知。所以只要聽一個人開口誦詩，就可以判斷他有沒有「讀通」。做教師、演員或演講人而不會誦詩，就得留心了。

　　誦詩其實也是一種藝術，其道介於「說」、「唱」之間。詩用語言來表達，無論如何不能失去口語的自然與活潑。另一方面，詩又是加工提煉的語言，有了節奏、韻律等等的優點，甚至組合成某種句法或詩體，所以具備了廣義的音樂性。因此詩的誦讀應該兼顧語言的順暢與音樂的動聽。

　　英文詩的誦讀也是如此，才能把英文的特色表現出來。首先，發音吐字必須清楚，例如 e 的長音與 i 的短音應該截然可分，feet 和 fit, greet 和 grit，不可相混。子音也要分別，例如 clash 和 crash, flight 和 fright 也不可糾纏。

　　語言經加工提煉而有了工整悅耳的節奏，誦讀起來就有自然的起伏波動。英詩裏最常用的節奏，就是前輕後重的二音節組合，例如 allow、delight、regard，術語稱爲 iamb

（形容詞為 iambic）。每一組合稱為音步（foot），若干
音步又組成一行（line）。且以華茲華斯名著〈水仙吟〉
（The Daffodils）為例：

I wandered lonely as a cloud
That floats on high o'er vales and hills,
When all at once I saw a crowd,
A host of golden daffodils;
Beside the lake, beneath the trees,
Fluttering and dancing in the breeze.

　　每行都含八個音節，重音落在二、四、六、八的音節。
第二行的 o'er 乃 over 之縮寫，因為如不縮寫而維持原來的
二音節，第二行就不是八音節而是九音節了，超出了八音
節的常態，亂了。第六行開頭的 fluttering 也是一例外：首
先它有三音節，使該行共有九音節，本不合格，但因它後
面的二音節（tering）都不重讀，實際的聽覺效果只相當於
一音節，所以可予通融。其次，就算它是二音節，聽來像
fluttring 吧，重音也是前重後輕，不合詩體規定。其實這種
偶發例外，不但無傷大雅，抑且有助變化，是可以破格而存
的。正如中國七言詩的平仄，也容許「一三五不論，二四六
分明」。
　　為了遵守每行八音節或十音節，不足時就得加上一音
節，超過時又得減去一音節，所以英詩就會偶見如此加減的

符號，例如濟慈《聖安妮節的前夕》第二十二段：

> Her falt'ring hand upon the balustrade,
> Old Angela was feeling for the stair,
> When Madeline, St. Agnes' charmèd maid,
> Rose, like a missioned spirit, unaware:
> With silver taper's light, and pious care,
> She turned, and down the agèd gossip led
> To a safe level matting ...

　　前引的這七行半中，就有三處音節的增減。減去的是 faltering 一字，因該行共有十一音節，所以減去 e，而以「,」標示刪減。增加的是 charmed 與 aged 二字，本來都是單音節，但該二行各欠一音節，乃各加上，於是 charmèd 與 agèd 就都變成了形容詞，也都念二音節了。這些調整音節數量的符號，常見於英詩，乃成了誦讀時發音困惑的「路障」。所以 ever 會縮成 e'er，whoever 會縮成 whoe'er，It is 會縮成 'Tis，thinkest 會縮成 think'st。諸如此類「音障」，專業讀者必須克服。濟慈名著〈希臘古甕頌〉第三段前四行，是另一佳例：

> Ah, happy, happy boughs! that cannot shed
> Your leaves, nor ever bid the Spring adieu;
> And, happy melodist, unwearièd,

For ever piping songs for ever new;

　　一般讀者，就算英文程度不錯，大概都會把第三行末字讀成三音節（略近 unweereed），那就錯了，因為如此一來，不但少了一個音節，使第三行聽覺欠足，而且更嚴重的，是和第一行的shed不能押韻。所以此字該讀足四個音節，略如 un-wee-ri-èd，始為內行。

　　詩體的格律，如果寫來完全按部就班，也會過分工整，失之單調，所以放在輕音部位的音節，加以重讀，反而覺得有力。大詩人也不免如此，且看莎翁商籟第一一六號是如何破空而來：

Let me not to the marriage of true minds
Admit impediments.

　　首行的 let 與 not 二字都出現在輕音部位，但是都不能不重讀：let 是文法上祈使句（imperative sentence）的起句語，not 是主宰文意的否定詞，分量都很重。其次，這一行半的詩句不但半途迴行，而且句式倒裝（正讀該是 Let me not admit impediments to the marriage of true minds.），所以蟠蜿騰挪，分外有力。再看雪萊〈西風頌〉的末五行：

Scatter, as from an unextinguished hearth,
Ashes and sparks, my words among mankind!

Be through my lips to unawakened earth
The trumpet of a prophecy! O Wind,
If Winter comes, can spring be far behind?

前三行的第一字都以重讀起頭，也很有力，卻是反規律的。又兩個完整句都各自插入了文法割裂的片語，更增延宕與跳接的變化。若用散文順序的句法來說，應該是：Scatter my words among mankind as ashes and sparks from an unextinguished hearth! / Be the trumpet of a prophecy to unawakened earth through my lips. 所以誦到 hearth 和 earth，爲了迴行的懸宕，不可停下（stop），卻應稍頓（pause）。

有些字眼，因爲意義重大，必須強調，所以無論放在何處，都應重讀。也就是說，英詩的節奏雖有前輕後重或前重後輕等等的格式，只是用來維持常態調整節奏的方法，誦讀時切勿拘泥，以免陷於刻板單調。諸如 all, so, no, never, too, most, must, do 等字眼，在散文中已舉足輕重，在詩中也一律不可草草掠過。例如濟慈這首〈艾爾金大理石雕觀後〉：

My spirit is <u>too</u> weak - mortality
<u>Weighs</u> heavily on me like unwilling sleep,
And each imagined pinnacle and steep
Of godike hardship tells me I <u>must</u> die

Like a sick Eagle looking at the sky.

Yet 'tis a gentle luxury to weep,

That I have not the cloudy winds to keep

<u>Fresh</u> for the opening of the morning's eye.

<u>Such</u> dim - conceivèd glories of the brain

<u>Bring</u> round the heart an undesc<u>ribable</u> feud;

<u>So do</u> these wonders a <u>most</u> dizzy pain

That mingles Grecian grandeur with the rude

<u>Wasting</u> of old <u>Time</u> – with a bil<u>lowy</u> main –

A sun – a shadow of a magnitude.

　　畫了底線的單音節字眼，詩人雖放在輕音部位，卻都必須重讀，才符合文意。其中 too, must, such, so, most 在任何場合都不能忽略；而動詞 weighs, bring，名詞 Time, wasting，形容詞 fresh，也都是此詩主題的關鍵字眼，不可隨便掠過。第十一行首的 so do 二字均應重讀，後面的 do 尤其更重，因爲它代替了前面的 bring。相鄰的兩個音節如果都輕讀就可連成一音節，例如 bable, lowy。

　　濟慈的長詩之中，我選譯了三首，其一是《亥貢亮之敗亡》，爲了讓讀者領略濟慈使用「無韻體」（blank verse）的功力。濟慈熟讀莎士比亞的戲劇和米爾頓的史詩，對「無韻體」絕不陌生；他自己寫《亥貢亮》時更採用此一詩體，後來寫《亥貢亮之敗亡》，仍用此體。所謂 blank verse，blank 表示不用韻，但是仍稱 verse，因爲保留了傳統詩的節

奏，採用了每行十音節五音步的「抑揚五步格」（lines in iambic pentameter）。這種詩體解除了韻的束縛，只能在句法的長短互濟開闔吞吐上求節奏之變化，所以最便於用來寫詩劇與史詩。解除了句末押韻的「等距呼應」，無韻的詩行（line）乃可忽短忽長，忽順寫忽倒裝，有時文法上的一整句可以橫跨四、五行甚至十多行，也正是米爾頓史詩的元氣所賴。年輕的濟慈要追摹米爾頓的氣勢，實在辛苦。中國古典詩中，從無類似的詩體，所以中文讀者的聽覺，不易欣賞如此的節奏：一大原因是在此體之中，文法上之句（sentence）與詩體上之行（line）交錯進展，互見出入，而非並駕齊驅。所以讀者念我的譯文，務必細心體會。

　　至於眞正誦讀時的腔調，應以「不列顛腔」（British accent）爲宜。此事當然不能強求，但是過分滑溜的「美國北佬腔」（Yankee accent）還是不妥。英語和美語發音不同，有時也會妨礙到押韻，例如 clerk 一字，英文發音與 dark 協韻，美語發音卻與 work 相押。

濟慈年表

1795　10月31日生於倫敦 Finsbury 的一家馬車行

1797　2月28日二弟喬治生

1799　11月18日三弟湯瑪斯生

1803　6月3日妹芬妮生

　　　8月進 Enfield 小學

1804　4月16日父親去世

　　　6月27日母親改嫁，兒女送去外公外婆家

1805　外公去世，隨外婆搬去 Edmonton

1810　3月20日母親因肺疾去世。外婆將眾孫交給 John Sandall 與

　　　Richard Abbey 監護

1811　濟慈跟外科醫師習醫

　　　譯魏吉爾的史詩《伊尼亞紀》（Aeneid）

1812　寫〈擬史賓塞體〉

1813　初識畫家塞文（Severn）

1814　開始寫詩

1815　知音編輯李衡（Leigh Hunt）出獄，寫詩慰問

　　　10月1日入 Guy's Hospital 習醫

1816　5月5日處女作十四行詩〈寂寞吟〉發表於李衡主編之刊物 The Examiner

7月25日通過「藥劑師學堂」考試,有資格行醫

10月寫十四行詩〈初窺柴譯荷馬〉

1817　3月3日處女集《詩集》出版

遍遊牛津、坎特布里、威島、馬爾蓋特各地

年底三次會見華茲華斯

1818　1月至2月,聽海斯立特之「英國詩人講座」

夏天遊蘇格蘭與湖區,並登大不列顛島最高峰奈維斯峰（Ben Nevis）

4月長篇寓言詩《恩迪米安》出版,9月遭受《評論季刊》惡評

此年長住倫敦北郊漢普斯台（Hampstead）

7月重感冒,9月、12月均苦喉痛

9月初識芬妮・布朗（Fanny Brawne）

12月1日三弟湯瑪斯死於肺病

1819　1月寫《聖安妮節前夕》

4月5月間寫〈無情的豔女〉與五大頌歌

10月寫〈秋之頌〉

11月寫《亥貴亮之敗亡》,未完

12月喉痛大發,但與芬妮訂婚

1820　2月3日腦溢血,臥病至月底

2月13日求芬妮解除婚約,芬妮不肯

6月22日咳血

7月重要詩集《蕾米亞、伊莎貝拉、聖安妮節前夕，及其他》出版

7月5日醫生吩咐速去意大利

8月雪萊邀去意大利同住，婉拒

9月18日由好友塞文陪同自格瑞夫升德啟航（Gravesend 有「墓派」之意，實非吉兆）。中途因氣候不佳，阻於樸茨茅斯，再續航時，未出英吉利海峽，濟慈在一本《莎翁詩卷》上寫下他最後的一首詩：十四行的〈亮星啊，願我能〉。

10月21日船抵那不勒斯，又因隔離檢疫不得上岸十日。終抵羅馬，已是11月15日

1821　　2月23日夜11時逝世

2月26日葬入羅馬新教徒公墓

3月17日噩耗傳回倫敦

The Sonnets

To Chatterton

O Chatterton! how very sad thy fate!
   Dear child of sorrow – son of misery!
   How soon the film of death obscured that eye,
Whence Genius wildly flashed, and high debate.
How soon that voice, majestic and elate,
   Melted in dying murmurs! Oh! how nigh
   Was night to thy fair morning. Thou didst die
A half-blown flower which cold blasts amate.
But this is past: thou art among the stars
   Of highest Heaven: to the rolling spheres
Thou sweetly singest: naught thy hymning mars,
   Above the ingrate world and human fears.
On earth the good man base detraction bars
   From thy fair name, and waters it with tears.

To one who has been long in city pent

To one who has been long in city pent,
   'Tis very sweet to look into the fair
   And open face of heaven – to breathe a prayer
Full in the smile of the blue firmament.
Who is more happy, when, with heart's content,
   Fatigued he sinks into some pleasant lair
   Of wavy grass, and reads a debonair
And gentle tale of love and languishment?
Returning home at evening, with an ear
   Catching the notes of Philomel – an eye
Watching the sailing cloudlet's bright career,
   He mourns that day so soon has glided by:
E'en like the passage of an angel's tear
   That falls through the clear ether silently.

On First Looking into Chapman's Homer

Much have I travelled in the realms of gold,
  And many goodly states and kingdoms seen;
  Round many western islands have I been
Which bards in fealty to Apollo hold.
Oft of one wide expanse had I been told
  That deep-browed Homer ruled as his demesne;
  Yet did I never breathe its pure serene
Till I heard Chapman speak out loud and bold:
Then felt I like some watcher of the skies
  When a new planet swims into his ken;
Or like stout Cortez when with eagle eyes
  He stared at the Pacific – and all his men
Looked at each other with a wild surmise –
  Silent, upon a peak in Darien.

Keen, fitful gusts are whispering here and there

Keen, fitful gusts are whispering here and there
  Among the bushes half leafless, and dry;
  The stars look very cold about the sky,
And I have many miles on foot to fare.
Yet feel I little of the cool bleak air,
  Or of the dead leaves rustling drearily,
  Or of those silver lamps that burn on high,
Or of the distance from home's pleasant lair:
For I am brimful of the friendliness
  That in a little cottage I have found;
Of fair-haired Milton's eloquent distress,
  And all his love for gentle Lycid drowned;
Of lovely Laura in her light green dress,
  And faithful Petrarch gloriously crowned.

On the Grasshopper and Cricket

The poetry of earth is never dead:

When all the birds are faint with the hot sun,

And hide in cooling trees, a voice will run

From hedge to hedge about the new-mown mead –

That is the Grasshopper's. He takes the lead

In summer luxury; he has never done

With his delights, for when tired out with fun

He rests at ease beneath some pleasant weed.

The poetry of earth is ceasing never:

On a lone winter evening, when the frost

Has wrought a silence, from the stove there shrills

The Cricket's song, in warmth increasing ever,

And seems to one in drowsiness half lost,

The Grasshopper's among some grassy hills.

Happy is England! I could be content

Happy is England! I could be content
　To see no other verdure than its own;
　To feel no other breezes than are blown
Through its tall woods with high romances blent:
Yet do I sometimes feel a languishment
　For skies Italian, and an inward groan
　To sit upon an Alp as on a throne,
And half forget what world or worldling meant.
Happy is England, sweet her artless daughters;
　Enough their simple loveliness for me,
　　Enough their whitest arms in silence clinging:
　Yet do I often warmly burn to see
　　Beauties of deeper glance, and hear their singing,
And float with them about the summer waters.

On Seeing the Elgin Marbles

My spirit is too weak – mortality
    Weighs heavily on me like unwilling sleep,
    And each imagined pinnacle and steep
Of godlike hardship, tells me I must die
Like a sick Eagle looking at the sky.
    Yet 'tis a gentle luxury to weep
    That I have not the cloudy winds to keep
Fresh for the opening of the morning's eye.
Such dim-conceivèd glories of the brain
        Bring round the heart an undescribable feud;
So do these wonders a most dizzy pain,
        That mingles Grecian grandeur with the rude
Wasting of old Time – with a billowy main –
A sun – a shadow of a magnitude.

On the Sea

It keeps eternal whisperings around
　　Desolate shores, and with its mighty swell
　　Gluts twice ten thousand caverns, till the spell
Of Hecate leaves them their old shadowy sound.
Often 'tis in such gentle temper found,
　　That scarcely will the very smallest shell
　　Be moved for days from where it sometime fell,
When last the winds of Heaven were unbound.
Oh ye! who have your eye-balls vexed and tired,
　　Feast them upon the wideness of the Sea –
　　　　Oh ye! whose ears are dinned with uproar rude,
　　Or fed too much with cloying melody –
　　　　Sit ye near some old cavern's mouth and brood,
Until ye start, as if the sea-nymphs quired!

On Sitting Down to Read *King Lear* Once Again

O golden-tongued Romance, with serence lute!
   Fair plumèd Syren, Queen of far-away!
   Leave melodizing on this wintry day,
Shut up thine olden pages, and be mute:
Adieu! for, once again, the fierce dispute
   Betwixt damnation and impassioned clay
   Must I burn through, once more humbly assay
The bitter-sweet of this Shakespearian fruit:
Chief Poet! and ye clouds of Albion,
   Begetters of our deep eternal theme!
When through the old oak forest I am gone,
   Let me not wander in a barren dream,
But, when I am consumèd in the fire,
Give me new Phoenix wings to fly at my desire.

When I have fears that I may cease to be

When I have fears that I may cease to be
  Before my pen has gleaned my teeming brain,
Before high-pilèd books, in charactery,
  Hold like rich garners the full-ripened grain;
When I behold, upon the night's starred face,
  Huge cloudy symbols of a high romance,
And think that I may never live to trace
  Their shadows, with the magic hand of chance;
And when I feel, fair creature of an hour!
  That I shall never look upon thee more,
Never have relish in the faery power
  Of unreflecting love! – then on the shore
Of the wide world I stand alone, and think
Till love and fame to nothingness do sink.

To —

Time's sea hath been five years at its slow ebb,
 Long hours have to and fro let creep the sand,
Since I was tangled in thy beauty's web,
 And snared by the ungloving of thy hand.
And yet I never look on midnight sky,
 But I behold thine eyes' well-memoried light;
I cannot look upon the rose's dye,
 But to thy cheek my soul doth take its flight;
I cannot look on any budding flower,
 But my fond ear, in fancy at thy lips,
And hearkening for a love-sound, doth devour
 Its sweets in the wrong sense: – Thou dost eclipse
Every delight with sweet remembering,
And grief unto my darling joys dost bring.

To the Nile

Son of the old moon-mountains African!
  Chief of the pyramid and crocodile!
  We call thee fruitful, and, that very while,
A desert fills our seeing's inward span.
Nurse of swart nations since the world began,
  Art thou so fruitful? or dost thou beguile
  Such men to honour thee, who, worn with toil,
Rest for a space 'twixt Cairo and Decan?
O may dark fancies err! They surely do.
  'Tis ignorance that makes a barren waste
Of all beyond itself. Thou dost bedew
  Green rushes like our rivers, and dost taste
The pleasant sun-rise. Green isles hast thou too,
  And to the sea as happily dost haste.

To J [ames] R [ice]

O that a week could be an age, and we

    Felt parting and warm meeting every week,

Then one poor year a thousand years would be,

    The flush of welcome ever on the cheek:

So could we live long life in little space,

    So time itself would be annihilate,

So a day's journey in oblivious haze

    To serve our joys would lengthen and dilate.

O to arrive each Monday morn from Ind!

    To land each Tuesday from the rich Levant!

In little time a host of joys to bind,

    And keep our souls in one eternal pant!

This morn, my friend, and yester-evening taught

Me how to harbour such a happy thought.

To Homer

Standing aloof in giant ignorance,
   Of thee I hear and of the Cyclades,
As one who sits ashore and longs perchance
   To visit dolphin-coral in deep seas.
So wast thou blind! – but then the veil was rent,
   For Jove uncurtained Heaven to let thee live,
And Neptune made for thee a spumy tent,
   And Pan made sing for thee his forest-hive;
Ay, on the shores of darkness there is light,
   And precipices show untrodden green;
There is a budding morrow in midnight;
   There is a triple sight in blindness keen;
Such seeing hadst thou, as it once befell
To Dian, Queen of Earth, and Heaven, and Hell.

To Ailsa Rock

Hearken, thou craggy ocean pyramid!
    Give answer by thy voice, the sea-fowls' screams!
    When were thy shoulders mantled in huge streams?
    When from the sun was thy broad forehead hid?
    How long is't since the mighty power bid
        Thee heave to airy sleep from fathom dreams?
        Sleep in the lap of thunder or sunbeams,
    Or when grey clouds are thy cold coverlid?
Thou answer'st not; for thou art dead asleep.
    Thy life is but two dead eternities –
    The last in air, the former in the deep,
        First with the whales, last with the eagle-skies.
    Drowned wast thou till an earthquake made thee steep,
        Another cannot wake thy giant size!

This mortal body of a thousand days

This mortal body of a thousand days
    Now fills, O Burns, a space in thine own room,
Where thou didst dream alone on budded bays,
    Happy and thoughtless of thy day of doom!
My pulse is warm with thine own barley-bree,
    My head is light with pledging a great soul,
My eyes are wandering, and I cannot see,
    Fancy is dead and drunken at its goal:
Yet can I stamp my foot upon thy floor,
    Yet can I ope thy window-sash to find
The meadow thou hast trampèd o'er and o'er,
    Yet can I think of thee till thought is blind,
Yet can I gulp a bumper to thy name –
O smile among the shades, for this is fame!

To Sleep

O soft embalmer of the still midnight,
    Shutting, with careful fingers and benign,
Our gloom-pleased eyes, embowered from the light,
    Enshaded in forgetfulness divine:
O soothest Sleep! if so it please thee, close
    In midst of this thine hymn, my willing eyes,
Or wait the 'Amen', ere thy poppy throws
    Around my bed its lulling charities.
Then save me, or the passèd day will shine
Upon my pillow, breeding many woes;
    Save me from curious conscience, that still hoards
Its strength for darkness, burrowing like the mole;
    Turn the key deftly in the oilèd wards,
And seal the hushèd casket of my soul.

If by dull rhymes our English must be chained

If by dull rhymes our English must be chained,

And, like Andromeda, the Sonnet sweet

Fettered, in spite of painèd loveliness,

Let us find out, if we must be constrained,

Sandals more interwoven and complete

To fit the naked foot of Poesy:

Let us inspect the lyre, and weigh the stress

Of every chord, and see what may be gained

By ear industrious, and attention meet;

Misers of sound and syllable, no less

Than Midas of his coinage, let us be

Jealous of dead leaves in the bay wreath crown;

So, if we may not let the Muse be free,

She will be bound with garlands of her own.

On Fame (I)

Fame, like a wayward girl, will still be coy
  To those who woo her with too slavish knees,
But makes surrender to some thoughtless boy,
  And dotes the more upon a heart at ease;
She is gipsy, will not speak to those
  Who have not learnt to be content without her;
A jilt, whose ear was never whispered close,
  Who thinks they scandal her who talk about her –
A very gipsy is she, Nilus-born,
  Sister-in-law to jealous Potiphar.
Ye love-sick bards! repay her scorn for scorn;
  Ye artists lovelorn! madmen that ye are,
Make your best bow to her and bid adieu –
Then, if she likes it, she will follow you.

Bright star! would I were steadfast as thou art

Bright star! would I were steadfast as thou art –
 Not in lone splendour hung aloft the night
And watching, with eternal lids apart,
 Like nature's patient, sleepless Eremite,
The moving waters at their priestlike task
 Of pure ablution round earth's human shores,
Or gazing on the new soft-fallen mask
 Of snow upon the mountains and the moors –
No – yet still steadfast, still unchangeable,
 Pillowed upon my fair love's ripening breast,
To feel for ever its soft swell and fall,
 Awake for ever in a sweet unrest,
Still, still to hear her tender-taken breath,
And so live ever – or else swoon to death.

The Lyrics

Lines on the Mermaid Tavern

Souls of Poets dead and gone,
What Elysium have ye known,
Happy field or mossy cavern,
Choicer than the Mermaid Tavern?
Have ye tippled drink more fine
Than mine host's Canary wine?
Or are fruits of Paradise
Sweeter than those dainty pies
Of venison? O generous food!
Dressed as though bold Robin Hood
Would, with his maid Marian,
Sup and bowse from horn and can.

I have heard that on a day
Mine host's sign-board flew away,
Nobody knew whither, till
An astrologer's old quill
To a sheepskin gave the story,
Said he saw you in your glory,
Underneath a new-old sign
Sipping beverage divine,
And pledging with contented smack
The Mermaid in the Zodiac.

Souls of Poets dead and gone,
What Elysium have ye known,
Happy field or mossy cavern,
Choicer than the Mermaid Tavern?

La Belle Dame sans Merci. A Ballad

1

O what can ail thee, knight-at-arms,
  Alone and palely loitering?
The sedge has withered from the lake,
  And no birds sing.

2

O what can ail thee, knight-at-arms,
  So haggard and so woe-begone?
The squirrel's granary is full,
  And the harvest's done.

3

I see a lily on thy brow,
  With anguish moist and fever-dew,
And on thy cheeks a fading rose
  Fast withereth too.

4

I met a lady in the meads,
  Full beautiful – a faery's child,
Her hair was long, her foot was light,

And her eyes were wild.

5

I made a garland for her head,
   And bracelets too, and fragrant zone;
She looked at me as she did love,
   And made sweet moan.

6

I set her on my pacing steed,
   And nothing else saw all day long,
For sidelong would she bend, and sing
   A faery's song.

7

She found me roots of relish sweet,
   And honey wild, and manna-dew,
And sure in language strange she said –
   'I love thee true'.

8

She took me to her elfin grot,
   And there she wept and sighed full sore,
And there I shut her wild wild eyes
   With kisses four.

9

And there she lullèd me asleep
  And there I dreamed – Ah! woe betide! –
The latest dream I ever dreamt
  On the cold hill side.

10

I saw pale kings and princes too,
  Pale warriors, death-pale were they all;
They cried – 'La Belle Dame sans Merci
  Thee hath in thrall!'

11

I saw their starved lips in the gloam,
  With horrid warning gapèd wide,
And I awoke and found me here,
  On the cold hill's side.

12

And this is why I sojourn here
  Alone and palely loitering,
Though the sedge is withered from the lake,
  And no birds sing.

The Odes

Ode to Psyche

O Goddess! hear these tuneless numbers, wrung
   By sweet enforcement and remembrance dear,
And pardon that thy secrets should be sung
   Even into thine own soft-conchèd ear:
Surely I dreamt to-day, or did I see
   The wingèd Psyche with awakened eyes?
I wandered in a forest thoughtlessly,
   And, on the sudden, fainting with surprise,
Saw two fair creatures, couchèd side by side
   In deepest grass, beneath the whispering roof
   Of leaves and tremblèd blossoms, where there ran
     A brooklet, scarce espied:
'Mid hushed, cool-rooted flowers, fragrant-eyed,
   Blue, silver-white, and budded Tyrian,
They lay calm-breathing on the bedded grass;
   Their arms embraced, and their pinions too;
   Their lips touched not, but had not bade adieu,
As if disjoined by soft-handed slumber,
And ready still past kisses to outnurnber
   At tender eye-dawn of aurorean love:
     The wingèd boy I knew;
   But who wast thou, O happy, happy dove?

His Psyche true!

O latest born and loveliest vision far
  Of all Olympus' faded hierarchy!
Fairer than Phoebe's sapphire-regioned star,
  Or Vesper, amorous glow-worm of the sky;
Fairer than these, though temple thou hast none,
    Nor altar heaped with flowers;
Nor virgin-choir to make delicious moan
    Upon the midnight hours;
No voice, no lute, no pipe, no incense sweet
  From chain-swung censer teeming;
No shrine, no grove, no oracle, no heat
  Of pale-mouthed prophet dreaming.

O brightest! though too late for antique vows,
  Too, too late for the fond believing lyre,
When holy were the haunted forest boughs,
  Holy the air, the water, and the fire;
Yet even in these days so far retired
  From happy pieties, thy lucent fans,
  Fluttering among the faint Olympians,
I see, and sing, by my own eyes inspired.
So let me be thy choir, and make a moan
    Upon the midnight hours;

Thy voice, thy lute, thy pipe, thy incense sweet

    From swingèd censer teeming –

Thy shrine, thy grove, thy oracle, thy heat

    Of pale-mouthed prophet dreaming.

Yes, I will be thy priest, and build a fane

    In some untrodden region of my mind,

Where branchèd thoughts, new grown with pleasant pain,

    Instead of pines shall murmur in the wind:

Far, far around shall those dark-clustered trees

    Fledge the wild-ridgèd mountains steep by steep;

And there by zephyrs, streams, and birds, and bees,

    The moss-lain Dryads shall be lulled to sleep;

And in the midst of this wide quietness

    A rosy sanctuary will I dress

With the wreathed trellis of a working brain,

    With buds, and bells, and stars without a name,

With all the gardener Fancy e'er could feign,

    Who breeding flowers, will never breed the same:

And there shall be for thee all soft delight

    That shadowy thought can win,

A bright torch, and a casement ope at night,

    To let the warm Love in!

Ode on a Grecian Urn

1

Thou still unravished bride of quietness,
  Thou foster-child of silence and slow time,
Sylvan historian, who canst thus express
  A flowery tale more sweetly than our rhyme:
What leaf-fringed legend haunts about thy shape
  Of deities or mortals, or of both,
    In Tempe or the dales of Arcady?
  What men or gods are these? What maidens loth?
What mad pursuit? What struggle to escape?
    What pipes and timbrels? What wild ecstasy?

2

Heard melodies are sweet, but those unheard
  Are sweeter; therefore, ye soft pipes, play on;
Not to the sensual ear, but, more endeared,
  Pipe to the spirit ditties of no tone:
Fair youth, beneath the trees, thou canst not leave
  Thy song, nor ever can those trees be bare;
    Bold Lover, never, never canst thou kiss,
Though winning near the goal – yet, do not grieve:
  She cannot fade, though thou hast not thy bliss,

For ever wilt thou love, and she be fair!

3

Ah, happy, happy boughs! that cannot shed
   Your leaves, nor ever bid the Spring adieu;
And, happy melodist, unwearièd,
   For ever piping songs for ever new;
More happy love! more happy, happy love!
   For ever warm and still to be enjoyed,
     For ever panting, and for ever young –
All breathing human passion far above,
   That leaves a heart high-sorrowful and cloyed,
     A burning forehead, and a parching tongue.

4

Who are these coming to the sacrifice?
   To what green altar, O mysterious priest,
Lead'st thou that heifer lowing at the skies,
   And all her silken flanks with garlands dressed?
What little town by river or sea shore,
   Or mountain-built with peaceful citadel,
     Is emptied of this folk, this pious morn?
And, little town, thy streets for evermore
   Will silent be; and not a soul to tell
     Why thou art desolate, can e'er return.

5

O Attic shape! Fair attitude! with brede

  Of marble men and maidens overwrought,

With forest branches and the trodden weed;

  Thou, silent form, dost tease us out of thought

As doth eternity: Cold Pastoral!

  When old age shall this generation waste,

    Thou shalt remain, in midst of other woe

Than ours, a friend to man, to whom thou say'st,

  'Beauty is truth, truth beauty, – that is all

    Ye know on earth, and all ye need to know.'

Ode to a Nightingale

1

My heart aches, and a drowsy numbness pains
   My sense, as though of hemlock I had drunk,
Or emptied some dull opiate to the drains
   One minute past, and Lethe-wards had sunk:
'Tis not through envy of thy happy lot,
   But being too happy in thine happiness –
      That thou, light-wingèd Dryad of the trees,
         In some melodious plot
Of beechen green, and shadows numberless,
   Singest of summer in full-throated ease.

2

O, for a draught of vintage! that hath been
   Cooled a long age in the deep-delvèd earth,
Tasting of Flora and the country green,
   Dance, and Provençal song, and sunburnt mirth!
O for a beaker full of the warm South,
   Full of the true, the blushful Hippocrene,
      With beaded bubbles winking at the brim,
         And purple-stainèd mouth,
That I might drink, and leave the world unseen,

And with thee fade away into the forest dim –

3

Fade far away, dissolve, and quite forget

  What thou among the leaves hast never known,

The weariness, the fever, and the fret

  Here, where men sit and hear each other groan;

Where palsy shakes a few, sad, last grey hairs,

    Where youth grows pale, and spectre-thin, and dies;

    Where but to think is to be full of sorrow

      And leaden-eyed despairs;

    Where Beauty cannot keep her lustrous eyes,

      Or new Love pine at them beyond to-morrow.

4

Away!away! for I will fly to thee,

  Not charioted by Bacchus and his pards,

But on the viewless wings of Poesy,

  Though the dull brain perplexes and retards.

Already with thee! tender is the night,

  And haply the Queen-Moon is on her throne,

    Clustered around by all her starry Fays;

      But here there is no light,

    Save what from heaven is with the breezes blown

      Through verdurous glooms and winding mossy ways.

5

I cannot see what flowers are at my feet,

Nor what soft incense hangs upon the boughs,

But, in embalmèd darkness, guess each sweet

Wherewith the seasonable month endows

The grass, the thicket, and the fruit-tree wild –

White hawthorn, and the pastoral eglantine;

Fast fading violets covered up in leaves;

And mid-May's eldest child,

The coming musk-rose, full of dewy wine,

The murmurous haunt of flies on summer eves.

6

Darkling I listen; and, for many a time

I have been half in love with easeful Death,

Called him soft names in many a musèd rhyme,

To take into the air my quiet breath;

Now more than ever seems it rich to die,

To cease upon the midnight with no pain,

While thou art pouring forth thy soul abroad

In such an ecstasy!

Still wouldst thou sing, and I have ears in vain –

To thy high requiem become a sod.

7

Thou wast not born for death, immortal Bird!
  No hungry generations tread thee down;
The voice I hear this passing night was heard
  In ancient days by emperor and clown:
Perhaps the self-same song that found a path
    Through the sad heart of Ruth, when, sick for home,
      She stood in tears amid the alien corn;
        The same that oft-times hath
      Charmed magic casements, opening on the foam
      Of perilous seas, in faery lands forlorn.

8

Forlorn! the very word is like a bell
  To toll me back from thee to my sole self!
Adieu! the fancy cannot cheat so well
  As she is famed to do, deceiving elf.
Adieu! adieu! thy plaintive anthem fades
    Past the near meadows, over the still stream,
      Up the hill-side; and now 'tis buried deep
      In the next valley-glades:
    Was it a vision, or a waking dream?
    Fled is that music – Do I wake or sleep?

Ode on Melancholy

1

No, no, go not to Lethe, neither twist

   Wolf's-bane, tight-rooted, for its poisonous wine:

Nor suffer thy pale forehead to be kissed

   By nightshade, ruby grape of Proserpine;

Make not your rosary of yew-berries,

    Nor let the beetle, nor the death-moth be

      Your mournful Psyche, nor the downy owl

A partner in your sorrow's mysteries;

    For shade to shade will come too drowsily,

      And drown the wakeful anguish of the soul.

2

But when the melancholy fit shall fall

   Sudden from heaven like a weeping cloud,

That fosters the droop-headed flowers all,

   And hides the green hill in an April shroud;

Then glut thy sorrow on a morning rose,

    Or on the rainbow of the salt sand-wave,

      Or on the wealth of globèd peonies;

Or if thy mistress some rich anger shows,

    Emprison her soft hand, and let her rave,

And feed deep, deep upon her peerless eyes.

3

She dwells with Beauty – Beauty that must die;

   And Joy, whose hand is ever at his lips

Bidding adieu; and aching Pleasure nigh,

   Turning to poison while the bee-mouth sips:

Ay, in the very temple of Delight

   Veiled Melancholy has her sovran shrine,

     Though seen of none save him whose strenuous tongue

   Can burst Joy's grape against his palate fine;

His soul shall taste the sadness of her might,

   And be among her cloudy trophies hung.

Ode on Indolence

'They toil not, neither do they spin.'

1

One morn before me were three figures seen,
    With bowèd necks, and joinèd hands, side-faced;
And one behind the other stepped serene,
    In placid sandals, and in white robes graced;
They passed, like figures on a marble urn,
    When shifted round to see the other side;
        They came again; as when the urn once more
Is shifted round, the first seen shades return;
    And they were strange to me, as may betide
        With vases, to one deep in Phidian lore.

2

How is it, Shadows! that I knew ye not?
    How came ye muffled in so hush a masque?
Was it a silent deep-disguisèd plot
    To steal away, and leave without a task
My idle days? Ripe was the drowsy hour;
    The blissful cloud of summer-indolence
        Benumbed my eyes; my pulse grew less and less;
Pain had no sting, and pleasure's wreath no flower:

O, why did ye not melt, and leave my sense

Unhaunted quite of all but – nothingness?

3

A third time passed they by, and, passing, turned

Each one the face a moment whiles to me;

Then faded, and to follow them I burned

And ached for wings because I knew the three;

The first was a fair Maid, and Love her name;

The second was Ambition, pale of cheek,

And ever watchful with fatiguèd eye;

The last, whom I love more, the more of blame

Is heaped upon her, maiden most unmeek –

I knew to be my demon Poesy.

4

They faded, and, forsooth! I wanted wings.

O folly! What is love! and where is it?

And, for that poor Ambition – it springs

From a man's little heart's short fever-fit.

For Poesy! – no, she has not a joy –

At least for me – so sweet as drowsy noons,

And evenings steeped in honeyed indolence.

O, for an age so sheltered from annoy,

That I may never know how change the moons,

Or hear the voice of busy common-sense!

5

A third time came they by – alas! wherefore?
My sleep had been embroidered with dim dreams;
My soul had been a lawn besprinkled o'er
With flowers, and stirring shades, and baffled beams:
The morn was clouded, but no shower fell,
Though in her lids hung the sweet tears of May;
The open casement pressed a new-leaved vine,
Let in the budding warmth and throstle's lay;
O Shadows! 'twas a time to bid farewell!
Upon your skirts had fallen no tears of mine.

6

So, ye three Ghosts, adieu! Ye cannot raise
My head cool-bedded in the flowery grass;
For I would not be dieted with praise,
A pet-lamb in a sentimental farce!
Fade softly from my eyes, and be once more
In masque-like figures on the dreamy urn.
Farewell! I yet have visions for the night,
And for the day faint visions there is store.
Vanish, ye Phantoms! from my idle sprite,
Into the clouds, and never more return!

To Autumn

1

Season of mists and mellow fruitfulness,
  Close bosom-friend of the maturing sun,
Conspiring with him how to load and bless
  With fruit the vines that round the thatch-eves run;
To bend with apples the mossed cottage-trees,
  And fill all fruit with ripeness to the core;
    To swell the gourd, and plump the hazel shells
  With a sweet kernel; to set budding more,
And still more, later flowers for the bees,
Until they think warm days will never cease,
    For Summer has o'er-brimmed their clammy cells.

2

Who hath not seen thee oft amid thy store?
  Sometimes whoever seeks abroad may find
Thee sitting careless on a granary floor,
  Thy hair soft-lifted by the winnowing wind;
Or on a half-reaped furrow sound asleep,
  Drowsed with the fume of poppies, while thy hook
    Spares the next swath and all its twinèd flowers;
And sometimes like a gleaner thou dost keep

Steady thy laden head across a brook;

Or by a cider-press, with patient look,

Thou watchest the last oozings hours by hours.

3

Where are the songs of Spring? Ay, where are they?

Think not of them, thou hast thy music too –

While barrèd clouds bloom the soft-dying day,

And touch the stubble-plains with rosy hue:

Then in a wailful choir the small gnats mourn

Among the river sallows, borne aloft

Or sinking as the light wind lives or dies;

And full-grown lambs loud bleat from hilly bourn;

Hedge-crickets sing; and now with treble soft

The red-breast whistles from a garden-croft;

And gathering swallows twitter in the skies.

Longer Poems

The Eve of St Agnes

1

St Agnes' Eve – Ah, bitter chill it was!

The owl, for all his feathers, was a-cold;

The hare limped trembling through the frozen grass,

And silent was the flock in woolly fold:

Numb were the Beadsman's fingers, while he told

His rosary, and while his frosted breath,

Like pious incense from a censer old,

Seemed taking flight for heaven, without a death,

Past the sweet Virgin's picture, while his prayer he saith.

2

His prayer he saith, this patient, holy man;

Then takes his lamp, and riseth from his knees,

And back returneth, meagre, barefoot, wan,

Along the chapel aisle by slow degrees:

The sculptured dead, on each side, seem to freeze,

Emprisoned in black, purgatorial rails;

Knights, ladies, praying in dumb orat'ries,

He passeth by; and his weak spirit fails

To think how they may ache in icy hoods and mails.

3

Northward he turneth through a little door,

And scarce three steps, ere Music's golden tongue

Flattered to tears this agèd man and poor;

But no – already had his deathbell rung:

The joys of all his life were said and sung:

His was harsh penance on St Agnes' Eve.

Another way he went, and soon among

Rough ashes sat he for his soul's reprieve,

And all night kept awake, for sinners' sake to grieve.

4

That ancient Beadsman heard the prelude soft;

And so it chanced, for many a door was wide,

From hurry to and fro. Soon, up aloft,

The silver, snarling trumpets 'gan to chide:

The level chambers, ready with their pride,

Were glowing to receive a thousand guests:

The carvèd angels, ever eager-eyed,

Stared, where upon their heads the cornice rests,

With hair blown back, and wings put cross-wise on their
breasts.

5

At length burst in the argent revelry,

With plume, tiara, and all rich array,

Numerous as shadows haunting faerily

The brain, new-stuffed, in youth, with triumphs gay

Of old romance. These let us wish away,

And turn, sole-thoughted, to one Lady there,

Whose heart had brooded, all that wintry day,

On love, and winged St Agnes' saintly care,

As she had heard old dames full many times declare.

6

They told her how, upon St Agnes' Eve,

Young virgins might have visions of delight,

And soft adorings from their loves receive

Upon the honeyed middle of the night,

If ceremonies due they did aright;

As, supperless to bed they must retire,

And couch supine their beauties, lily white;

Nor look behind, nor sideways, but require

Of Heaven with upward eyes for all that they desire.

7

Full of this whim was thoughtful Madeline:

The music, yearning like a God in pain,

She scarcely heard: her maiden eyes divine,

Fixed on the floor, saw many a sweeping train

Pass by – she heeded not at all: in vain

Came many a tip-toe, amorous cavalier,

And back retired – not cooled by high disdain,

But she saw not: her heart was otherwhere.

She sighed for Agnes' dreams, the sweetest of the year.

8

She danced along with vague, regardless eyes,

Anxious her lips, her breathing quick and short:

The hallowed hour was near at hand: she sighs

Amid the timbrels, and the thronged resort

Of whisperers in anger, or in sport;

'Mid looks of love, defiance, hate, and scorn,

Hoodwinked with faery fancy – all amort,

Save to St Agnes and her lambs unshorn,

And all the bliss to be before to-morrow morn.

9

So, purposing each moment to retire,

She lingered still. Meantime, across the moors,

Had come young Porphyro, with heart on fire

For Madeline. Beside the portal doors,

Buttressed from moonlight, stands he, and implores

All saints to give him sight of Madeline

But for one moment in the tedious hours,

That he might gaze and worship all unseen;

Perchance speak, kneel, touch, kiss – in sooth such things

   have been.

10

He ventures in – let no buzzed whisper tell,

All eyes be muffled, or a hundred swords

Will storm his heart, Love's fev'rous citadel:

For him, those chambers held barbarian hordes,

Hyena foemen, and hot-blooded lords,

Whose very dogs would execrations howl

Against his lineage: not one breast affords

Him any mercy, in that mansion foul,

Save one old beldame, weak in body and in soul.

11

Ah, happy chance! the agèd creature came,

Shuffling along with ivory-headed wand,

To where he stood, hid from the torch's flame,

Behind a broad hall-pillar, far beyond

The sound of merriment and chorus bland:

He startled her; but soon she knew his face,

And grasped his fingers in her palsied hand,

Saying, 'Mercy, Porphyro! hie thee from this place:

They are all here to-night, the whole blood-thirsty race!

12

'Get hence! get hence! there's dwarfish Hildebrand –
He had a fever late, and in the fit
He cursèd thee and thine, both house and land:
Then there's that old Lord Maurice, not a whit
More tame for his grey hairs – Alas me! flit!
Flit like a ghost away.' 'Ah, gossip dear,
We're safe enough; here in this arm-chair sit,
And tell me how –' 'Good Saints! not here, not here;
Follow me, child, or else these stones will be thy bier.'

13

He followed through a lowly archèd way,
Brushing the cobwebs with his lofty plume,
And as she muttered, 'Well-a – well-a-day!'
He found him in a little moonlight room,
Pale, latticed, chill, and silent as a tomb.
'Now tell me where is Madeline,' said he,
'O tell me, Angela, by the holy loom
Which none but secret sisterhood may see,
When they St Agnes' wool are weaving piously.'

14

'St Agnes? Ah! it is St Agnes' Eve –
Yet men will murder upon holy days:

Thou must hold water in a witch's sieve,

And be liege-lord of all the Elves and Fays,

To venture so: it fills me with amaze

To see thee, Porphyro! – St Agnes' Eve!

God's help! my lady fair the conjuror plays

This very night. Good angels her deceive!

But let me laugh awhile, I've mickle time to grieve.'

15

Feebly she laugheth in the languid moon,

While Porphyro upon her face doth look,

Like puzzled urchin on an agèd crone

Who keepeth closed a wondrous riddle-book,

As spectacled she sits in chimney nook.

But soon his eyes grew brilliant, when she told

His lady's purpose; and he scarce could brook

Tears, at the thought of those enchantments cold,

And Madeline asleep in lap of legends old.

16

Sudden a thought came like a full-blown rose,

Flushing his brow, and in his painèd heart

Made purple riot; then doth he propose

A stratagem, that makes the beldame start:

'A cruel man and impious thou art:

Sweet lady, let her pray, and sleep, and dream

Alone with her good angels, far apart

From wicked men like thee. Go, go! – I deem

Thou canst not surely be the same that thou didst seem.'

17

'I will not harm her, by all saints I swear,'

Quoth Porphyro: 'O may I ne'er find grace

When my weak voice shall whisper its last prayer,

If one of her soft ringlets I displace,

Or look with ruffian passion in her face:

Good Angela, believe me by these tears,

Or I will, even in a moment's space,

Awake, with horrid shout, my foemen's ears,

And beard them, though they be more fanged than wolves

and bears.'

18

'Ah! why wilt thou affright a feeble soul?

A poor, weak, palsy-stricken, churchyard thing,

Whose passing-bell may ere the midnight toll;

Whose prayers for thee, each morn and evening,

Were never missed.' – Thus plaining, doth she bring

A gentler speech from burning Porphyro,

So woeful, and of such deep sorrowing,

That Angela gives promise she will do
Whatever he shall wish, betide her weal or woe.

19

Which was, to lead him, in close secrecy,
Even to Madeline's chamber, and there hide
Him in a closet, of such privacy
That he might see her beauty unespied,
And win perhaps that night a peerless bride,
While legioned faeries paced the coverlet,
And pale enchantment held her sleepy-eyed.
Never on such a night have lovers met,
Since Merlin paid his Demon all the monstrous debt.

20

'It shall be as thou wishest,' said the Dame:
'All cates and dainties shall be storèd there
Quickly on this feast-night; by the tambour frame
Her own lute thou wilt see. No time to spare,
For I am slow and feeble, and scarce dare
On such a catering trust my dizzy head.
Wait here, my child, with patience; kneel in prayer
The while. Ah! thou must needs the lady wed,
Or may I never leave my grave among the dead.'

21

So saying, she hobbled off with busy fear.

The lover's endless minutes slowly passed;

The dame returned, and whispered in his ear

To follow her; with agèd eyes aghast

From fright of dim espial. Safe at last,

Through many a dusky gallery, they gain

The maiden's chamber, silken, hushed, and chaste;

Where Porphyro took covert, pleased amain.

His poor guide hurried back with agues in her brain.

22

Her faltering hand upon the balustrade,

Old Angela was feeling for the stair,

When Madeline, St Agnes' charmèd maid,

Rose, like a missioned spirit, unaware:

With silver taper's light, and pious care,

She turned, and down the agèd gossip led

To a safe level matting. Now prepare,

Young Porphyro, for gazing on that bed –

She comes, she comes again, like ring-dove frayed and fled.

23

Out went the taper as she hurried in;

Its little smoke, in pallid moonshine, died:

She closed the door, she panted, all akin
To spirits of the air, and visions wide –
No uttered syllable, or, woe betide!
But to her heart, her heart was voluble,
Paining with eloquence her balmy side;
As though a tongueless nightingale should swell
Her throat in vain, and die, heart-stiflèd, in her dell.

24

A casement high and triple-arched there was,
All garlanded with carven imag'ries
Of fruits, and flowers, and bunches of knot-grass,
And diamonded with panes of quaint device,
Innumerable of stains and splendid dyes,
As are the tiger-moth's deep-damasked wings;
And in the midst, 'mong thousand heraldries,
And twilight saints, and dim emblazonings,
A shielded scutcheon blushed with blood of queens and
    kings.

25

Full on this casement shone the wintry moon,
And threw warm gules on Madeline's fair breast,
As down she knelt for heaven's grace and boon;
Rose-bloom fell on her hands, together pressed,

And on her silver cross soft amethyst,

And on her hair a glory, like a saint:

She seemed a splendid angel, newly dressed,

Save wings, for Heaven – Porphyro grew faint;

She knelt, so pure a thing, so free from mortal taint.

26

Anon his heart revives; her vespers done,

Of all its wreathèd pearls her hair she frees;

Unclasps her warmèd jewels one by one;

Loosens her fragrant bodice; by degrees

Her rich attire creeps rustling to her knees:

Half-hidden, like a mermaid in sea-weed,

Pensive awhile she dreams awake, and sees,

In fancy, fair St Agnes in her bed,

But dares not look behind, or all the charm is fled.

27

Soon, trembling in her soft and chilly nest,

In sort of wakeful swoon, perplexed she lay,

Until the poppied warmth of sleep oppressed

Her soothèd limbs, and soul fatigued away –

Flown, like a thought, until the morrow-day;

Blissfully havened both from joy and pain;

Clasped like a missal where swart Paynims pray;

Blinded alike from sunshine and from rain,

As though a rose should shut, and be a bud again.

28

Stolen to this paradise, and so entranced,

Porphyro gazed upon her empty dress,

And listened to her breathing, if it chanced

To wake into a slumbrous tenderness;

Which when he heard, that minute did he bless,

And breathed himself: then from the closet crept,

Noiseless as fear in a wide wilderness,

And over the hushed carpet, silent, stept,

And 'tween the curtains peeped, where, lo! – how fast she

slept.

29

Then by the bed-side, where the faded moon

Made a dim, silver twilight, soft he set

A table, and, half anguished, threw thereon

A cloth of woven crimson, gold, and jet –

O for some drowsy Morphean amulet!

The boisterous, midnight, festive clarion,

The kettle-drum, and far-heard clarinet,

Affray his ears, though but in dying tone;

The hall door shuts again, and all the noise is gone.

30

And still she slept an azure-lidded sleep,

In blanchèd linen, smooth, and lavendered,

While he from forth the closet brought a heap

Of candied apple, quince, and plum, and gourd,

With jellies soother than the creamy curd,

And lucent syrups, tinct with cinnamon;

Manna and dates, in argosy transferred

From Fez; and spicèd dainties, every one,

From silken Samarkand to cedared Lebanon.

31

These delicates he heaped with glowing hand

On golden dishes and in baskets bright

Of wreathèd silver; sumptuous they stand

In the retirèd quiet of the night,

Filling the chilly room with perfume light.

'And now, my love, my seraph fair, awake!

Thou art my heaven, and I thine eremite:

Open thine eyes, for meek St Agnes' sake,

Or I shall drowse beside thee, so my soul doth ache.'

32

Thus whispering, his warm, unnervèd arm

Sank in her pillow. Shaded was her dream

By the dusk curtains – 'twas a midnight charm
Impossible to melt as icèd stream:
The lustrous salvers in the moonlight gleam;
Broad golden fringe upon the carpet lies.
It seemed he never, never could redeem
From such a steadfast spell his lady's eyes;
So mused awhile, entoiled in woofèd fantasies.

33

Awakening up, he took her hollow lute,
Tumultuous, and, in chords that tenderest be,
He played an ancient ditty, long since mute,
In Provence called, 'La belle dame sans mercy',
Close to her ear touching the melody –
Wherewith disturbed, she uttered a soft moan:
He ceased – she panted quick – and suddenly
Her blue affrayèd eyes wide open shone.
Upon his knees he sank, pale as smooth-sculptured stone.

34

Her eyes were open, but she still beheld,
Now wide awake, the vision of her sleep –
There was a painful change, that nigh expelled
The blisses of her dream so pure and deep.
At which fair Madeline began to weep,

And moan forth witless words with many a sigh,

While still her gaze on Porphyro would keep;

Who knelt, with joinèd hands and piteous eye,

Fearing to move or speak, she looked so dreamingly.

35

'Ah, Porphyro!' said she, 'but even now

Thy voice was at sweet tremble in mine ear,

Made tuneable with every sweetest vow,

And those sad eyes were spiritual and clear:

How changed thou art! How pallid, chill, and drear!

Give me that voice again, my Porphyro,

Those looks immortal, those complainings dear!

O leave me not in this eternal woe,

For if thou diest, my Love, I know not where to go.'

36

Beyond a mortal man impassioned far

At these voluptuous accents, he arose,

Ethereal, flushed, and like a throbbing star

Seen mid the sapphire heaven's deep repose;

Into her dream he melted, as the rose

Blendeth its odour with the violet –

Solution sweet. Meantime the frost-wind blows

Like Love's alarum pattering the sharp sleet

Against the window-panes; St Agnes' moon hath set.

37

'Tis dark: quick pattereth the flaw-blown sleet.

'This is no dream, my bride, my Madeline!'

'Tis dark: the icèd gusts still rave and beat.

'No dream, alas! alas! and woe is mine!

Porphyro will leave me here to fade and pine. –

Cruel! what traitor could thee hither bring?

I curse not, for my heart is lost in thine,

Though thou forsakest a deceivèd thing –

A dove forlorn and lost with sick unprunèd wing.'

38

'My Madeline! sweet dreamer! lovely bride!

Say, may I be for aye thy vassal blessed?

Thy beauty's shield, heart-shaped and vermeil dyed?

Ah, silver shrine, here will I take my rest

After so many hours of toil and quest,

A famished pilgrim – saved by miracle.

Though I have found, I will not rob thy nest

Saving of thy sweet self; if thou think'st well

To trust, fair Madeline, to no rude infidel.

39

'Hark! 'tis an elfin-storm from faery land,

Of haggard seeming, but a boon indeed:

Arise – arise! the morning is at hand.

The bloated wassaillers will never heed –

Let us away, my love, with happy speed –

There are no ears to hear, or eyes to see,

Drowned all in Rhenish and the sleepy mead;

Awake! arise! my love, and fearless be,

For o'er the southern moors I have a home for thee.'

40

She hurried at his words, beset with fears,

For there were sleeping dragons all around,

At glaring watch, perhaps, with ready spears –

Down the wide stairs a darkling way they found.

In all the house was heard no human sound.

A chain-drooped lamp was flickering by each door;

The arras, rich with horseman, hawk, and hound,

Fluttered in the besieging wind's uproar;

And the long carpets rose along the gusty floor.

41

They glide, like phantoms, into the wide hall;

Like phantoms, to the iron porch, they glide;

Where lay the Porter, in uneasy sprawl,

With a huge empty flaggon by his side:

The wakeful bloodhound rose, and shook his hide,

But his sagacious eye an inmate owns.

By one, and one, the bolts, full easy slide –

The chains lie silent on the footworn stones –

The key turns, and the door upon its hinges groans.

42

And they are gone – ay, ages long ago

These lovers fled away into the storm.

That night the Baron dreamt of many a woe,

And all his warrior-guests, with shade and form

Of witch, and demon, and large coffin-worm,

Were long be-nightmared. Angela the old

Died palsy-twitched, with meagre face deform;

The Beadsman, after thousand aves told,

For aye unsought for slept among his ashes cold.

Lamia

PART I

Upon a time, before the faery broods

Drove Nymph and Satyr from the prosperous woods,

Before King Oberon's bright diadem,

Sceptre, and mantle, clasped with dewy gem,

Frighted away the Dryads and the Fauns

From rushes green, and brakes, and cowslipped lawns,

The ever-smitten Hermes empty left

His golden throne, bent warm on amorous theft:

From high Olympus had he stolen light,

On this side of Jove's clouds, to escape the sight

Of his great summoner, and made retreat

Into a forest on the shores of Crete.

For somewhere in that sacred island dwelt

A nymph, to whom all hoofèd Satyrs knelt,

At whose white feet the languid Tritons poured

Pearls, while on land they withered and adored.

Fast by the springs where she to bathe was wont,

And in those meads where sometime she might haunt,

Were strewn rich gifts, unknown to any Muse,

Though Fancy's casket were unlocked to choose.

Ah, what a world of love was at her feet!

So Hermes thought, and a celestial heat
Burnt from his wingèd heels to either ear,
That from a whiteness, as the lily clear,
Blushed into roses 'mid his golden hair,
Fallen in jealous curls about his shoulders bare.

From vale to vale, from wood to wood, he flew,
Breathing upon the flowers his passion new,
And wound with many a river to its head
To find where this sweet nymph prepared her secret bed.
In vain; the sweet nymph might nowhere be found,
And so he rested, on the lonely ground,
Pensive, and full of painful jealousies
Of the Wood-Gods, and even the very trees.
There as he stood, he heard a mournful voice,
Such as, once heard, in gentle heart destroys
All pain but pity; thus the lone voice spake:
'When from this wreathèd tomb shall I awake!
When move in a sweet body fit for life,
And love, and pleasure, and the ruddy strife
Of hearts and lips! Ah, miserable me!'
The God, dove-footed, glided silently
Round bush and tree, soft-brushing, in his speed,
The taller grasses and full-flowering weed,
Until he found a palpitating snake,

Bright, and cirque-couchant in a dusky brake.

    She was a gordian shape of dazzling hue,
Vermilion-spotted, golden, green, and blue;
Striped like a zebra, freckled like a pard,
Eyed like a peacock, and all crimson barred;
And full of silver moons, that, as she breathed,
Dissolved, or brighter shone, or interwreathed
Their lustres with the gloomier tapestries –
So rainbow-sided, touched with miseries,
She seemed, at once, some penanced lady elf,
Some demon's mistress, or the demon's self.
Upon her crest she wore a wannish fire
Sprinkled with stars, like Ariadne's tiar;
Her head was serpent, but ah, bitter-sweet!
She had a woman's mouth with all its pearls complete;
And for her eyes – what could such eyes do there
But weep, and weep, that they were born so fair,
As Proserpine still weeps for her Sicilian air?
Her throat was serpent, but the words she spake
Came, as through bubbling honey, for Love's sake,
And thus – while Hermes on his pinions lay,
Like a stooped falcon ere he takes his prey –

    'Fair Hermes, crowned with feathers, fluttering light,

I had a splendid dream of thee last night:

I saw thee sitting, on a throne of gold,

Among the Gods, upon Olympus old,

The only sad one; for thou didst not hear

The soft, lute-fingered Muses chanting clear,

Nor even Apollo when he sang alone,

Deaf to his throbbing throat's long, long melodious moan.

I dreamt I saw thee, robed in purple flakes,

Break amorous through the clouds, as morning breaks,

And, swiftly as a bright Phoebean dart,

Strike for the Cretan isle; and here thou art!

Too gentle Hermes, hast thou found the maid?'

Whereat the star of Lethe not delayed

His rosy eloquence, and thus inquired:

'Thou smooth-lipped serpent, surely high inspired!

Thou beauteous wreath, with melancholy eyes,

Possess whatever bliss thou canst devise,

Telling me only where my nymph is fled –

Where she doth breathe!' 'Bright planet, thou hast said,'

Returned the snake, 'but seal with oaths, fair Gold!'

'I swear,' said Hermes, 'by my serpent rod,

And by thine eyes, and by thy starry crown!'

Light flew his earnest words, among the blossoms blown.

Then thus again the brilliance feminine:

'Too frail of heart! for this lost nymph of thine,

Free as the air, invisibly, she strays

About these thornless wilds; her pleasant days

She tastes unseen; unseen her nimble feet

Leave traces in the grass and flowers sweet;

From weary tendrils, and bowed branches green,

She plucks the fruit unseen, she bathes unseen;

And by my power is her beauty veiled

To keep it unaffronted, unassailed

By the love-glances of unlovely eyes

Of Satyrs, Fauns, and bleared Silenus' sighs.

Pale grew her immortality, for woe

Of all these lovers, and she grievèd so

I took compassion on her, bade her steep

Her hair in weïrd syrops, that would keep

Her loveliness invisible, yet free

To wander as she loves, in liberty.

Thou shalt behold her, Hermes, thou alone,

If thou wilt, as thou swearest, grant my boon!'

Then, once again, the charmèd God began

An oath, and through the serpent's ears it ran

Warm, tremulous, devout, psalterian.

Ravished, she lifted her Circean head,

Blushed a live damask, and swift-lisping said,

'I was a woman, let me have once more

A woman's shape, and charming as before.

I love a youth of Corinth – O the bliss!

Give me my woman's form, and place me where he is.

Stoop, Hermes, let me breathe upon thy brow,

And thou shalt see thy sweet nymph even now.'

The God on half-shut feathers sank serene,

She breathed upon his eyes, and swift was seen

Of both the guarded nymph near-smiling on the green.

It was no dream; or say a dream it was,

Real are the dreams of Gods, and smoothly pass

Their pleasures in a long immortal dream.

One warm, flushed moment, hovering, it might seem

Dashed by the wood-nymph's beauty, so he burned;

Then, lighting on the printless verdure, turned

To the swooned serpent, and with languid arm,

Delicate, put to proof the lithe Caducean charm.

So done, upon the nymph his eyes he bent

Full of adoring tears and blandishment,

And towards her stepped: she, like a moon in wane,

Faded before him, cowered, nor could restrain

Her fearful sobs, self-folding like a flower

That faints into itself at evening hour:

But the God fostering her chillèd hand,

She felt the warmth, her eyelids opened bland,

And, like new flowers at morning song of bees,

Bloomed, and gave up her honey to the lees.

Into the green-recessèd woods they flew;

Nor grew they pale, as mortal lovers do.

   Left to herself, the serpent now began

To change; her elfin blood in madness ran,

Her mouth foamed, and the grass, therewith besprent,

Withered at dew so sweet and virulent;

Her eyes in torture fixed, and anguish drear,

Hot, glazed, and wide, with lid-lashes all sear,

Flashed phosphor and sharp sparks, without one cooling
    tear.

The colours all inflamed throughout her train,

She writhed about, convulsed with scarlet pain:

A deep volcanian yellow took the place

Of all her milder-moonèd body's grace;

And, as the lava ravishes the mead,

Spoilt all her silver mail, and golden brede;

Made gloom of all her frecklings, streaks and bars,

Eclipsed her crescents, and licked up her stars.

So that, in moments few, she was undressed

Of all her sapphires, greens, and amethyst,

And rubious-argent; of all these bereft,

Nothing but pain and ugliness were left.

Still shone her crown; that vanished, also she

Melted and disappeared as suddenly;

And in the air, her new voice luting soft,

Cried, 'Lycius! gentle Lycius!' – Borne aloft

With the bright mists about the mountains hoar

These words dissolved: Crete's forests heard no more.

Whither fled Lamia, now a lady bright,

A full-born beauty new and exquisite?

She fled into that valley they pass o'er

Who go to Corinth from Cenchreas' shore;

And rested at the foot of those wild hills,

The rugged founts of the Peræan rills,

And of that other ridge whose barren back

Stretches, with all its mist and cloudy rack,

South-westward to Cleone. There she stood

About a young bird's flutter from a wood,

Fair, on a sloping green of mossy tread,

By a clear pool, wherein she passionèd

To see herself escaped from so sore ills,

While her robes flaunted with the daffodils.

Ah, happy Lycius! – for she was a maid

More beautiful than ever twisted braid,

Or sighed, or blushed, or on spring-flowered lea

Spread a green kirtle to the minstrelsy:

A virgin purest lipped, yet in the lore

Of love deep learnèd to the red heart's core;
Not one hour old, yet of sciential brain
To unperplex bliss from its neighbour pain;
Define their pettish limits, and estrange
Their points of contact, and swift counterchange;
Intrigue with the specious chaos, and dispart
Its most ambiguous atoms with sure art;
As though in Cupid's college she had spent
Sweet days a lovely graduate, still unshent,
And kept his rosy terms in idle languishment.

Why this fair creature chose so faerily
By the wayside to linger, we shall see;
But first 'tis fit to tell how she could muse
And dream, when in the serpent prison-house,
Of all she list, strange or magnificent:
How, ever, where she willed, her spirit went;
Whether to faint Elysium, or where
Down through tress-lifting waves the Nereids fair
Wind into Thetis' bower by many a pearly stair;
Or where God Bacchus drains his cups divine,
Stretched out, at ease, beneath a glutinous pine;
Or where in Pluto's gardens palatine
Mulciber's columns gleam in far piazzian line.
And sometimes into cities she would send

Her dream, with feast and rioting to blend;

And once, while among mortals dreaming thus,

She saw the young Corinthian Lycius

Charioting foremost in the envious race,

Like a young Jove with calm uneager face,

And fell into a swooning love of him.

Now on the moth-time of that evening dim

He would return that way, as well she knew,

To Corinth from the shore; for freshly blew

The eastern soft wind, and his galley now

Grated the quaystones with her brazen prow

In port Cenchreas, from Egina isle

Fresh anchored; whither he had been awhile

To sacrifice to Jove, whose temple there

Waits with high marble doors for blood and incense rare.

Jove heard his vows, and bettered his desire;

For by some freakful chance he made retire

From his companions, and set forth to walk,

Perhaps grown wearied of their Corinth talk:

Over the solitary hills he fared,

Thoughtless at first, but ere eve's star appeared

His fantasy was lost, where reason fades,

In the calmed twilight of Platonic shades.

Lamia beheld him coming, near, more near –

Close to her passing, in indifference drear,

His silent sandals swept the mossy green;

So neighboured to him, and yet so unseen

She stood: he passed, shut up in mysteries,

His mind wrapped like his mantle, while her eyes

Followed his steps, and her neck regal white

Turned – syllabling thus, 'Ah, Lycius bright,

And will you leave me on the hills alone?

Lycius, look back! and be some pity shown.'

He did – not with cold wonder fearingly,

But Orpheus-like at an Eurydice –

For so delicious were the words she sung,

It seemed he had loved them a whole summer long.

And soon his eyes had drunk her beauty up,

Leaving no drop in the bewildering cup,

And still the cup was full – while he, afraid

Lest she should vanish ere his lip had paid

Due adoration, thus began to adore

(Her soft look growing coy, she saw his chain so sure):

'Leave thee alone! Look back! Ah, Goddess, see

Whether my eyes can ever turn from thee!

For pity do not this sad heart belie –

Even as thou vanisheth so shall I die.

Stay! though a Naiad of the rivers, stay!

To thy far wishes will thy streams obey.

Stay! though the greenest woods be thy domain,

Alone they can drink up the morning rain:
Though a descended Pleiad, will not one
Of thine harmonious sisters keep in tune
Thy spheres, and as thy silver proxy shine?
So sweetly to these ravished ears of mine
Came thy sweet greeting, that if thou shouldst fade
Thy memory will waste me to a shade –
For pity do not melt!' – 'If I should stay,'
Said Lamia, 'here, upon this floor of clay,
And pain my steps upon these flowers too rough,
What canst thou say or do of charm enough
To dull the nice remembrance of my home?
Thou canst not ask me with thee here to roam
Over these hills and vales, where no joy is –
Empty of immortality and bliss!
Thou art a scholar, Lycius, and must know
That finer spirits cannot breathe below
In human climes, and live. Alas! poor youth,
What taste of purer air hast thou to soothe
My essence? What serener palaces,
Where I may all my many senses please,
And by mysterious sleights a hundred thirsts appease?
It cannot be – Adieu!' So said, she rose
Tip-toe with white arms spread. He, sick to lose
The amorous promise of her lone complain,

Swooned, murmuring of love, and pale with pain.

The cruel lady, without any show

Of sorrow for her tender favourite's woe,

But rather, if her eyes could brighter be,

With brighter eyes and slow amenity,

Put her new lips to his, and gave afresh

The life she had so tangled in her mesh;

And as he from one trance was wakening

Into another, she began to sing,

Happy in beauty, life, and love, and every thing,

A song of love, too sweet for earthly lyres,

While, like held breath, the stars drew in their panting fires.

And then she whispered in such trembling tone,

As those who, safe together met alone

For the first time through many anguished days,

Use other speech than looks; bidding him raise

His drooping head, and clear his soul of doubt,

For that she was a woman, and without

Any more subtle fluid in her veins

Than throbbing blood, and that the self-same pains

Inhabited her frail-strung heart as his.

And next she wondered how his eyes could miss

Her face so long in Corinth, where, she said,

She dwelt but half retired, and there had led

Days happy as the gold coin could invent

Without the aid of love; yet in content
Till she saw him, as once she passed him by,
Where 'gainst a column he leant thoughtfully
At Venus' temple porch, 'mid baskets heaped
Of amorous herbs and flowers, newly reaped
Late on that eve, as 'twas the night before
The Adonian feast; whereof she saw no more,
But wept alone those days, for why should she adore?
Lycius from death awoke into amaze,
To see her still, and singing so sweet lays;
Then from amaze into delight he fell
To hear her whisper woman's lore so well;
And every word she spake enticed him on
To unperplexed delight and pleasure known.
Let the mad poets say whate'er they please
Of the sweets of Faeries, Peris, Goddesses,
There is not such a treat among them all,
Haunters of cavern, lake, and waterfall,
As a real woman, lineal indeed
From Pyrrha's pebbles or old Adam's seed.
Thus gentle Lamia judged, and judged aright,
That Lycius could not love in half a fright,
So threw the goddess off, and won his heart
More pleasantly by playing woman's part,
With no more awe than what her beauty gave,

That, while it smote, still guaranteed to save.

Lycius to all made eloquent reply,

Marrying to every word a twinborn sigh;

And last, pointing to Corinth, asked her sweet,

If 'twas too far that night for her soft feet.

The way was short, for Lamia's eagerness

Made, by a spell, the triple league decrease

To a few paces; not at all surmised

By blinded Lycius, so in her comprised.

They passed the city gates, he knew not how,

So noiseless, and he never thought to know.

   As men talk in a dream, so Corinth all,

Throughout her palaces imperial,

And all her populous streets and temples lewd,

Muttered, like tempest in the distance brewed,

To the wide-spreaded night above her towers.

Men, women, rich and poor, in the cool hours,

Shuffled their sandals o'er the pavement white,

Companioned or alone; while many a light

Flared, here and there, from wealthy festivals,

And threw their moving shadows on the walls,

Or found them clustered in the corniced shade

Of some arched temple door, or dusky colonnade.

Muffling his face, of greeting friends in fear,
Her fingers he pressed hard, as one came near
With curled grey beard, sharp eyes, and smooth bald crown,
Slow-stepped, and robed in philosophic gown:
Lycius shrank closer, as they met and passed,
Into his mantle, adding wings to haste,
While hurried Lamia trembled: 'Ah,' said he,
'Why do you shudder, love, so ruefully?
Why does your tender palm dissolve in dew?' –
'I'm wearied,' said fair Lamia, 'tell me who
Is that old man? I cannot bring to mind
His features – Lycius! wherefore did you blind
Yourself from his quick eyes?' Lycius replied,
''Tis Apollonius sage, my trusty guide
And good instructor; but tonight he seems
The ghost of folly haunting my sweet dreams.'

While yet he spake they had arrived before
A pillared porch, with lofty portal door,
Where hung a silver lamp, whose phosphor glow
Reflected in the slabbèd steps below,
Mild as a star in water; for so new,
And so unsullied was the marble hue,
So through the crystal polish, liquid fine,
Ran the dark veins, that none but feet divine

Could e'er have touched there. Sounds Aeolian

Breathed from the hinges, as the ample span

Of the wide doors disclosed a place unknown

Some time to any, but those two alone,

And a few Persian mutes, who that same year

Were seen about the markets: none knew where

They could inhabit; the most curious

Were foiled, who watched to trace them to their house.

And but the flitter-wingèd verse must tell,

For truth's sake, what woe afterwards befell,

'Twould humour many a heart to leave them thus,

Shut from the busy world of more incredulous.

PART II

Love in a hut, with water and a crust,

Is – Love, forgive us! – cinder, ashes, dust;

Love in a palace is perhaps at last

More grievous torment than a hermit's fast.

That is a doubtful tale from faery land,

Hard for the non-elect to understand.

Had Lycius lived to hand his story down,

He might have given the moral a fresh frown,

Or clenched it quite: but too short was their bliss

To breed distrust and hate, that make the soft voice hiss.

Besides, there, nightly, with terrific glare,

Love, jealous grown of so complete a pair,

Hovered and buzzed his wings, with fearful roar,

Above the lintel of their chamber door,

And down the passage cast a glow upon the floor.

For all this came a ruin: side by side

They were enthronèd, in the eventide,

Upon a couch, near to a curtaining

Whose airy texture, from a golden string,

Floated into the room, and let appear

Unveiled the summer heaven, blue and clear,

Betwixt two marble shafts. There they reposed,

Where use had made it sweet, with eyelids closed,

Saving a tithe which love still open kept,

That they might see each other while they almost slept;

When from the slope side of a suburb hill,

Deafening the swallow's twitter, came a thrill

Of trumpets – Lycius started – the sounds fled,

But left a thought, a buzzing in his head.

For the first time, since first he harboured in

That purple-linèd palace of sweet sin,

His spirit passed beyond its golden bourne

Into the noisy world almost forsworn.

The lady, ever watchful, penetrant,

Saw this with pain, so arguing a want

Of something more, more than her empery

Of joys; and she began to moan and sigh

Because he mused beyond her, knowing well

That but a moment's thought is passion's passing - bell.

'Why do you sigh, fair creature?'whispered he:

'Why do you think?'returned she tenderly,

'You have deserted me – where am I now?

Not in your heart while care weighs on your brow:

No, no, you have dismissed me; and I go

From your breast houseless – ay, it must be so.'

He answered, bending to her open eyes,

Where he was mirrored small in paradise,

'My silver planet, both of eve and morn!

Why will you plead yourself so sad forlorn,

While I am striving how to fill my heart

With deeper crimson, and a double smart?

How to entangle, trammel up and snare

Your soul in mine, and labyrinth you there

Like the hid scent in an unbudded rose?

Ay, a sweet kiss – you see your mighty woes.

My thoughts! shall I unveil them? Listen then!

What mortal hath a prize, that other men

May be confounded and abashed withal,

But lets it sometimes pace abroad majestical,

And triumph, as in thee I should rejoice

Amid the hoarse alarm of Corinth's voice.

Let my foes choke, and my friends shout afar,

While through the throngèd streets your bridal car

Wheels round its dazzling spokes.'– The lady's cheek

Trembled; she nothing said, but, pale and meek,

Arose and knelt before him, wept a rain

Of sorrows at his words; at last with pain

Beseeching him, the while his hand she wrung,

To change his purpose. He thereat was stung,

Perverse, with stronger fancy to reclaim

Her wild and timid nature to his aim:

Besides, for all his love, in self-despite,

Against his better self, he took delight

Luxurious in her sorrows, soft and new.

His passion, cruel grown, took on a hue

Fierce and sanguineous as 'twas possible

In one whose brow had no dark veins to swell.

Fine was the mitigated fury, like

Apollo's presence when in act to strike

The serpent – Ha, the serpent! Certes, she

Was none. She burnt, she loved the tyranny,

And, all subdued, consented to the hour

When to the bridal he should lead his paramour.

Whispering in midnight silence, said the youth,

'Sure some sweet name thou hast, though, by my truth,

I have not asked it, ever thinking thee
Not mortal, but of heavenly progeny,
As still I do. Hast any mortal name,
Fit appellation for this dazzling frame?
Or friends or kinsfolk on the citied earth,
To share our marriage feast and nuptial mirth?'
'I have no friends,'said Lamia,'no, not one;
My presence in wide Corinth hardly known:
My parents' bones are in their dusty urns
Sepulchred, where no kindled incense burns,
Seeing all their luckless race are dead, save me,
And I neglect the holy rite for thee.
Even as you list invite your many guests;
But if, as now it seems, your vision rests
With any pleasure on me, do not bid
Old Apollonius – from him keep me hid.'
Lycius, perplexed at words so blind and blank,
Made close inquiry; from whose touch she shrank,
Feigning a sleep; and he to the dull shade
Of deep sleep in a moment was betrayed.

    It was the custom then to bring away
The bride from home at blushing shut of day,
Veiled, in a chariot, heralded along
By strewn flowers, torches, and a marriage song,

With other pageants: but this fair unknown
Had not a friend. So being left alone,
(Lycius was gone to summon all his kin)
And knowing surely she could never win
His foolish heart from its mad pompousness,
She set herself, high-thoughted, how to dress
The misery in fit magnificence.
She did so, but 'tis doubtful how and whence
Came, and who were her subtle servitors.
About the halls, and to and from the doors,
There was a noise of wings, till in short space
The glowing banquet-room shone with wide-archèd grace.
A haunting music, sole perhaps and lone
Supportress of the faery-roof, made moan
Throughout, as fearful the whole charm might fade.
Fresh carvèd cedar, mimicking a glade
Of palm and plantain, met from either side,
High in the midst, in honour of the bride;
Two palms and then two plantains, and so on,
From either side their stems branched one to one
All down the aislèd place; and beneath all
There ran a stream of lamps straight on from wall to wall.
So canopied, lay an untasted feast
Teeming with odours. Lamia, regal dressed,
Silently paced about, and as she went,

In pale contented sort of discontent,

Missioned her viewless servants to enrich

The fretted splendour of each nook and niche.

Between the tree-stems, marbled plain at first,

Came jasper panels; then anon, there burst

Forth creeping imagery of slighter trees,

And with the larger wove in small intricacies.

Approving all, she faded at self-will,

And shut the chamber up, close, hushed and still,

Complete and ready for the revels rude,

When dreadful guests would come to spoil her solitude.

The day appeared, and all the gossip rout.

O senseless Lycius! Madman! wherefore flout

The silent-blessing fate, warm cloistered hours,

And show to common eyes these secret bowers?

The herd approached; each guest, with busy brain,

Arriving at the portal, gazed amain,

And entered marvelling – for they knew the street,

Remembered it from childhood all complete

Without a gap, yet ne'er before had seen

That royal porch, that high-built fair demesne.

So in they hurried all, mazed, curious and keen –

Save one, who looked thereon with eye severe,

And with calm-planted steps walked in austere.

'Twas Apollonius: something too he laughed,
As though some knotty problem, that had daffed
His patient thought, had now begun to thaw,
And solve and melt – 'twas just as he foresaw.

He met within the murmurous vestibule
His young disciple.''Tis no common rule,
Lycius,' said he,'for uninvited guest
To force himself upon you, and infest
With an unbidden presence the bright throng
Of younger friends; yet must I do this wrong,
And you forgive me.'Lycius blushed, and led
The old man through the inner doors broad-spread;
With reconciling words and courteous mien
Turning into sweet milk the sophist's spleen.

Of wealthy lustre was the banquet-room,
Filled with pervading brilliance and perfume:
Before each lucid panel fuming stood
A censer fed with myrrh and spicèd wood,
Each by a sacred tripod held aloft,
Whose slender feet wide-swerved upon the soft
Wool-woofèd carpets; fifty wreaths of smoke
From fifty censers their light voyage took
To the high roof, still mimicked as they rose

Along the mirrored walls by twin-clouds odorous.

Twelve spherèd tables, by silk seats ensphered,

High as the level of a man's breast reared

On libbard's paws, upheld the heavy gold

Of cups and goblets, and the store thrice told

Of Ceres' horn, and, in huge vessels, wine

Come from the gloomy tun with merry shine.

Thus loaded with a feast the tables stood,

Each shrining in the midst the image of a God.

　　When in an antechamber every guest

Had felt the cold full sponge to pleasure pressed,

By ministering slaves, upon his hands and feet,

And fragrant oils with ceremony meet

Poured on his hair, they all moved to the feast

In white robes, and themselves in order placed

Around the silken couches, wondering

Whence all this mighty cost and blaze of wealth could spring.

　　Soft went the music the soft air along,

While fluent Greek a vowelled undersong

Kept up among the guests, discoursing low

At first, for scarcely was the wine at flow;

But when the happy vintage touched their brains,

Louder they talk, and louder come the strains

Of powerful instruments. The gorgeous dyes,

The space, the splendour of the draperies,

The roof of awful richness, nectarous cheer,

Beautiful slaves, and Lamia's self, appear,

Now, when the wine has done its rosy deed,

And every soul from human trammels freed,

No more so strange; for merry wine, sweet wine,

Will make Elysian shades not too fair, too divine.

Soon was God Bacchus at meridian height;

Flushed were their cheeks, and bright eyes double bright:

Garlands of every green, and every scent

From vales deflowered, or forest-trees branch-rent,

In baskets of bright osiered gold were brought

High as the handles heaped, to suit the thought

Of every guest – that each, as he did please,

Might fancy-fit his brows, silk-pillowed at his ease.

What wreath for Lamia? What for Lycius?

What for the sage, old Apollonius?

Upon her aching forehead be there hung

The leaves of willow and of adder's tongue;

And for the youth, quick, let us strip for him

The thyrsus, that his watching eyes may swim

Into forgetfulness; and, for the sage,

Let spear-grass and the spiteful thistle wage

War on his temples. Do not all charms fly
At the mere touch of cold philosophy?
There was an awful rainbow once in heaven:
We know her woof, her texture; she is given
In the dull catalogue of common things.
Philosophy will clip an Angel's wings,
Conquer all mysteries by rule and line,
Empty the haunted air, and gnomèd mine –
Unweave a rainbow, as it erewhile made
The tender-personed Lamia melt into a shade.

By her glad Lycius sitting, in chief place,
Scarce saw in all the room another face,
Till, checking his love trance, a cup he took
Full brimmed, and opposite sent forth a look
'Cross the broad table, to beseech a glance
From his old teacher's wrinkled countenance,
And pledge him. The bald-head philosopher
Had fixed his eye, without a twinkle or stir
Full on the alarmèd beauty of the bride,
Brow-beating her fair form, and troubling her sweet pride.
Lycius then pressed her hand, with devout touch,
As pale it lay upon the rosy couch:
'Twas icy, and the cold ran through his veins;
Then sudden it grew hot, and all the pains

Of an unnatural heat shot to his heart.

'Lamia, what means this? Wherefore dost thou start?

Know'st thou that man?'Poor Lamia answered not.

He gazed into her eyes, and not a jot

Owned they the lovelorn piteous appeal;

More, more he gazed; his human senses reel;

Some hungry spell that loveliness absorbs;

There was no recognition in those orbs.

'Lamia!'he cried – and no soft-toned reply.

The many heard, and the loud revelry

Grew hush; the stately music no more breathes;

The myrtle sickened in a thousand wreaths.

By faint degrees, voice, lute, and pleasure ceased;

A deadly silence step by step increased,

Until it seemed a horrid presence there,

And not a man but felt the terror in his hair.

'Lamia!'he shrieked; and nothing but the shriek

With its sad echo did the silence break.

'Begone, foul dream!'he cried, gazing again

In the bride's face, where now no azure vein

Wandered on fair-spaced temples; no soft bloom

Misted the cheek; no passion to illume

The deep-recessèd vision. All was blight;

Lamia, no longer fair, there sat a deadly white.

'Shut, shut those juggling eyes, thou ruthless man!

Turn them aside, wretch! or the righteous ban

Of all the Gods, whose dreadful images

Here represent their shadowy presences,

May pierce them on the sudden with the thorn

Of painful blindness; leaving thee forlorn,

In trembling dotage to the feeblest fright

Of conscience, for their long offended might,

For all thine impious proud-heart sophistries,

Unlawful magic, and enticing lies.

Corinthians! look upon that grey-beard wretch!

Mark how, possessed, his lashless eyelids stretch

Around his demon eyes! Corinthians, see!

My sweet bride withers at their potency.'

'Fool!'said the sophist, in an undertone

Gruff with contempt; which a death-nighing moan

From Lycius answered, as heart-struck and lost,

He sank supine beside the aching ghost.

'Fool! Fool!'repeated he, while his eyes still

Relented not, nor moved;'From every ill

Of life have I preserved thee to this day,

And shall I see thee made a serpent's prey?'

Then Lamia breathed death-breath; the sophist's eye,

Like a sharp spear, went through her utterly,

Keen, cruel, perceant, stinging: she, as well

As her weak hand could any meaning tell,

Motioned him to be silent; vainly so,

He looked and looked again a level – *No!*

'A Serpent!' echoed he; no sooner said,

Than with a frightful scream she vanishèd:

And Lycius' arms were empty of delight,

As were his limbs of life, from that same night.

On the high couch he lay! – his friends came round –

Supported him – no pulse, or breath they found,

And, in its marriage robe, the heavy body wound.

The Fall of Hyperion. A Dream

CANTO I

Fanatics have their dreams, wherewith they weave

A paradise for a sect; the savage too

From forth the loftiest fashion of his sleep

Guesses at Heaven: pity these have not

Traced upon vellum or wild Indian leaf

The shadows of melodious utterance.

But bare of laurel they live, dream, and die;

For Poesy alone can tell her dreams,

With the fine spell of words alone can save

Imagination from the sable charm

And dumb enchantment. Who alive can say,

'Thou are no Poet – mayst not tell thy dreams'?

Since every man whose soul is not a clod

Hath visions, and would speak, if he had loved,

And been well nurtured in his mother tongue.

Whether the dream now purposed to rehearse

Be Poet's or Fanatic's will be known

When this warm scribe my hand is in the grave.

Methought I stood where trees of every clime,

Palm, myrtle, oak, and sycamore, and beech,

With plantain, and spice-blossoms, made a screen –
In neighbourhood of fountains, by the noise
Soft-showering in mine ears, and, by the touch
Of scent, not far from roses. Turning round,
I saw an arbour with a drooping roof
Of trellis vines, and bells, and larger blooms,
Like floral censers, swinging light in air;
Before its wreathèd doorway, on a mound
Of moss, was spread a feast of summer fruits,
Which, nearer seen, seemed refuse of a meal
By angel tasted, or our Mother Eve;
For empty shells were scattered on the grass,
And grape-stalks but half bare, and remnants more,
Sweet-smelling, whose pure kinds I could not know.
Still was more plenty than the fabled horn
Thrice emptied could pour forth at banqueting
For Proserpine returned to her own fields,
Where the white heifers low. And appetite
More yearning than on earth I ever felt
Growing within, I ate deliciously;
And, after not long, thirsted, for thereby
Stood a cool vessel of transparent juice,
Sipped by the wandered bee, the which I took,
And, pledging all the mortals of the world,
And all the dead whose names are in our lips,

Drank. That full draught is parent of my theme.

No Asian poppy, nor elixir fine

Of the soon-fading jealous Caliphat;

No poison gendered in close monkish cell,

To thin the scarlet conclave of old men,

Could so have rapt unwilling life away.

Among the fragrant husks and berries crushed,

Upon the grass I struggled hard against

The domineering potion; but in vain –

The cloudy swoon came on, and down I sunk,

Like a Silenus on an antique vase.

How long I slumbered 'tis a chance to guess.

When sense of life returned, I started up

As if with wings; but the fair trees were gone,

The mossy mound and arbour were no more.

I looked around upon the carvèd sides

Of an old sanctuary with roof august,

Builded so high, it seemed that filmèd clouds

Might spread beneath, as o'er the stars of heaven.

So old the place was, I remembered none

The like upon the earth: what I had seen

Of grey cathedrals, buttressed walls, rent towers,

The superannuations of sunk realms,

Or Nature's rocks toiled hard in waves and winds,

Seemed but the faulture of decrepit things

To that eternal domèd monument.
Upon the marble at my feet there lay
Store of strange vessels and large draperies,
Which needs had been of dyed asbestos wove,
Or in that place the moth could not corrupt,
So white the linen; so, in some, distinct
Ran imageries from a sombre loom.
All in a mingled heap confused there lay
Robes, golden tongs, censer and chafing-dish,
Girdles, and chains, and holy jewelleries –

Turning from these with awe, once more I raised
My eyes to fathom the space every way –
The embossèd roof, the silent massy range
Of columns north and south, ending in mist
Of nothing, then to eastward, where black gates
Were shut against the sunrise evermore.
Then to the west I looked, and saw far off
An Image, huge of feature as a cloud,
At level of whose feet an altar slept,
To be approached on either side by steps,
And marble balustrade, and patient travail
To count with toil the innumerable degrees.
Towards the altar sober-paced I went,
Repressing haste, as too unholy there;

And, coming nearer, saw beside the shrine
One ministering; and there arose a flame.
When in mid-May the sickening East wind
Shifts sudden to the south, the small warm rain
Melts out the frozen incense from all flowers,
And fills the air with so much pleasant health
That even the dying man forgets his shroud –
Even so that lofty sacrificial fire,
Sending forth Maian incense, spread around
Forgetfulness of everything but bliss,
And clouded all the altar with soft smoke,
From whose white fragrant curtains thus I heard
Language pronounced:'If thou canst not ascend
These steps, die on that marble where thou art.
Thy flesh, near cousin to the common dust,
Will parch for lack of nutriment – thy bones
Will wither in few years, and vanish so
That not the quickest eye could find a grain
Of what thou now art on that pavement cold.
The sands of thy short life are spent this hour,
And no hand in the universe can turn
Thy hourglass, if these gummèd leaves be burnt
Ere thou canst mount up these immortal steps.'
I heard, I looked: two senses both at once,
So fine, so subtle, felt the tyranny

Of that fierce threat, and the hard task proposed.

Prodigious seemed the toil; the leaves were yet

Burning – when suddenly a palsied chill

Struck from the pavèd level up my limbs,

And was ascending quick to put cold grasp

Upon those streams that pulse beside the throat.

I shrieked; and the sharp anguish of my shriek

Stung my own ears – I strove hard to escape

The numbness, strove to gain the lowest step.

Slow, heavy, deadly was my pace: the cold

Grew stifling, suffocating, at the heart;

And when I clasped my hands I felt them not.

One minute before death, my iced foot touched

The lowest stair; and as it touched, life seemed

To pour in at the toes: I mounted up,

As once fair Angels on a ladder flew

From the green turf to Heaven.'Holy Power,'

Cried I, approaching near the hornèd shrine,

'What am I that should so be saved from death?

What am I that another death come not

To choke my utterance sacrilegious, here?'

Then said the veilèd shadow:'Thou hast felt

What 'tis to die and live again before

Thy fated hour. That thou hadst power to do so

Is thy own safety; thou hast dated on

Thy doom.''High Prophetess,'said I,'purge off,

Benign, if so it please thee, my mind's film.'

'None can usurp this height,'returned that shade,

'But those to whom the miseries of the world

Are misery, and will not let them rest.

All else who find a haven in the world,

Where they may thoughtless sleep away their days,

If by a chance into this fane they come,

Rot on the pavement where thou rotted'st half.'

'Are there not thousands in the world, 'said I,

Encouraged by the sooth voice of the shade,

'Who love their fellows even to the death;

Who feel the giant agony of the world;

And more, like slaves to poor humanity,

Labour for mortal good? I sure should see

Other men here: but I am here alone.'

'They whom thou spak'st of are no visionaries,'

Rejoined that voice –'They are no dreamers weak,

They seek no wonder but the human face;

No music but a happy-noted voice –

They come not here, they have no thought to come –

And thou art here, for thou art less than they –

What benefit canst thou do, or all thy tribe,

To the great world? Thou art a dreaming thing,

A fever of thyself. Think of the Earth;

What bliss even in hope is there for thee?
What haven? Every creature hath its home;
Every sole man hath days of joy and pain,
Whether his labours be sublime or low –
The pain alone; the joy alone; distinct:
Only the dreamer venoms all his days,
Bearing more woe than all his sins deserve.
Therefore, that happiness be somewhat shared,
Such things as thou art are admitted oft
Into like gardens thou didst pass erewhile,
And suffered in these temples; for that cause
Thou standest safe beneath this statue's knees.'
'That I am favoured for unworthiness,
By such propitious parley medicined
In sickness not ignoble, I rejoice –
Ay, and could weep for love of such award.'
So answered I, continuing,'If it please,
Majestic shadow, tell me: sure not all
Those melodies sung into the world's ear
Are useless: sure a poet is a sage,
A humanist, physician to all men.
That I am none I feel, as vultures feel
They are no birds when eagles are abroad.
What am I then? Thou spakest of my tribe:
What tribe?'– The tall shade veiled in drooping white

Then spake, so much more earnest, that the breath
Moved the thin linen folds that drooping hung
About a golden censer from the hand
Pendent. —'Art thou not of the dreamer tribe?
The poet and the dreamer are distinct,
Diverse, sheer opposite, antipodes.
The one pours out a balm upon the world,
The other vexes it.' Then shouted I,
Spite of myself, and with a Pythia's spleen,
'Apollo! faded, far-flown Apollo!
Where is thy misty pestilence to creep
Into the dwellings, through the door crannies,
Of all mock lyrists, large self-worshippers
And careless hectorers in proud bad verse.
Though I breathe death with them it will be life
To see them sprawl before me into graves.
Majestic shadow, tell me where I am,
Whose altar this; for whom this incense curls;
What image this, whose face I cannot see,
For the broad marble knees; and who thou art,
Of accent feminine so courteous?'

Then the tall shade, in drooping linens veiled,
Spake out, so much more earnest, that her breath
Stirred the thin folds of gauze that drooping hung

About a golden censer from her hand

Pendent; and by her voice I knew she shed

Long-treasured tears.'This temple, sad and lone,

Is all spared from the thunder of a war

Foughten long since by giant hierarchy

Against rebellion; this old image here,

Whose carvèd features wrinkled as he fell,

Is Saturn's; I Moneta, left supreme

Sole priestess of his desolation.'

I had no words to answer, for my tongue,

Useless, could find about its roofèd home

No syllable of a fit majesty

To make rejoinder to Moneta's mourn.

There was a silence, while the altar's blaze

Was fainting for sweet food: I looked thereon,

And on the pavèd floor, where nigh were piled

Faggots of cinnamon, and many heaps

Of other crispèd spice-wood – then again

I looked upon the altar, and its horns

Whitened with ashes, and its languorous flame,

And then upon the offerings again;

And so by turns – till sad Moneta cried:

'The sacrifice is done, but not the less

Will I be kind to thee for thy goodwill.

My power, which to me is still a curse,

Shall be to thee a wonder; for the scenes

Still swooning vivid through my globèd brain,

With an electral changing misery,

Thou shalt with those dull mortal eyes behold,

Free from all pain, if wonder pain thee not.'

As near as an immortal's spherèd words

Could to a mother's soften, were these last:

But yet I had a terror of her robes,

And chiefly of the veils, that from her brow

Hung pale, and curtained her in mysteries

That made my heart too small to hold its blood.

This saw that Goddess, and with sacred hand

Parted the veils. Then saw I a wan face,

Not pined by human sorrows, but bright-blanched

By an immortal sickness which kills not;

It works a constant change, which happy death

Can put no end to; deathwards progressing

To no death was that visage; it had passed

The lily and the snow; and beyond these

I must not think now, though I saw that face –

But for her eyes I should have fled away.

They held me back, with a benignant light,

Soft-mitigated by divinest lids

Half-closed, and visionless entire they seemed

Of all external things – they saw me not,

But in blank splendour beamed like the mild moon,

Who comforts those she sees not, who knows not

What eyes are upward cast. As I had found

A grain of gold upon a mountain's side,

And twinged with avarice strained out my eyes

To search its sullen entrails rich with ore,

So at the view of sad Moneta's brow

I ached to see what things the hollow brain

Behind enwombèd; what high tragedy

In the dark secret chambers of her skull

Was acting, that could give so dread a stress

To her cold lips, and fill with such a light

Her planetary eyes; and touch her voice

With such a sorrow –'Shade of Memory!'

Cried I, with act adorant at her feet,

'By all the gloom hung round thy fallen house,

By this last temple, by the golden age,

By great Apollo, thy dear foster child,

And by thyself, forlorn divinity,

The pale Omega of a withered race,

Let me behold, according as thou said'st,

What in thy brain so ferments to and fro.'

No sooner had this conjuration passed

My devout lips, than side by side we stood

(Like a stunt bramble by a solemn pine)

Deep in the shady sadness of a vale,

Far sunken from the healthy breath of morn,

Far from the fiery noon and eve's one star.

Onward I looked beneath the gloomy boughs,

And saw, what first I thought an image huge,

Like to the image pedestalled so high

In Saturn's temple. Then Moneta's voice

Came brief upon mine ear:'So Saturn sat

When he had lost his realms.' Whereon there grew

A power within me of enormous ken

To see as a God sees, and take the depth

Of things as nimbly as the outward eye

Can size and shape pervade. The lofty theme

At those few words hung vast before my mind,

With half-unravelled web. I set myself

Upon an eagle's watch, that I might see,

And seeing ne'er forget. No stir of life

Was in this shrouded vale, not so much air

As in zoning of a summer's day

Robs not one light seed from the feathered grass,

But where the dead leaf fell there did it rest.

A stream went voiceless by, still deadened more

By reason of the fallen divinity

Spreading more shade; the Naiad 'mid her reeds

Pressed her cold finger closer to her lips.

Along the margin-sand large footmarks went
No farther than to where old Saturn's feet
Had rested, and there slept – how long a sleep!
Degraded, cold, upon the sodden ground
His old right hand lay nerveless, listless, dead,
Unsceptred; and his realmless eyes were closed,
While his bowed head seemed listening to the Earth,
His ancient mother, for some comfort yet.

It seemed no force could wake him from his place;
But there came one who, with a kindred hand
Touched his wide shoulders, after bending low
With reverence, though to one who knew it not.
Then came the grieved voice of Mnemosyne,
And grieved I hearkened. 'That divinity
Whom thou saw'st step from yon forlornest wood,
And with slow pace approach our fallen King,
Is Thea, softest-natured of our brood.'
I marked the Goddess in fair statuary
Surpassing wan Moneta by the head,
And in her sorrow nearer woman's tears.
There was a listening fear in her regard,
As if calamity had but begun;
As if the vanward clouds of evil days
Had spent their malice, and the sullen rear

Was with its storèd thunder labouring up.

One hand she pressed upon that aching spot

Where beats the human heart, as if just there,

Though an immortal, she felt cruel pain;

The other upon Saturn's bended neck

She laid, and to the level of his hollow ear

Leaning with parted lips, some words she spake

In solemn tenor and deep organ tune,

Some mourning words, which in our feeble tongue

Would come in this-like accenting – how frail

To that large utterance of the early Gods! –

'Saturn! look up – and for what, poor lost King?

I have no comfort for thee, no – not one;

I cannot cry, *Wherefore thus sleepest thou?*

For Heaven is parted from thee, and the Earth

Knows thee not, so afflicted, for a God;

And Ocean too, with all its solemn noise,

Has from thy sceptre passed, and all the air

Is emptied of thine hoary Majesty.

Thy thunder, captious at the new command,

Rumbles reluctant o'er our fallen house;

And thy sharp lightning, in unpractised hands,

Scorches and burns our once serene domain.

With such remorseless speed still come new woes

That unbelief has not a space to breathe.

Saturn! sleep on. Me thoughtless, why should I
Thus violate thy slumbrous solitude?
Why should I ope thy melancholy eyes?
Saturn, sleep on, while at thy feet I weep.'

As when, upon a trancèd summer-night,
Forests, branch-charmèd by the earnest stars,
Dream, and so dream all night without a noise,
Save from one gradual solitary gust,
Swelling upon the silence; dying off;
As if the ebbing air had but one wave –
So came these words, and went; the while in tears
She pressed her fair large forehead to the earth,
Just where her fallen hair might spread in curls,
A soft and silken mat for Saturn's feet.
Long, long those two were postured motionless,
Like sculpture builded-up upon the grave
Of their own power. A long awful time
I looked upon them: still they were the same;
The frozen God still bending to the earth,
And the sad Goddess weeping at his feet,
Moneta silent. Without stay or prop,
But my own weak mortality, I bore
The load of this eternal quietude,
The unchanging gloom, and the three fixèd shapes

Ponderous upon my senses a whole moon.

For by my burning brain I measured sure

Her silver seasons shedded on the night,

And every day by day methought I grew

More gaunt and ghostly. Oftentimes I prayed

Intense, that death would take me from the vale

And all its burthens. Gasping with despair

Of change, hour after hour I cursed myself –

Until old Saturn raised his faded eyes,

And looked around and saw his kingdom gone,

And all the gloom and sorrow of the place,

And that fair kneeling Goddess at his feet.

As the moist scent of flowers, and grass, and leaves,

Fills forest dells with a pervading air

Known to the woodland nostril, so the words

Of Saturn filled the mossy glooms around,

Even to the hollows of time-eaten oaks,

And to the windings in the foxes' hole,

With sad low tones, while thus he spake, and sent

Strange musings to the solitary Pan:

'Moan, brethren, moan; for we are swallowed up

And buried from all godlike exercise

Of influence benign on planets pale,

And peaceful sway above man's harvesting,

And all those acts which deity supreme

Doth ease its heart of love in. Moan and wail.

Moan, brethren, moan; for lo! the rebel spheres

Spin round, the stars their ancient courses keep,

Clouds still with shadowy moisture haunt the earth,

Still suck their fill of light from sun and moon,

Still buds the tree, and still the sea-shores murmur.

There is no death in all the universe,

No smell of death – there shall be death – moan, moan,

Moan, Cybele, moan; for thy pernicious babes

Have changed a God into a shaking palsy.

Moan, brethren, moan, for I have no strength left,

Weak as the reed – weak – feeble as my voice –

O, O, the pain, the pain of feebleness.

Moan, moan, for still I thaw – or give me help:

Throw down those imps, and give me victory.

Let me hear other groans, and trumpets blown

Of triumph calm, and hymns of festival,

From the gold peaks of heaven's high-pilèd clouds –

Voices of soft proclaim, and silver stir

Of strings in hollow shells; and let there be

Beautiful things made new for the surprise

Of the sky-children – ' So he feebly ceased,

With such a poor and sickly sounding pause,

Methought I heard some old man of the earth

Bewailing earthly loss; nor could my eyes

And ears act with that pleasant unison of sense

Which marries sweet sound with the grace of form

And dolorous accent from a tragic harp

With large-limbed visions. More I scrutinized:

Still fixed he sat beneath the sable trees,

Whose arms spread straggling in wild serpent forms,

With leaves all hushed; his awful presence there

(Now all was silent) gave a deadly lie

To what I erewhile heard – only his lips

Trembled amid the white curls of his beard.

They told the truth, though, round, the snowy locks

Hung nobly, as upon the face of heaven

A midday fleece of clouds. Thea arose,

And stretched her white arm through the hollow dark,

Pointing some whither; whereat he too rose

Like a vast giant, seen by men at sea

To grow pale from the waves at dull midnight.

They melted from my sight into the woods;

Ere I could turn, Moneta cried:'These twain

Are speeding to the families of grief,

Where roofed in by black rocks they waste, in pain

And darkness, for no hope.'– And she spake on,

As ye may read who can unwearied pass

Onward from the antechamber of this dream,

Where even at the open doors awhile

I must delay, and glean my memory

Of her high phrase – perhaps no further dare.

CANTO II

'Mortal, that thou mayst understand aright,

I humanize my sayings to thine ear,

Making comparisons of earthly things;

Or thou mightst better listen to the wind,

Whose language is to thee a barren noise,

Though it blows legend-laden through the trees –

In melancholy realms big tears are shed,

More sorrow like to this, and such-like woe,

Too huge for mortal tongue, or pen of scribe.

The Titans fierce, self-hid or prison-bound,

Groan for the old allegiance once more,

Listening in their doom for Saturn's voice.

But one of our whole eagle-brood still keeps

His sovereignty, and rule, and majesty;

Blazing Hyperion on his orbèd fire

Still sits, still snuffs the incense teeming up

From man to the sun's God – yet unsecure.

For as upon the earth dire prodigies

Fright and perplex, so also shudders he:

Nor at dog's howl or gloom-bird's even screech,

Or the familiar visitings of one

Upon the first toll of his passing-bell:

But horrors, portioned to a giant nerve,

Make great Hyperion ache. His palace bright,

Bastioned with pyramids of glowing gold,

And touched with shade of bronzèd obelisks,

Glares a blood-red through all the thousand courts,

Arches, and domes, and fiery galleries;

And all its curtains of Aurorian clouds

Flush angerly: when he would taste the wreaths

Of incense breathed aloft from sacred hills,

Instead of sweets, his ample palate takes

Savour of poisonous brass and metals sick.

Wherefore, when harboured in the sleepy West,

After the full completion of fair day,

For rest divine upon exalted couch

And slumber in the arms of melody,

He paces through the pleasant hours of ease

With strides colossal, on from hall to hall;

While far within each aisle and deep recess

His wingèd minions in close clusters stand

Amazed, and full of fear; like anxious men,

Who on a wide plain gather in sad troops,

When earthquakes jar their battlements and towers.

Even now, while Saturn, roused from icy trance,

Goes, step for step, with Thea from yon woods,

Hyperion, leaving twilight in the rear,

Is sloping to the threshold of the West –

Thither we tend.'– Now in clear light I stood,

Relieved from the dusk vale. Mnemosyne

Was sitting on a square-edged polished stone,

That in its lucid depth reflected pure

Her priestess-garments. My quick eyes ran on

From stately nave to nave, from vault to vault,

Through bowers of fragrant and enwreathèd light

And diamond-pavèd lustrous long arcades.

Anon rushed by the bright Hyperion;

His flaming robes streamed out beyond his heels,

And gave a roar, as if of earthly fire,

That scared away the meek ethereal Hours,

And made their dove-wings tremble. On he flared...

余光中作品集

　　余光中一生從事詩、散文、評論、翻譯，自稱為寫作的四度空間，詩風與文風的多變、多產、多樣，盱衡同輩晚輩，幾乎少有匹敵者。從舊世紀到新世紀，對現代文學影響既深且遠，遍及兩岸三地的華人世界。他筆下揮灑成形的恢弘氣象，既是個人豐饒生命的投影，也是當代歷史魂魄的縮影，半個多世紀以來，一直是臺灣文學最重要的代表性人物。

詩集

　　余光中的詩，詠人如畫家為人造像；詠物能實能虛，由實入虛，妙得雙關。他把中國的古風與西方的無韻體融為一體，從頭到尾連綿不斷，一氣呵成，顯示詩人的布局與魄力。《白玉苦瓜》是他盛年的代表作，亦是詩與歌完美的結合，有〈鄉愁〉、〈鄉愁四韻〉、〈民歌〉等，風行四方，又屢屢改編歌曲，帶動校園民歌風潮，也是學生讀余光中詩作的首選，最新詩集《藕神》更證明詩心不老，繆思永遠眷顧。

　　0110203　高樓對海 220元
　　0110206　白玉苦瓜　200元
　　0110209　藕神(平裝) 240元
　　0110200　藕神(精裝) 360元
　　F0342　　守夜人（中英對照） 290元

散文

　　余光中散文最迷人之處，在於閱讀中可以聽見聲音，聞到氣味，發現顏色，造成觸覺。當他寫景，會邀請你與他同行，感覺視覺的遠近，天地的深淺；當他寫人，會牽動你隱而不見的情緒；當他寫事，你會隨著文章節奏而忙碌，而悠閒，而疲憊。《逍遙遊》是他青春盛年時期最具代表性的文集，文體兼具知性與感性，同時開創現代散文新流派；創作中期代表作《聽聽那冷雨》，從書評、序言到詩論、樂評，既抒情又幽默，有知識更有情趣；《望鄉的牧神》展現青年余光中的藝術天分與熱情，也開創了臺灣旅遊文學的先河。

0110201　青銅一夢　270元
0110205　聽聽那冷雨　230元
0110207　望鄉的牧神　250元
0110208　憑一張地圖　220元
0110212　余光中跨世紀散文　陳芳明編　420元
0110214　日不落家　250元
0110215　青青邊愁　300元
0106006　余光中精選集　320元
F0283　　隔水呼渡　220元
F0575　　逍遙遊　220元

評論

　　余光中的評論有學者的淵博，更具作家的經驗與真知，他「以文為論」，靈光一閃，常見生動的比喻，富於形象思維。《從徐霞客到梵谷》論山水遊記，又論西方繪畫，莫不說理透徹，情趣盎然。

翻譯

余光中將國外名家的作品翻譯成中文，帶領讀者認識文學家、藝術家以及劇作家的文字與生命。《梵谷傳》看梵谷用畫寫人生，史東以小說細繪梵谷在宗教、藝術、愛情中熊熊燃燒的藝術家靈魂。本書由余光中翻譯、審訂，並有余光中手繪梵谷一生行程圖、為梵谷而寫的詩作，是認識梵谷最完整最精彩的著作。

0130043　梵谷傳(平裝)　600元
0130044　梵谷傳(精裝)　伊爾文・史東Irving Stone著　680元
0110211　不要緊的女人　王爾德Oscar Wilde著　200元

余光中作品集 16

濟慈名著譯述

譯者	余光中
責任編輯	莊文松
發行人	蔡文甫
出版發行	九歌出版社有限公司
	臺北市105八德路3段12巷57弄40號
	電話／02-25776564・傳真／02-25789205
	郵政劃撥／0112295-1
九歌文學網	www.chiuko.com.tw
印刷	晨捷印製股份有限公司
法律顧問	龍躍天律師・蕭雄淋律師・董安丹律師
初版	2012 (民國101) 年4月
定價	平裝380元　藏詩版460元

書號	0110216
ISBN	978-957-444-794-7 (平裝)
ISBN	978-957-444-821-0 (藏詩版)

國家圖書館出版品預行編目資料

濟慈名著譯述 / 余光中. -- 初版. -- 臺北
市：九歌, 民101.04
面； 公分. -- (余光中作品集 ; 16)

ISBN 978-957-444-794-7(平裝)
ISBN 978-957-444-821-0(藏詩版)

873.4   100019097